Breakfast with Friends

By

Mary Lee Peck

Reading Research Institute

Westerville, Ohio

Mary Lee Peck earned her Ph.D. in Education from The Ohio State University. She has taught at all levels from preschool to graduate school. She is the author of *The Mansion* and *Raven's Call* and will soon release the sequel to *Raven's Call.* She has also authored several children's books and a college textbook in reading instruction.

Published by Reading Research Institute, Westerville, Ohio

E-book ISBN
ISBN:10: 1-931365-05-9
ISBN:13: 978-1-931365-05-5

Print Version ISBN
ISBN: 10: 1-931365-04-0
ISBN:13: 978-1-931365-04-8

Print Version Library of Congress Control Number:
2011913209

This book is dedicated to those who take risks to protect the ones they love.

Breakfast With Friends

Gina leaned against the counter and gazed idly through the large glass window of the diner. It was about time for Sam Weston to come wheeling in with his new, red pick-up. He was always their first customer every day, even on Sundays. She liked Sam. He was genuine. She had been worrying about him lately, though. "Hey, Frank," she called out. "How old do you think Sam is?"

"I haven't the faintest idea—somewhere in his seventies, I guess. Why?"

"No reason. Just curious. I've noticed he walks a little slower these days. I worry about him being out there all alone on that big ol' farm working with those humongous cows he breeds."

Frank sighed and continued to wipe down the grill. "You worry too much. You're always worrying about someone else. You'd better start worrying about yourself and those jerks you drag home with you from your karaoke bars. How many black eyes have you had so far this year? I've lost count."

"I sure know how to pick 'em, don't I? I need to figure out a way to get rid of my latest dependent, Greg. He's just like all the others—abusive and lazy—and I'm tired of supporting losers."

"Well, it's about time," said Frank as he pushed past her and headed into the storage room.

"Well, at least I keep looking for love. You run from it."

"Don't go there, Gina," he warned as he shoved past her to the back room. He shot her one of his glances that she had come to recognize over the years as an admonition that she was about to cross his privacy line.

She smiled and moved to the other side of the counter to get out of his way as he scurried back and forth from the back room to the grill filling up the trays and bins with the things he kept at his fingertips for grilling. She would offer to help him, but she knew he preferred to do it himself.

Frank was not just her boss; he was a loyal friend. He pretended to be gruff, but she knew he was a softie at heart. He worried as much as she did about their customer-friends and about her and his other waitresses, Jan and Kelley. She stared at him as he hustled past her carrying multiple trays and containers. His sandy colored hair was turning gray at the temples, but at almost fifty, he still was trim and fit. The muscles in his back bulged under his white tee shirt as he reached for the heavy metal container of fresh eggs stored in the cooler next to the prep-area and easily lifted the container with one hand. He carefully placed the container on the left side of his grill—eggs, meat, and cheese on the left; potatoes, pancake batter, and plates on the right — he'd been arranging the food around the grill in the same way since the day he opened the diner. "You're like a robot in front

6

of that grill, Frank," she commented.

"What do you mean by that?"

"It's like your hands just automatically reach for whatever you need, and your eyes stay fixed on the grill."

"After twenty years of doing the same thing every day, I should be able to do it unconsciously, don't you think?"

"Yea, I guess, but don't you ever get bored coming in here every day and fixing the same stuff?"

Frank chuckled. "What? Are you kidding? People like you and Sam keep me entertained all the time. You guys have a different mess to talk about every day. This place is like living in the middle of a big soap opera." He stood back to examine the arrangement of items around the grill. "What about you? You bored?"

Gina hesitated for a minute before answering. "No, not really. I like our customers and Jan and Kelley."

"So, what am I? Chopped liver?"

Gina laughed. "I didn't mean to hurt your feelings. Of course, I like you. You're like the grouchy, big brother I never had."

Frank turned around and looked at her. "You know, if I was really your big brother, I'd be kicking your tiny, little butt out of here and sending you and your cowgirl boots to Nashville," he retorted. "When are you going to get the nerve to go for it?"

"Someday, maybe." Gina heaved a deep sigh. She knew that Frank was right. She was headed nowhere with her singing talent, and she had lost hope of making it in the world of country music. Success in a career like that just didn't happen to people like her.

"If you'd stop squandering your money on those jerks you drag home with you, you'd have enough to at least get you started," grumbled Frank.

"Are you trying to get rid of me, Frank?" she joked, even though she knew that wasn't the reason for his criticism. He was right as usual. She was wasting her life, and she did squander her money on jerks — always hoping that the next one would do what he promised to do — *turn his life around and take care of her.*

"Of course not, who would I fight with every day?" He smiled and turned back toward the grill. "Grill's hot. We're ready for Sam," he announced.

Gina glanced up at the clock—almost six. She liked being up early in the morning, especially in the summer. The fresh, warm breeze and the chirping of the birds made the mornings happy. "Do you like mornings, Frank?" she asked as he headed into the back room again.

"Do I like mornings?" He stopped at the swinging café doors and stared at her. "Gina, where do you come up with such questions?"

"What's wrong with asking if you like mornings? Don't you ever think about things like that?"

"I can't say that I do," he said as he continued into the storage room.

"Well, you should," she called after him. "You shouldn't just float through life without thinking about things like that. You're not getting any younger, you know. You should take time to enjoy something besides work."

Frank came back into the diner carrying the frozen steaks that some of the regulars ordered every day. "There you go again, worrying about someone else's life instead of your own. You're hopeless."

"And you're like talking to a dead man," she said as she stomped to the door to unlock it.

Frank watched her angrily flip over the *Closed* sign on the door. "I'm sorry, kiddo. I didn't mean to hurt your feelings—especially not on such a lovely, summer morning with the birds singing and the warm breeze carrying the sweet smell of roses across the city," he said teasingly.

"You're impossible," she snapped. "Here comes Jan. I bet she noticed the birds singing this morning."

Gina watched Frank's deep, brown eyes light up as he smiled and waved at Jan. *Why in the heck don't they get married*, she wondered. *They obviously care about one another. Makes no sense to me why two people who enjoy being together and who have the same likes and dislikes are afraid to admit that they're in love.* She sighed and picked up her apron. *Maybe they're smarter than me. I'm always following my heart and not my head. No wonder I'm always in some sort of messy, going-*

9

nowhere relationship.

Gina admired Jan Clark. She was still a knock out at forty, even though life hadn't always treated her fairly. Jan was like a surrogate mother to her—taking the place of her own mom, who died several years ago. Her real mother had never been much of a mother figure—always drunk or high on drugs—but not Jan. She was a loving mother to her nineteen-year-old daughter, Olivia. *I would give anything to have someone like Jan as my mom*, she thought. *I would never treat her the way Olivia does. Don't go there*, she warned. *You're alone; suck it up and realize that it's never going to be any different for you— end of pity party.* "Morning, Jan. You look as fresh and lovely as ever. I swear you must use a whole can of spray starch on your blouses to make them look so crisp. I'm lucky if I get mine out of the dryer and on to a hanger before they get all wrinkled."

"From the looks of the blouse you're wearing, Gina," said Frank, "it doesn't look like you got to the dryer soon enough."

Gina faked a laugh and pretended to check the napkin dispensers on the counter, trying to hide the pain that Frank's light-hearted response about her blouse had unintentionally caused. He was right. She couldn't get near the dryer last night. She had spent the night locked up in the bathroom to get away from Greg's jealous rampage. She had to wait until she heard him hit the floor, passed out in a drunken stupor, before she dared to come out. She had actually grabbed her clothes and had spent the rest of the night in her car.

She had no idea what she was going to do about Greg.

10

That's tonight's problem. She sighed. She was safe at the diner, and there were other things to think about here.

"Gina looks just as perky as ever," said Jan reaching across the counter to squeeze Frank's hand. "You need to stop teasing her, Frank."

Gina watched them exchange affectionate smiles and couldn't stop herself from blurting out what she'd been thinking. "Why don't you two get married? I don't understand it. You obviously care for one another."

The sparkle in Frank's eyes quickly changed to burning fury. "Why don't you mind your own business? I swear, Gina, you're always trying to run everyone's life but your own. Someone should put a muzzle on that mouth of yours." He whipped around and pretended to be searching for something in the storage cabinet next to the grill.

Jan just shrugged her shoulders and winked at Gina as she headed into the back room to grab an apron.

"Here comes Sam." Gina glanced up at the clock. "He's running two minutes late today." She watched out the window as Sam carefully climbed out of his truck. To lower himself to the ground, he stepped on to the grooved running board, and held on to the door. Once on the ground, he stood next to his truck for several moments, jiggling his legs up and down as if he were trying to get circulation to his arthritic feet. Finally, he limped toward the diner and waved at her through the window. She was glad to see him. He was always good for a laugh and a friendly argument. "Good morning,

Sam. You're late today."

"Morning, Sam," mumbled Frank, who obviously was still pouting about Gina's earlier comment.

"Howdy, Frank. Good morning, Gina. It's Sunday. I'm allowed to sleep in on Sundays. Phew, it's going to be a hot one today," he said swinging his stiff leg astride the single-pedestal stool. "What's the temperature supposed to be anyway?" He leaned across the counter to pick up part of the newspaper that was within his reach. "It's way too hot for June," he complained as he took off his ball cap and wiped his forehead with a handkerchief that he pulled from his back jeans pocket. "Too much heat messes up my breeding cycle."

"Yours or the cows'?" responded Gina as she automatically shoved him a steaming cup of coffee and a plate of rye toast, light on the butter—just the way he liked it.

Sam laughed. "You know what I meant, you ornery thing."

"Two or three eggs today?" she asked.

"Just two. I don't have any heavy work today, so I gotta cut back some."

"Yeah, right—like one less egg is going to help you deflate that ring of flab you're carryin' 'round your middle. If you'd lose some of that weight, you wouldn't mind the heat so much."

12

"Gina," barked Frank, looking up from the grill. "Leave Sam alone and take down the rest of the chairs."

"Are you blind? I already took down the chairs, for gosh sakes. Where's your mind been all morning?" snapped Gina. "Jeez, what a grump."

For the next hour, the early-morning customers streamed into the diner. Most of them had been coming into the diner for years, and Gina knew them all. Occasionally, there was a first-time customer that she didn't know, like the middle-age couple who was just coming through the door. "Howdy, folks," she cheerfully greeted them. "Find yourself a seat, and one of us will be right with you."

"Why is it that newcomers always look so confused when they walk in here?" whispered Jan on her way to the kitchen with a tub of dirty dishes.

"I guess nowadays they're used to having a hostess at the door to lead them to a table. Maybe we should get Frank to spring for a *Seat Yourself* sign to cut down on the deer-in-the-headlights look they get when they first come in."

"Are you kidding? Frank hasn't spent a dime on this place since he opened twenty years ago," said Jan. "Anyway, I think he gets a kick out of watching new customers squirm when they're not sure what to do. Why they ever come back, is a mystery to me."

"It's because of our charming ways and good looks; don't you know that by now?" Gina answered. Glancing out of the window, she watched as Kelley Johnson came dragging across the parking lot. "Here comes Kelley.

13

She's not looking too lively today. One of the kids was probably up all night."

"She'd better get her act together," responded Jan looking up at the large Coca Cola clock above the grill. "She has just about two seconds to get her apron on before Frank will start griping about her always being late."

"She's got a lot on her mind," said Gina. "Thank goodness Carl is due home pretty soon —the sooner the better. Did she tell you that they cut off her phone last week? Poor thing, she just got it turned back on yesterday. I don't know how she's managed this past year—him gone and four little ones under the age of five. It's really taken a toll on her. She looks as worn out as some of our older customers."

"Orders up," shouted Frank. "Or, are you two still on your break?"

"What's a break, Frank?" retorted Gina. "Hey, Kelley," she said as Kelley dragged herself through the door of the diner. "Look at that, Frank. She's right on time." Gina pointed up at the clock and winked at Kelley. "Hurry up, sweetie. We're about to get slammed with the early church crowd."

"Hey, Gina," responded Kelley. She winked at Gina, obviously grateful to her for attempting to protect her from Frank's concern about her lateness. "I'm on it. Hey, Sam," she said patting him on the shoulder as she headed into the back room to grab an apron.

"Hi, good lookin'," replied Sam. "What's the news from
14

Afghanistan? Carl still fighting for our freedom?"

Kelley sighed. "Only about two more weeks, I can't wait until he's back here fighting some of our own battles."

As Jan was clearing the table next to the window, the distinctive sound of a motorcycle attracted her attention. "Hey ladies, look at what just pulled up on a new *Harley*—combat boots and all."

"Whew-ee!" responded Gina. "I bet he has *Semper Fi* tattooed somewhere on that gorgeous torso. Oh, how I'd like a chance to hunt for it. Now that's what I call a hunk."

"Close your mouth, Gina. You're about to drool all over my eggs," chided Sam.

The handsome, young biker sat in the parking lot seemingly unaware that anyone was watching him. Gina noticed that, for some reason, he was hesitant about getting off the bike. "Come on in; come on in," she whispered. "Please, come in and brighten my day."

Sam laughed. "You do realize your lusting all over the place, don't you?"

"Shush, Sam. Let me enjoy the view in silence." She gawked at the biker's broad, well-defined shoulders under the tan t-shirt that clung to him like a second skin. His arms were strong and tanned, most likely from riding across the country in the open air. "My, oh my, they couldn't sculpt one any better than him. He's obviously military from the dog tags around his neck and his camouflage pants. I bet he's just passing through Columbus on his way to some military base out West.

15

Just my luck." She sighed, disappointed that the handsome biker was probably just a one-time visitor at the diner.

As she continued to admire his well-built torso, he grabbed a package out of the tote bag on the back of his cycle and headed for the door. "Yes!" she cheered as she rushed toward the door. "Find a seat wherever you'd like," she greeted before he was halfway in the diner. There was no way she was going to let Frank get a kick out of embarrassing this one. Unfortunately, she forgot about Sam and his obsession over the diner seating-chart, and, as fate would have it, her soldier headed straight for the stool next to Sam's.

"Sorry, buddy," said Sam. "That there stool is for my friend Leroy Collins, and the one on my right is for Howard Lacey. I reckon Leroy will be pulling up here in about three minutes, and Howard is due back from his winter vacation today. So, if you don't mind, you might take the stool down there at the end. It's usually vacant during this time on Sundays."

Gina was horrified as she watched her young biker freeze in midair, halfway between standing and sitting on the barstool. She was relieved when he seemed to accept Sam's mandate without any fuss. He simply smiled and moved down to the end of the counter, laying his package on the floor under his assigned stool.

"From around here or just passing by?" asked Sam. "Haven't seen you in here before. I'm Sam Weston. Welcome to *Frank's Diner*. We could use some new faces up at the counter here, but you just gotta get used to who sits where."

16

"Nice to meet you, sir. My name's Mark Tyler," answered the young man.

"Who made you the Welcome Wagon, Sam?" interrupted Gina. "Don't mind him, gorgeous. He thinks that because he lives here, he owns the place. What can I get for you?"

"May I see a menu?"

"You name it; we'll fix it," answered Gina. "What do you normally have for Sunday breakfast?"

"I don't usually eat breakfast."

"Son," interrupted Sam, "hasn't anyone ever told you that breakfast is the most important meal of the day? You can't expect to be at your peak without a good, hearty breakfast."

"Try the steak and eggs," suggested the customer sitting on the stool next to Mark. "Steak's pretty thin, but it has a good taste — and it's tender too. I'm Tom McGinnis. Welcome to *Frank's,*" said Tom offering his hand.

"No, don't listen to him," interjected Sam. "The hot-cakes are better. They'll stick with you longer. Is your bike new?" he asked without pausing for a breath. He turned around to stare at the shiny, black Harley parked next to his truck.

"Yes, sir. It's new." Then, turning his attention to Gina, Mark said, "I'll just have some oatmeal with brown sugar and butter. That is, if you've got oatmeal," he added looking up at her as he took off his mirrored sunglasses.

Gina felt her knees buckle and her heart skip a beat. His eyes were bluer than any pool of tropical waters she'd ever seen in pictures. "You have the bluest eyes I've ever seen, but then I guess everyone tells you that. It's just that, with such dark hair, I was kind of expecting your eyes to be dark too — not that it matters much, though." Embarrassed by her uncontrollable babbling, she turned to Frank and shouted, "One large bowl of oatmeal smothered with brown sugar and topped with butter — milk on the side."

Sam laughed as Mark almost jumped off his stool. "You've gotta brace yourself when Gina hollers out your order. She'll bust your eardrums."

"Why are you telling me that order, Gina?" Frank growled. "You know where the oatmeal is. It's not something I fix on the grill for Pete's sake. What's wrong with you?"

"Just thought you'd like to know," she quickly retorted. "You're always yelling about keeping track of the stupid inventory." She stormed off to get the oatmeal unwilling to admit that she was distracted by Mark's good looks.

The bell on the door of the diner jingled against the glass, and Sam quickly turned around to greet his friend. "Hey, Leroy, where've you been?" he asked.

"What do you mean? I'm right on the minute," responded Leroy as he slapped his old railroad buddy on the shoulder. "It's eight o'clock on the dot. You'd better fix your watch or your eyes 'cause one of them is broken.

18

Never 'twas the brakeman who caused the train to be late; 'twas always the engineer." He lightly poked Sam in the side with his elbow as he slid onto the barstool next to him.

"Well, well, Ol' buddy," whispered Sam, gesturing toward the door with a toss of his head. "Take a gander at who just followed you in here. Now that's a real lady."

Leroy turned toward the door as a woman about their age came into the diner. "Not bad, not bad at all," he agreed. "She looks a little familiar to me, does she to you?" he asked.

Sam crinkled his nose and squinted his eyes to get a clearer look at the woman entering the diner. "Hmm, maybe. But, I think I would have remembered meeting her."

"Good morning, sweetie," Gina greeted. "There's a table over there by the window if you'd like." Gina could see why Sam and Leroy were impressed. For her age, the woman was extremely attractive. Her hair was snowy white in front and dark in the back. She wore it short, and it fell softly around her face. Her skin was smooth and tanned. The pale blue, linen dress that she was wearing and the matching cardigan that she had draped casually across her shoulders matched the blue of her eyes. She was thin with straight, proud posture. *I agree with Leroy,* Gina decided. *She does look familiar, but I don't think she's been here as a customer.*

~~~~~

"Thank you," Meredith replied softly. All morning she had

19

stewed about whether or not to come to the diner. She hated to eat alone in public, and besides, this had been Howard's place, not hers. She had almost decided that she wouldn't go but then changed her mind because she had promised Howard that she would come here today.

From her seat by the window, she could see the entire diner. It was smaller than she thought it would be. Five round tables were scattered in the middle of the open, square room, and three more lined the wide, front windows, which didn't provide much of a view other than that of the parking lot and a glimpse between the parked cars at the busy street in front of the diner. She noticed that today there were fewer cars speeding toward the freeway entrance located nearby. *Of course*, she reminded herself, *it would be a little less busy on Sundays.*

She continued to glance around at the diner. Six booths with high wooden backs hugged the walls along the right side of the room and partially across the back wall, stopping at the doors leading to the restrooms. A long, curved counter with eight backless, swivel-top bar stools surrounded the grill up front. A comforting aroma of fried bacon, hot cakes, and freshly brewed coffee hovered in the air and reminded her that she hadn't actually eaten a decent meal in over a week. Lately, she preferred just to grab some tidbit from the refrigerator and to eat it as she wandered from room to room in her house, not feeling comfortable anywhere. The soft murmur of casual conversation and the constant whirr of the fans above the grill provided a comforting atmosphere that offered a respite from the oppressive silence of her house.

Although she had never actually been in the diner before

20

this morning, it was familiar to her. She recognized its distinguishing features that Howard had described to her. On the front wall, above the counter, she spotted the large, black and white photograph. It was an enlarged snapshot of a bride and groom waving from the back seat of a car. According to Howard, it was the wedding picture of Frank's parents.

Frank Fitzpatrick was the owner of the diner. From the model of the car, the picture must have been taken in the late 50's. The couple in the picture looked like they were about eighteen years old—*the same age Howard and I were when we got married*. She looked down at the table, willing herself not to cry.

The story that Howard told her about the picture was a sad one. When Frank was seven years old, his mom disappeared with his infant brother and some man she knew from high school. Frank never got over his mother leaving him behind and taking only his brother. He had the photo enlarged and kept it on the front wall of the diner so that everyone coming in the door could see it. Howard said that Frank keeps hoping that someday his brother will stop in and recognize the girl in the picture as their mother. Then, maybe he would get the chance to reunite with him again.

Next to the photograph, there was a large, cheap frame holding the first occupancy license issued when Frank started the restaurant more than twenty years ago. Surrounding the license were the first one, five, ten, and twenty-dollar bills he received during the first week he was open. There was space for a fifty and a hundred in the circle of bills, but he had either never gotten one of those, or he had never bothered to add them to the

21

collage.

Above the booths, the back and side walls of the diner were lined with familiar black and white prints of Elvis Pressley, Marilyn Monroe, Frank Sinatra, and other stars of the 50's. Even though the diner was located in a small strip center in Ohio, once you were inside, it had the feel of one found along the Route 66 corridor out West during the fifties and sixties.

It didn't look like Frank had done much remodeling in the past twenty years. The once white ceiling tiles were yellowed and stained. She doubted they had been replaced since the restaurant opened. Huge water spots created a strange combination of cloud-like shapes and shadows above her. The black and white, linoleum floor tiles were clearly the original flooring. They were cracked and worn thin in several places, but they were clean. According to Howard, Frank built the booths and tables. They were made of oak that he hadn't bothered to stain. He had just splashed them with heavy lacquer that had partially worn off from years of surface cleaning. Some of the cheap, red vinyl seats in the booths and on the chairs were split in several places. *This is a man's diner — clean, but with minimal attention to atmosphere. The rough, well-used look would appeal to Howard—no wonder he enjoyed coming here,* she thought.

Glancing around at the people seated at the counter and at the 'gals,' as Howard used to call the waitresses, she could readily identify his breakfast friends. Sam was undoubtedly the relatively robust man seated at the counter. Howard called him the chatterbox of the counter-crowd. Unlike most men of his age, Sam had a full head of dark hair that was only slightly streaked with gray at the temples and with no thinning bald spot in the back. He was casually dressed in a pair of jeans and a plaid, cotton shirt with a button-down-collar. His shirt was tucked haphazardly around his bulging waist, and his boots were scuffed and worn. *All that's missing is a Stetson.* She smiled as she noticed the ball cap lying next to him on the counter.

She remembered Howard telling her that Sam owned a large farm located just north of the diner where he raised and bred cattle. Howard used to go there to fish in the pond that Sam kept well-stocked just for him. Although she could only see his profile, Sam had a handsome, kind appearance and seemed to be thoroughly enjoying himself. Howard particularly liked him. *'You can always depend on Sam,'* he used to say. *'He'll do anything for anyone.'* It seemed strange that, at some time during the years that Howard had been coming into the diner, she had never had the opportunity to actually meet Sam.

Seated next to Sam, she recognized Leroy Corbett — Sam's thin pal who always arrived and left the diner at precisely the same time every day. In appearance, Leroy offered quite a contrast to Sam. He was smartly dressed in a soft cotton golf-shirt and neatly pressed tan trousers. He was almost totally bald with a thin band of closely cropped white hair forming a u-shape around his head. He wore highly polished loafers and tan socks that matched his pants.

According to what Howard had told her, Sam and Leroy worked together for a while on the railroad before Sam left to take over his family's cow-breeding operation. Sam had been an engineer on the Penn Central; Leroy had been a brakeman. For years, the two of them had worked together on the same run between Columbus and Logansport, Indiana. Now, they met every morning at *Frank's* and exchanged stories about the good-old days when railroad was king and argued over everything, including who had the most prestigious job—the engineer or the brakeman. *It's strange how much I know about them, even though I've never actually met them,* she thought.

At the end of the counter, she noticed a nice looking, younger man who looked to be in his mid-thirties. His lean torso and athletic gear helped her to identify him as Tom, who, as far as the other counter-mates knew, had never held a full-time job in his life. He didn't talk much according to Howard, preferring to listen to the stories of the others. No one knew much about him—only that, regardless of the weather, he came to *Frank's* every day after a long, early morning run and always ordered steak and eggs. He was the most recent member of the counter-crowd having just joined them about a year ago.

The younger man sitting on the stool next to Tom, wasn't familiar to her. *Perhaps, he's a first-time visitor like me,* she guessed. *He must be sitting on what Howard and the others designated as the 'visitor's stool.'* Most likely, Sam, who Howard said was the self-appointed maître de in charge of the seating arrangements at the counter, had directed him to that seat.

As she continued to scan the diner for other regulars that Howard had talked about, she spotted an elderly couple at a table in the center of the room. *They must be the O'Connors,* she decided. Howard described Mrs. O'Connor as a bubbly, talkative lady who chatted constantly to those around her. Her husband was the quiet, shy man—the fallen hero in all of her stories. She smiled as she watched Mrs. O'Connor happily babbling away to the diners on both sides of her table while her husband quietly sipped his coffee.

In the back of the diner, she located the two off-duty police officers Howard talked about—Jeff and Colin. Jeff was the younger one in shorts. He always rode his bike around his beat in good weather. She had actually seen him before, when Howard had pointed him out at the Fourth of July celebration last year. Colin was the older officer. He and Jeff covered the same beat, but Colin drove a cruiser. Their shift ended at seven in the morning, and for years, they had been stopping at *Frank's* for breakfast on their way home. Colin was reaching retirement age and would eventually be joining the others at the counter. *He will probably take Howard's assigned stool*, she thought.

Next, seated all alone in the first booth, she noticed a strange, young man who appeared to be in his early twenties. She had almost forgotten about him. Howard had told her that the guys at the counter called him *Unabomber 2. Other than his long, unruly brown hair, he certainly doesn't look like Ted Kaczynski*, she thought. According to Howard, he was a loner and never talked to anyone in the diner. He came in every morning, headed straight for his booth, and immediately took out a yellow pad from his grubby backpack. The whole time he was in the diner, he would scribble numbers all over the pages. She had noticed a bicycle outside with all sorts of baskets and junk strapped to the front and rear fenders. *It probably belongs to him*, she decided. She watched as his mud-stained hands flew across the page, writing numbers with lightening speed. He never looked up from his yellow pad even when the waitress refilled

25

his coffee. *I wonder what his true story is,* she mused.

Meredith turned her attention to the waitresses. She decided that Gina Meyers must be the taller, thin waitress with the multiple piercings in both ears and a tiny rose tattoo on her wrist. Howard liked her. *'She's got spunk,'* he used to say. *'Not afraid to put ol' Frank in his place whenever he steps across her line.'* Meredith watched her as Gina flew around the room, smiling and chatting with everyone, even Unabomber 2. Of course, he never looked up or answered her, but that didn't seem to bother Gina. She just babbled away at him every time she refilled his coffee. Everyone was obviously her friend.

Gina's light blonde hair was pulled back and twisted into a straggly knot that was held in place by a large comb-clip. She wore almost no makeup except for a slight hint of pink on her lips. There was no affectation about her; she appeared to be totally wholesome, inside and out. The apron she had tied around her tiny waist hung down below the hemline of her short skirt, and it looked like she was wearing an apron that belonged to her mother. *She wouldn't be described as the most beautiful girl in the world,* Meredith decided. *But, the twinkle in her soft, brown eyes; her well-proportioned, athletic figure; and her dainty facial features definitely put her in the pretty and cute category.*

While Gina was cleaning off a table nearby, Meredith could hear her softly singing along with one of the country songs that was playing from a small radio up in the front of the diner. She obviously liked country music and appeared to know the words to every song they played on the radio.

26

As she continued to watch Gina, a middle-age waitress whispered something in Gina's ears, and the two of them laughed. *She must be Jan Clark*, Meredith decided. Howard described her as the mother hen of the others and the buffer between Frank and them. She appeared to be in her forties and was particularly attractive. Her dark brown, wavy hair was gathered into a neat, short updo with wispy, curly tresses dangling at her temples and at the base of her neck. She was conservatively dressed in khaki slacks, a neatly pressed white, short-sleeve blouse, and black flats. Meredith studied her for a moment and decided that she had way too much class for *Frank's*. Yet, according to Howard, she'd worked at the diner for years. She'd come to work here about the same time Howard started coming to the diner—soon after it had first opened. Her beautiful, brown eyes had a gentle, sad look. Several years ago, Jan's husband died rather suddenly, leaving her alone to raise her teen-age daughter.

Meredith admired Jan's quiet, friendly approach with customers. She also noticed that Frank glanced up at Jan every time she delivered an order and that she always smiled affectionately at him whenever their eyes met. There was obviously a caring relationship between Jan and Frank. *Maybe they will eventually get around to pursuing marriage,* she hoped. *There is no greater institution in life. But, of course, my marriage to Howard had been idyllic—one of those rare relationships between two people who thought and acted as one.* She had never cared that Howard couldn't give her a child, until now. *It would be nice to have family who could help me get through this*, she thought. She swallowed hard to hold back the rush of tears.

Trying to get her mind off herself, she continued looking

around for other people she could recognize. She finally spotted Kelley Johnson. Howard called her *'the little mother of four.'* Hers was a story full of challenge and stress, according to him. Her young husband was in the military and serving his third tour in the Middle East. Watching her as she chatted with the O'Connor's, Meredith couldn't help but notice her slumping shoulders, the dark circles under her eyes, and her lackluster smile. She looked like she was carrying around the weight of the world and was about to collapse at any moment.

Last Christmas, Meredith had helped Howard select some gifts for Kelley's kids— one girl, the youngest sister of three little boys. The oldest of the four was a five-year-old boy. *'My little man'* was what Kelley called him. Howard always had a soft spot for him because his situation reminded him of his own childhood. Howard's dad had been killed during WWII when Howard was only six and the oldest of four. He never actually had a childhood after that, and he hoped that Kelley's brave, little son wouldn't have the same experience.

"Hey, Frank," shouted Sam, trying to get Frank's attention over the roaring fans above the grills. "Wasn't Howard supposed to be back today? I thought he planned to get back in town on the sixth."

"Yeah, that's what he said," muttered Frank. "Something must have come up, or he would've been in here by now."

"Strange," said Leroy, "he always came back on time before."

28

As the counter conversation interrupted her reverie, Meredith gasped, and an uncontrollable flood of tears escaped down her cheeks.

"Are you okay, mam?" asked Gina, slipping into the chair next to her and putting her arm around Meredith's shoulder. Immediately, Jan seated herself in the other chair, and the two waitresses stared at her with genuine concern.

"I'm sorry," sobbed Meredith. "I'm Meredith Lacey, Howard's widow."

~~~~

A hush fell over the entire diner. Gina noticed that even Frank turned around, dropping his spatula on the floor. Sam and Leroy whipped around on their stools, and Mrs. O'Connor and Kelley flew across the room to join them at Meredith's table. As usual, Sam was the first to break the silence.

"Now I know why I recognized you. Howard used to show us pictures of the two of you from your trips." He hesitated for a moment, and then stammered, "Did, did I hear you right? Did you just say you were Howard's widow?"

That's where I know her from, remembered Gina. *Sam is right. Howard showed them pictures of their Florida winters every year. He was always so proud of Meredith, bragging to them about how lucky he was to have such a gorgeous wife.* Gina's heart sank, and she had to fight to hold back her own tears. Howard was such a gentle soul. He loved coming in to the diner and arguing good-

29

naturedly with his counter-mates. They would all miss him terribly. *Poor Meredith*, she thought. *I can't imagine the heartbreak she must be feeling.*

"I'm sorry to blurt it out like that," said Meredith. "Howard made me promise I would come here today to tell you all good-bye for him. You were all very important to him —his *breakfast* family he used to call you." She dabbed at her eyes with a tissue as the tears began to flow again. "Other than me, you were the only family he had left."

"What happened?" asked Gina softly with tears swelling in her eyes.

"His heart just gave out. He died just before we were to head back up here from Florida. He was cremated, and I scattered his ashes in the bay outside of our condo— just the way he wanted. In the hospital, he made me promise I'd take this to you today." From her bag, she pulled out a cup with Howard's picture and name embossed on it. "He wanted you to have this," she whispered.

Jan reached out and gently took the cup from her. "We used to tease him because he always carried in his own cup. We'll take good care of it for him," she promised.

"Now, if you don't mind, I think I'll just go back home," sighed Meredith.

"No, you won't," insisted Sam, sliding off his stool, and huffing and puffing his way to her table. "You just bring your things and sit up here with Leroy and me. We'll take good care of you. I'm sure Howard would expect us to do that. When was the last time you had a decent meal?" he chattered.

Gina helped Sam usher Meredith to Howard's stool and quickly went to get her some coffee and a glass of water while Jan looked around for a spot for Howard's cup. She finally placed it on a small shelf on the wall next to the big picture of Frank's parents. Kelley stood next to Meredith patting her on the shoulder, and Frank went to work on the grill fixing Howard's favorite breakfast for her.

Gina smiled as she watched Mrs. O'Connor flit from table to table explaining to everyone what was happening and asking for their patience in getting their orders. On his way out the door, Unabomber 2 utterly astounded her and everyone else when he dropped a piece of wrapped candy on the counter next to Meredith's plate. "What a nice thing to do," Gina called out to him as he hurried out the door without turning around. She was proud of the compassion that everyone was showing to Meredith.

~~~~~

At the end of the counter, Tom and Mark sat in silence. Tom felt a deep pang of sadness as he watched the genuine closeness of the mixed group of people caring for one of their own. Even though, by choice, he had remained secretive and purposely aloof, he was drawn to each of them. They were all so different, but when any of them was hurting, they thought and acted as one. He had never before experienced such closeness among people who were bound together only because of a place where they ate their breakfast.

31

If they only knew about the future plans for this building, he thought with a deep sigh. It was obvious that they hadn't heard the news from the leasing company yet. He wished that Dick Tobin, a former tenant in the center where the diner was located, hadn't told him about the planned destruction of the strip center. Knowing the future of the diner made the morning even sadder. *What will happen to them*, he wondered. He especially worried about Frank. The diner was his life. And, what about the waitresses—the diner was not only their livelihood, it was their family, too.

He quietly slipped off his stool and headed outside. He drew in a deep breath of the warm, morning air, and slowly began jogging toward his workshop. *I'm just a few weeks away from fulfilling my promise,* he thought. *I know I can do it, but if I allow myself to get sucked into the problem with the future of the diner, then I will lose.*

Chapter 2

Mark sat quietly and watched as the others fussed over Meredith. He knew the pain that she was feeling. He had lost two people he loved—first his dad; and just recently, his grandfather who had raised him.

"Here, Meredith," said Gina, "these are phone numbers where you can reach me if you need something or just want to talk." She handed Meredith a paper napkin with the numbers written on it.

"You make sure you come here for breakfast," said Sam. "Leroy and I are here every day. Eating alone can be hard. Believe me, I know."

"You've all been so kind," replied Meredith. "I intend to move back to Florida as soon as I can sell the house up here. I don't like the cold weather, and I think I will feel closer to Howard down there. I'll come for breakfast until I get everything settled, and I'm ready to move. I can't thank you all enough. I don't feel quite so alone now— thanks to all of you. I'm sure that's why Howard made me promise to bring you his silly old cup. He'd only drink his coffee out of that cup. He took it with him to Florida every fall and lugged it back each spring."

When all of the regulars had left the diner, and the waitresses were busily wiping down the tables and sweeping up, Mark seized the opportunity to deliver his package. "Excuse me, sir," he said to Frank. "I know this is going to sound strange, but I have a package for you."

"For me?" quizzed Frank.

"Yes, sir. It's from my grandfather. He passed away last week. Just before he died, he gave me this envelope and made me promise to deliver it to you. He gave me the address of the diner and told me to 'take it to *Frank's Diner* and personally hand it to Frank Fitzpatrick.' I assume that's you." Mark reached down to pick up the package and laid it on the counter.

"Yes, that's me," said Frank cautiously. "What is it?"

"I don't know," answered Mark. "My grandfather insisted that I shouldn't open it, so I didn't. He used to live in Ohio a long time ago. I apologize if this is all some sort of mistake. He wasn't always lucid the last couple of years, but he seemed completely clear on the day he gave this to me."

Frank wiped his hands on his greasy apron and accepted the package with a foreboding look. "Do I know you from somewhere?"

Mark shifted on his stool. He could feel the intensity in Frank's stare. "No, sir. I grew up in West Virginia. My grandfather raised me after my Dad was killed in the Gulf. I never knew my mom. She ran off right after I was born." Mark looked down at the counter as Frank continued to stare at him. "I just graduated from The Citadel," he continued, "and I'm headed for Camp LeJeune this fall. Right now, I'm cycling across the country before I report for duty. It's something I used to do every summer with my dad and later with my grandpa

34

before he got so sick."

Finally, Frank looked away and tore open the envelope. Pictures dropped out from it and scattered on the counter. They both stared at the small black and white photo that landed face up on top of the others.

"Huh," muttered Mark, "that looks like the same picture that you have up there on your wall. Who are those people?"

Frank didn't answer. One-by-one, he flipped over the other photos.

"That's a picture of my Dad with my grandpa. Do you recognize either of them?" asked Mark.

Frank stared at the picture in silence.

"Are you okay, sir? You look a little pale. Let me get you something to drink." Mark stood up and easily vaulted over the counter. As he headed for the prep area to get a glass of water, he glanced across the room at the three waitresses. He was startled to see Gina heading toward him with her broom held up in the air as if she was ready to strike him with a deadly blow. He was relieved when Jan grabbed hold of her arm and signaled for her to stay away and not to say anything. *Gina must have thought I was going to rob the place.* He smiled. *She's certainly not afraid of anything, even if her only weapon is a flimsy, little broom. The girl's got guts. I wouldn't mind having her in my platoon.* He filled a glass with water and offered it to Frank.

He could feel Gina's stare burning into the back of his

head as he hopped back to the other side of the counter and sat back down on his stool. He remained silent as Frank picked up each of the photos, stared at it for a while, and then carefully laid it back down. Mark noticed that he stared longest at the pictures of his dad. Occasionally, after staring at one of his dad's early photos, Frank would glance up and stare at him without saying a word. "I think there's a letter that dropped on the floor when you opened the envelope." He bent down to retrieve the handwritten note for Frank. "Maybe it will explain what this all means."

"The pictures tell the story," said Frank. "I'd like to explain some of this to you, if you could spend time with me this afternoon. I think we have a lot in common." Frank smiled as he motioned for the three waitresses to join them. "Come on up here, ladies. I can tell you're all dying to know what's going on. I'd like to introduce you to my nephew. By the way, what the heck's your name again?" He laughed and reached out to shake Mark's hand.

"Mark, my name is Mark Tyler," stuttered Mark, "but you must have me confused with someone else. I'm not your nephew. I don't have any living relatives, at least that I know about, and I've never seen you before in my life."

"Well, son, I'm certain that I'm your father's older brother. I'm real sorry to hear about your dad. I can't say the same about your grandpa, but I obviously owe him for at least sending you to me."

"My dad never had an older brother," protested Mark, who was now the one turning pale.

Gina quickly passed him a cup of coffee. "Wow," she exclaimed, "this is just like one of my crazy soap operas."

Jan reached out and squeezed Frank's hand. "How about that? After all these years, that crazy picture finally paid off."

"Kelley, flip over the *Open* sign," said Frank. "We're closing early for the first time. Mark and I have some catching up to do, and I'm sure you ladies could find some way to spend the rest of your day." Then glancing at Kelley, he added, "Don't worry, Kelley. I'll pay all of you for the hour you're being shorted."

"Just give mine to Kelley," said Jan.

"Mine too," said Gina. "Kelley, why don't you take off and go to the movies or something? I'll stop by the house and send your babysitter home. I'd love to spend some time with the kids anyway, and I think you need to spend some time away from them."

Mark sat in stunned silence as Jan practically pushed the others out the door. It only took a few minutes for the three of them to gather their belongings and leave the two men alone in the diner. He closely observed Frank as he grabbed a cup of coffee and walked around the counter to sit next to him. Frank spread the pictures out in front of the two of them and opened the letter. He began reading it aloud.

> *"Dear Frank,*
>
> *First, let me introduce myself. My name is Ralph Tyler, and in case you don't*

37

recognize the name, I'm the person that your mother left with years ago. I know I owe you a long, over-due apology. Let me start out by saying that, for what it is worth, I loved your mom very much. I am only sorry that we didn't have much time together. I assume you know that she died in an automobile accident just a week after we left Ohio. I hope that your dad explained everything to you. But in case he didn't, let me tell you the truth.

Your mom told him that she was leaving. We didn't just abandon you. He refused to let her take you with us. She cried all the way to West Virginia about leaving you. She planned to come back and settle things with your dad and intended to beg him to let you come with us. Unfortunately, her accident happened before she could return to Ohio.

I let your dad know about her death. I don't know if he told you or not, but I guess that doesn't matter now. I didn't send your brother back to you because I knew your dad was struggling with an alcohol problem, and it wouldn't have been fair for you to have to take care of a baby and your dad. I also selfishly admit that I wanted some part of your mom to be with me, and he looked so much like her. I never told Mike that he had an older brother. Your dad signed papers to let me adopt him, and the facts of his birth family were never discussed. I know now that was selfish of

38

me.

You would have been proud of your brother. He had a compassionate spirit and was quite an athlete. The only mistake he ever made was getting married right out of high school. A year later, Mark was born, but Mike's wife wasn't ready to be a mom, so she ran off with someone else. Watching Mike suffer, tortured me because it made me realize how you and your dad must have felt when we left. Again, I am truly sorry for that.

I kept track of you through the years, and I came back to Ohio right after Mike was killed. I intended then to tell you about him. I actually came to the diner and saw the picture of your mom and dad. One of the waitresses told me why it was hanging there, and I just couldn't bring myself to tell you about Mike's death. I guess I thought it was better for you to keep thinking he was still out there somewhere. Anyway, I've made lots of mistakes in my life; many of them hurt you most of all. I hope you will forgive me somehow.

I'm sending Mark to you now. Please watch over him. He's a lot like his dad, and I hate to leave this world thinking he will have no one to turn to if things should get tough. I know you will do what's right by him.

I am truly sorry for the pain I have caused you.

Ralph Tyler"

For a long while, the two men sat in silence with their heads bowed. Attempting to conceal the tears swelling in his eyes, Frank shuffled the pictures around, staring at them without actually seeing them. "I really can't tell you much more than what was in the letter, Mark," he muttered in a voice raspy from his attempt to choke back tears. "But I would sure appreciate it if you would tell me about your dad. I had always hoped that someday he would come into the diner and see that stupid picture, and we could be together again." He hesitated and cleared his throat before he went on. "Anyway," he continued, "after Mom left, I cried myself to sleep every night for years, always wishing she would bring him back home. I didn't know she had died. Dad never told me. I'm not sure why. I guess he was so hurt that he didn't want to think about her ever again. Who knows what goes through a man's mind that has lost half of his family?"

"I'm sorry. I never knew anything about this part of my dad's story," Mark apologized. "I guess my dad was too young to remember anything about it, and my grandfather obviously never told him. What my grandfather said in his letter about my dad was true. My dad was terrific. I never knew my mom. I don't even know if she's still alive. I was just happy being with my dad and my grandpa. My dad was a quarter back in high school."

Mark fumbled through the pictures and pulled out one of

40

his dad in a football uniform. He handed it to Frank. "He worked with me from the time I was old enough to hold a football. After he died, grandpa continued coaching me. He was a football player too, maybe you already knew that about him. Anyway, that's how I got a scholarship to The Citadel—through football I mean. Otherwise, we'd never been able to afford it." He took in a deep breath. "It also helped that my dad was a decorated military hero," he said softly. He brushed a tear from his cheek. "He, uh.., he was killed in the first group of Marines that landed in Iraq on the 23rd of February, 1991. He saved his platoon by throwing himself across an in-coming. I was just seven when he died, and I missed him every day—still do."

"I guess that's another thing we have in common. I've missed him for years too. Tell me everything you can remember about him," Frank urged. "You look so much like him in these pictures. He had your blue eyes and dark hair, didn't he? I can remember everyone talking about how blue his eyes were when he was a baby."

"Yeah, we did look a lot alike. I have some pictures of him as a young boy. I'll send you some of him and some of me. You won't be able to tell which ones are him and which ones are me from our early pictures."

"So now you intend to follow his lead by joining the Marines. Was he career military?"

"Yes, the military was his life. He loved it. He joined the Marines right out of high school. He moved around a lot, but until the Gulf War, he was mostly stationed in the States, and I lived with my grandfather. My dad never had a chance to see me play high school or college ball."

41

"I'm sure he would have been very proud. Hell, I'm proud of you just hearing about your scholarship and all," said Frank reaching over and patting Mark on the shoulder.

"Thanks. Wow, this has been quite a day. I can't believe all that has happened in the last two hours." Mark picked up some of the pictures and put them back into the big envelope. He was still trying to sort out everything in his mind and had no idea what to say to his uncle. Finally, he muttered, "I was really impressed with how you all took care of that lady who lost her husband. You seem to be a very close group."

"Yeah, in a strange way, I guess we are. But honestly, the diner is all we have in common. We argue about everything under the sun, and we all lead our separate lives, but when something happens to one of us, the others are right there to lend a helping hand. Poor Meredith—Howard was a great guy. We're going to miss him around here. Every year he always came back from Florida with a story about the biggest fish he ever caught right off his dock. He did love it down there. I think the only reason he ever came back up here in the summer was to be with Sam and Leroy. The three of them made quite a trio."

"How'd you ever come to start up a diner?"

"To make a very long story, short," Frank answered, "as your grandpa indicated in the letter, my dad had an alcohol problem—one that he never licked. I went into the military straight out of high school and sent him all my money, which, of course, he blew on whiskey." Frank drew in a deep breath before continuing. "While I was

42

completing my first term in the Army, he got real sick, and I didn't re-enlist, so I could come home to take care of him. When I got back, I had to find work anywhere I could to pay for his doctor bills. I worked nights at a Waffle House and as a manager at Kroger during the day. I never went out, and I saved every penny I could. Eventually, I had saved enough money to take out a lease on this property, and as they say, the rest is history. I have a twenty-five-year lease that actually has to be renewed next year. Man, how time flies."

"Did you ever marry?"

"Nope. Came pretty close once, but I never really built up much trust in marriage. I think the letter sort of explains why that might be." He chuckled. "How long can you stay? I have an apartment nearby, and I'd love to hear more about you and your dad. I guess your grandpa actually isn't the evil person I pictured all these years, so I wouldn't mind hearing some more about him too."

"Honestly," said Mark, "he would have fit right in here with Leroy and Sam. He would have loved having some place like this to hang out. He got pretty lonely after I went off to college. We emailed and talked on the phone all the time, but after he got sick, I was never sure if he really knew who I was. I hated that. I missed him. It was hard to watch his mind come and go. It was like losing him over and over again."

"Yeah," said Frank with a look of sympathy. "I know what that's like. My dad had alcohol-induced dementia. I was never sure if he knew who I was either."

"I guess I could stay the night," said Mark. "I don't have any schedule other than that I have to report in at LeJeune by the first of September. I *would* like to get to know you better."

Franks eyes lit up. "Fantastic." He removed his apron and tossed it across the counter. "Let me just make sure all the grills and fans are turned off, and we can get out of here."

Strange, Mark thought to himself, *grandpa has never stopped taking care of me. God, I miss him.* He ran his hand nervously through his thick, wavy hair and put his sunglasses on to hide the tears in his eyes. He shrugged his shoulders and moved his head from side to side to relieve the tension building up in his body. "Can I help you with anything?" he asked as he followed Frank into the back room.

"Nope, I've got it. I could do this in my sleep." The lights in the dining room went off as Frank flipped several of the switches. "Why don't you wheel your bike in the front door? It'll be safer in here than parked out in front of my apartment. The neighborhood has been getting a little rough. I'm afraid I'm going to have to move into some place a little safer pretty soon. It's a shame, though. It's close to the diner, and I'm not one for too much change as you probably have guessed by now."

Mark looked at the empty space around the tables. The bike would take up a lot of that space. "Are you sure it's okay if I bring the cycle inside?"

"Sure, who cares? I'll wheel it out in the morning at five when I come in," answered Frank. He turned off the fan

44

above the grill and came around the counter to move a couple of tables to make enough room for Mark's bike.

"You start at five in the morning? That's like being in the Marines." Mark chuckled.

"Sort of, but my day ends at two in the afternoon. I love to fish in the summer and ski in the winter, and I like my evenings free. I'm a fan of football and NASCAR, so I've always kept the same hours for the diner—open to customers at six; close by two. That way, I only have to worry about breakfast and lunch meals. Evening meals are too expensive to serve, and customers are harder to please—something I learned while working at the Waffle House."

Mark already liked Frank. They had so many things in common it was uncanny. He and his dad also loved skiing, fishing, football, and auto racing. *Surely that kind of stuff isn't passed on through the genes.* He laughed. *Nah, that's just a male-thing.*

Chapter 3

As always, the traffic around the mall was heavy, and Jan was glad when she finally reached the entrance. Since the diner had closed early, she arranged to meet her daughter Olivia for lunch. Olivia had finally gotten a job at a small, retail store after weeks of trying to find someone who would hire her. She was bright and beautiful, but after her father's death, she started hanging out with the wrong crowd during her last year in high school. Until now, she hadn't held a job longer than a week because she would never show up on-time or simply would not show up at all. Jan had lost track of the number of times she had been fired. Olivia was belligerent and ignored everything Jan said or asked her to do. Somewhere in her twisted mind, Jan suspected that Olivia blamed her for Robert's death, even though Jan had done everything she could to make sure he got the best medical care available.

Olivia simply wouldn't admit that Robert's life style was the major cause for his poor health. He refused to go to the doctor, and he was terribly overweight. He simply was unable and unwilling to curb his appetite until it was too late. Eating was his escape from the reality that he had failed in other realms of his life. He was always scheming and chasing rainbows that ended in failure. Yet, he truly believed that each new venture would bring him wealth, but nothing ever came of any of his attempts.

46

Olivia always sided with her dad and blamed the world for taking advantage of his generous nature, cheating him out of millions of dollars that were his due. On his part, Robert made sure that Olivia had the best of everything, even if it meant using the money that should have paid their bills. Whatever she asked for, Olivia got. Reality had never touched her life until her dad's death. Then, she was forced to come face-to-face with the fact that he had left nothing for them but unpaid bills. Jan even had to borrow money to bury him.

As she pulled into a parking spot, she wondered what sort of mood Olivia would be in today. Her mood swings always went from dripping sweetness to horrid hatefulness. There was no middle ground with Olivia. Jan had arranged for her to get counseling after Robert died, but even that didn't work the way she had hoped. Olivia accused her of thinking that she was crazy, and at first, she refused to attend any of the counseling sessions. A month ago, she was involved with some friends in a stolen car incident, and a judge required her to attend counseling as part of her sentencing. She was now on medication to even-out her mood swings, but so far, Jan had not seen any real improvement in her behavior.

Jan made her way through the crowded mall to the shop where Olivia now worked. Olivia was busy with a customer, and Jan waited near the counter until she was finished.

"Hi, Mom," chirped Olivia. Jan smiled at her petite, young daughter. Olivia's blue eyes sparkled in the small spotlight that was shining down from the black ceiling, and her long eyelashes cast a shadow on her cheeks.

Olivia had Jan's curls, but she was blonde like her dad. She wore her hair short because it was too much effort to control the curls when it was long. Today she had a twisted scarf tied around her head with the ends dangling over her left ear—part of her Bohemian look that she still clung to, having vehemently rejected the more professional look that Jan had suggested to her.

When Olivia got her new job, Jan bought her some cute, short skirts and some feminine blouses that she had hoped she would wear to work, but they were still hanging in Olivia's closet with the tags still dangling from them. *I guess I should probably return them and get my money back*, Jan decided. She tried not to show her disapproval of Olivia's clothes, especially because her appearance blended in perfectly with the merchandise sold in the shop. The shop was full of gadgets and trinkets, adult games, glow-in-the dark velvet pictures, lava lamps, black lights, and other useless junk, but at least the owners were willing to take a chance on hiring her considering her track-record with other employers.

Jan knew that Frank had made this job possible for Olivia, but he would never admit it. The owner of the shop, Dick Tobin, had started out with a store in the same strip center where the diner was located. About six months ago, he moved his shop to the mall. When Frank suggested to Jan that Olivia apply at Dick's mall store, and she was immediately hired, Jan knew he had arranged this opportunity for her. She prayed that Olivia didn't blow it, but she was not optimistic.

"Hi, honey," responded Jan, relieved that she would be eating lunch with the sweet Olivia today.

48

"I'll just be a minute," Olivia responded.

"Take your time. I'll just look around."

"Mom, don't bother. You know there's nothing in here that you'd want." Olivia laughed at Jan's pretense of looking around at the cheap ear and toe rings. "You're much too straight-laced to enjoy the things we sell."

Jan knew that Olivia was right, but she retorted by sticking her tongue out at her and proceeded to look around the store as if she was interested in the merchandise. At last, Olivia rescued her, and they headed to the food court.

"Tell me," asked Olivia, "what in the world possessed Frank to close the diner early? Is he sick?"

Jan laughed. "No, he never gets sick; you know that. You'll never believe it, but you know that big picture of his parents that he hung in the front of the store?"

"Yeah, duh? How can you miss it? Don't tell me his long lost brother finally came into the diner and recognized their mom."

"No, not exactly." Jan told Olivia as much of the details as she knew about Frank and his nephew.

"Is he cute?" asked Olivia.

Jan laughed, not entirely surprised that Olivia had missed the sentimentalism of the reunion. "Well, Gina called him a hunk," she answered.

"We both know that Gina has poor taste when it comes to guys." Olivia sighed. "How would you categorize him on a scale from one to ten?"

"Hmm," said Jan. "I would say he's at least a 9, maybe a 10. He has beautiful, blue eyes and lots of dark, wavy hair, and he's a college graduate, headed for Camp LeJeune."

"Camp LeJeune? Where's that?"

"It's in South Carolina, I think. He's going into the Marines."

"Just my luck—I guess I won't waste my time checking him out."

"Why not?" asked Jan. "I think he would be a real catch, especially..."

"Especially, what?" shouted Olivia, causing the crowded food court to glance their way. "Especially for someone with as few options as me?" she screeched.

"Olivia, lower your voice. No, that was not what I was going to say, for heaven's sake. I was going to say, especially because he seems to be a nice guy. Jeez, why do you always have to assume that I'm thinking the worst of you?"

"Because you do!" snapped Olivia.

"No, sweetheart, you're the one who thinks so little of you, not me. I know the beautiful heart that's under the

50

coldness that you try to project. I just wish you could let yourself be you."

"Well, this turned out just great. Thanks, Mom." Olivia shoved back her chair and stormed out of the food court, leaving Jan sitting with a room full of staring shoppers.

Fighting back tears, she gathered up the uneaten food and headed for the shop. Olivia was nowhere in sight when she entered the store, so she left her food with another of the sales people who politely told her that Olivia was in the back.

"If you don't mind, just give her the food," replied Jan. "Tell her I had to go, and I'll see her later. Thanks," she muttered as she headed into the mall. Tears blurred her vision and smothered sobs threatened to choke her.

She sat in the car for a while gazing at the shoppers as they came and went through the large pillared entrance of the mall. *Why does it always end this way between us? Why does she shut me out? This is certainly not how I envisioned my life. I was going to be a college English professor, for god's sake. How'd this happen to me?* As tears flowed down her cheeks, the movie of her life ran through her mind.

At eighteen, she had taken a job as a waitress at a private club for the summer in her small hometown. She had just graduated from high school and had enrolled for fall classes at the local liberal arts college. Her life was carefully planned; the way she did everything. Then she met Robert. He was the manager of the food and beverage division of the club. He was handsome, energetic, and genuinely interested in her future. He was

51

also ten years older than she was and married with a family.

She looked forward to going to work every day, so she could be around him. He was much more sophisticated than the other waiters and college guys who constantly tried to get her to go out with them. Robert always paid more attention to her than he did to the other servers, causing them to gossip about her behind her back. He gave her the top tables and the most hours, so she would get the biggest tips, which made the others jealous.

Halfway through the summer, he told her that he was moving to California. He had been hired at a huge hotel on the beach as the general manager. He was elated, but she was crushed. The thought that she would never see him again was unbearable, so she did the unthinkable. She asked him if he would take her with him. He immediately agreed that it would do her some good to experience life outside of Pennsylvania.

Her parents were devastated, especially her father. *'How could you think about throwing away your plans for your future,'* he had shouted at her. *'You are bright. You have a dream. Why are you willing to disgrace yourself and us by chasing across the country after some older, married man? If you do this, don't ever think about coming back, we're through with you.'*

Her father and her older brother had gone to the club threatening to have Robert fired, but by pouring on his charm and engaging his ability to smooth talk his way out of anything, Robert easily calmed their anger. He assured them that he had only Jan's future in mind when he agreed to take her with him. '*After all,*' he had pointed out, '*how could Jan ever expect to be an accomplished writer or a skilled teacher if she has never been any further away than fifty miles from home?*' He had continued his defense by appealing to her brother to support her. '*Surely, as her brother, you recognize the importance of having some life experience before starting to college. Didn't you join the Navy for several years before finishing your degree?*'

Robert had also assured her family that he was happily married and would gladly arrange for them to have dinner with his wife and kids if that would ease their mind about his intentions. He also promised that he would arrange for Jan to take some classes at the University of California once she was settled in California. He was so convincing that Jan had been a little disappointed as she listened to the reasons that he was willing to take her with him—but not so disappointed that it stopped her from going with him.

Reluctantly, her parents had agreed to let her go, and by September, she found herself living in a small apartment in California. Robert's hotel was part of a huge, luxury chain with plush rooms and several large dining areas overlooking the ocean. Robert got her a job as a hotel maid, which gave her consistent hours. He had cautioned her not to let the others at the hotel know about their former relationship so as not to cast any suspicions on either of them.

Her attendance at the university was not mentioned, but she didn't care. She just enjoyed her strange, new life in California. The lifestyle there was totally opposite to that of upper Pennsylvania, and the weather was perfect.

53

The only disappointment about her new surroundings was that she rarely saw Robert. He was extremely busy as the general manager.

He and his family lived in an apartment in the hotel, so she saw his wife and kids as they came and went. Their paths had never crossed at the club in Pennsylvania, so they had no idea about her earlier relationship with Robert. The other maids and staff at the hotel gossiped about Robert and his family. According to the rumors, Robert and his wife often fought with one another. His wife was genuinely unhappy about living in the hotel. Despite the luxuries that hotel living afforded them, it was not the kind of environment she wanted for her kids. At one point, his wife left to go back to Ohio to visit relatives. That's when Robert began visiting her at her apartment.

At first, their meetings were platonic. He explained that he just needed a place to crash for a few hours to escape from the craziness of the hotel. She understood the pressure he had, and when she knew he was coming, she made it a point to have something healthful for him to eat and a tranquil atmosphere created by soft lighting and aromatic candles.

He talked a lot about his failing marriage and complained that his wife didn't understand the need for patience until he had established himself with the company. Jan's love and compassion for him continued to grow, but she kept her feelings to herself until one evening as he was leaving her apartment. He lingered at the door for a moment, then whirled around and took her into his arms. The next thing she knew, they were locked in a passionate embrace. Sometime in the night, he left her apartment while she lay exhausted—lost in

54

erotic dreams.

After that night, he spent more and more time with her at her apartment. His desire for her was insatiable, and she was more than willing to satisfy his needs. Eventually, his absence from the hotel began to arouse suspicions among his wife, his assistant, and the other hotel staff. Ultimately, he was fired, and she followed him to Texas. For the next several years, she followed him and his family from hotel to hotel, always living in a shabby apartment nearby and working at odd jobs, mostly in small restaurants. When her father suffered a heart attack, she told Robert she wanted to go home. He insisted on taking her there himself. She knew he was afraid she wouldn't come back, and he would have been right if things had been different at home.

They flew to Pennsylvania with the intention of returning the same day to Tennessee where Robert was currently the manager of a small Holiday Inn. She hated the deception that she was living. It made her feel cheap, but she was still very much in love with Robert and couldn't force herself to leave him. Whenever she would try to leave, he would beg her to stay, and she would.

When they landed at the airport in Pennsylvania, Robert rented a car to drive her to her parent's house. He dropped her off at the door and waited up the street from the house in the rental car. As Jan entered the front door of her parent's home, her mother met her in the hallway, screaming for her to get out and accusing her of causing her dad's heart attack. '*He has worried about you every day for years. You let us all down, especially him*,' her mother screeched.

Jan pushed past her mom and forced her way into her dad's room. When she saw him looking so frail and lost in the tall poster-bed, she threw herself across his chest and tried to hug him. He pushed her away and turned his head. "I'm so sorry, Dad. I know I've disappointed you."

Her father made no effort to reply or to even look at her, so she finally forced herself to leave. She fled from the house toward the rental car. Robert jumped out of the car and met her as she stumbled blindly down the street. He held her tightly and helped her into the car. She sobbed hysterically in his arms for a long time. He offered several times to go back to the house with her, but she'd told him that it would only make matters worse.

The flight home was spent in silence with intermittent sobs consuming her. Once they were back in her apartment, she finally said what she should have said years ago. "Robert, I can't go on this way. My mother was right. I have wasted my youth chasing you across the country and holding on to false hopes and dreams. I've hurt your family and mine, and I can't do that anymore. Please leave, and don't come back."

Robert had begged her to give him time enough to get a divorce. He promised that he would leave his family, and they could build a new life together. He begged her to wait for just another month. Not actually having many alternatives available to her, she had agreed. This time he kept his word. By the end of the month, he had filed for divorce, and they left together for Ohio. She got a job at the diner, and Robert worked as the food and beverage manager at another small Holiday Inn. They were married in a private ceremony at the diner and were

56

thrilled when she got pregnant with Olivia. Things went smoothly for them for a while, but Robert wasn't satisfied very long with working at the small hotel. He eventually talked some of his friends into investing in a bar, in a small town near Columbus. For several years, he was happy running the bar, and money was plentiful. He told her she could quit her job at the diner, but she didn't. She enjoyed the extra independence that the money gave her, and the hours allowed her to be home when Olivia got out of school.

Like his other ventures, the bar finally closed after Robert admitted to stealing money from it. After the bar closed, money was always an issue between them. Her salary covered the cost of their rent and utilities, and Robert worked at different small hotels in varying positions for the money he spent on Olivia.

When he got sick, he was forced to quit working. He died within a year of the discovery that he had pancreatic cancer. She buried him two years ago and had been trying to keep the roof over Olivia's head on her own. She knew that Olivia's life had been drastically changed. Her loveable, doting dad had been taken away, and she was left without any money or much hope for her future. Jan understood all of that, but it wasn't her fault. She wanted more for Olivia than she had settled for in her own life, but she had no idea how to give her what she wanted to give her.

Jan finally pulled herself together and backed the car out of the parking spot to head for home. As she was leaving the shopping mall, she wondered if Olivia would come home tonight. "I doubt it," she said aloud.

Chapter 4

Frank and Mark spent half of the night talking about their pasts. Frank learned a lot about the compassion of Ralph Tyler that he wished he had known before. It would have made his life a lot less bitter if he could have known that he was not actually a child that his mother didn't love enough to take with her and that his brother was being raised by someone who truly loved him. Useless anger and resentment about the secrets his father purposefully kept from him swelled and threatened to overcome the relief that Mark's arrival had brought him.

After Mark went to bed, Frank sat outside on his patio and let the tears that he had kept bottled up all day flow like raging rivers down his cheeks, soaking his shirt. Years of disappointment and feelings of rejection washed away, as he shamelessly sobbed like a child. At daybreak, he forced himself to go into the house to shower and shave. By the time he came out of his bedroom, Mark met him in the hallway. He was already dressed and had made a fresh pot of coffee.

"Good morning, Uncle Frank," he said. "You look like hell. Didn't you sleep at all last night?"

"I had a lot of bad memories that I had to shed last night, so this morning I feel like I obviously look. I suspect that this is going to be an extremely long day."

58

"Can I help you out at the diner? I've done my share of working in the dining hall at The Citadel. In addition to my scholarship, I was in a work-study program that required me to do at least twenty hours a week in some sort of college service. I spent most of my time working in the dining hall kitchen."

"Sure, if you feel like you want to spend your day doing that, we can always use the help," said Frank. "After we close, I'll take you fishing up at the dam."

"Sounds, great," replied Mark.

The two of them arrived at the diner at five o'clock, and while Frank fired up the grill, Mark moved his motorcycle outside and then started pulling the chairs down from the tables. "I take it you have a cleaning service that comes in to do the floors after you close. I bet they were surprised to see my motorcycle parked in here."

"No doubt. Did they move it or just mop around it, can you tell?"

Mark looked carefully at the tiles where his motorcycle had been parked. "It looks like they just mopped around it. They probably didn't want to run the risk of turning it over."

"Maybe not, but I don't think they're doing as good a job as they did when they first started out. That happens all the time. This is, at least, the fifth cleaning company I've had. I just don't get it. They start out great and then just seem to dwindle to almost nothing as time goes on."

"What can I do next?" asked Mark.

59

"You can grab a couple pounds of the bacon and four sausage steaks out of the freezer in the back. Bring up about five of the beefsteaks too. That's about how many we serve on a Monday morning."

"You really know your customers."

"Yeah, I rarely have any waste at the end of the day. We have a lot of regulars who eat the same thing day after day, so I pretty well can predict exactly what inventory I need to have ready, give or take a couple of surprises from newcomers."

For the next half hour, the two of them worked side-by-side doing the prep work. Frank was surprised at how efficiently Mark worked. With his help, the prep work went a lot faster. When Gina and Jan arrived, everything was done, and the two men were sitting at the counter enjoying a plate of eggs and bacon and sharing the newspaper.

"Well," said Gina, "this is something I've never seen before—Frank sitting at the counter reading the newspaper. Normally right about now, you're flying around here barking orders as we come through the door. Even the chairs are down. Did you two spend the night here?"

"Good morning, Gina," answered Frank, ignoring her insults.

"Don't get him used to having help, Mark," she said as she headed toward the back room. "You'll just make our life more miserable after you leave."

Frank was aware of Jan's careful scrutiny of him. She had obviously noticed his swollen, red eyes. He stared down at the newspaper, pretending to be engrossed in what he was reading.

"You look like hell, Frank," she whispered as she sat down next to him. "Are you okay?"

"I'm okay," he mumbled, finally looking directly at her. "Your eyes look a little swollen too. Did Olivia stay out all night again?"

Jan dropped her head, but Frank could still see the tears about to spill over onto her cheeks.

"Yes," she whispered. "I went to have lunch with her at the mall, and, as usual, she flew off the handle and stormed off. I just hope she doesn't do something stupid again. I hate it when I know she's out all night with her friends. Individually, most of them are okay, but when they get together, they always end up in some sort of trouble. Recently, she's picked up a couple of new friends that I don't know much about. I just hope she shows up at work today."

"I'll find out from Dick if he comes in today for lunch." Frank smiled and squeezed her hand.

"Here comes, Sam," announced Gina. She struggled with the long ties on her apron and ended up crossing it in the back and tying it around her tiny waist in the front. "It must be six o'clock."

"Good morning, everyone," boomed Sam as he came through the door. "Well, well, look at you," he said

61

noticing that Mark was sitting at the counter and was already eating. "Don't tell me I have competition for the first customer of the day award."

"Sam, I'd like you to meet my nephew, Mark Tyler," said Frank as he headed behind the counter. "It's a long story so don't ask. He just graduated from The Citadel, and he's headed for Camp LeJeune this September. Meanwhile, he's touring the country on his bike."

"Your nephew, huh?" remarked Sam. "Well, that must mean he's your brother's son, unless you have a long-lost-sister we haven't heard about. You realize, of course, that I've got to hear the details, so while you start frying my hot cakes, fill me in."

"Me, too," said Gina. "Do tell us the juicy little details. All of my soap operas eventually unfold the hidden little secrets. You can't keep us all guessing."

"I'll let Mark fill you in while I start Sam's pancakes. And, don't forget that this is a working diner, Gina. I don't expect to find you lingering around up here for more than a few minutes."

"Yes sir, commander," she answered, giving him a quick salute.

"Nice salute." Mark laughed. "I still have some trouble getting my arm to snap up like that."

Frank turned his back to the counter and scooped the pancake batter on to the hot grill. He listened as Mark began to explain to the others why he came to the diner. He enjoyed hearing Mark tell the story of their reunion in

62

his own words and smiled as he glanced over at Gina, who seemed to be mesmerized by either Mark or the story; he couldn't tell which. *Amazing*, he thought. *I've never seen her quiet for such a stretch of time.* He was impressed that Mark avoided disclosing to the others their shared emotional reaction to the letter and about his all-night crying fest. Mark simply related the facts about the letter and pictures and briefly told them about Frank's mom, her death, and his brother's adoption. He ended by telling them a little about his grandfather and his dad and about how he wished his grandfather could have had a place like the diner to go to every day. When he had finished the story, Frank turned around to face the others at the counter. The three of them just stood there looking at him in stunned silence.

Finally, Gina blurted out, "Wow, Frank. You must have gone through some pretty serious emotions when you heard all of this—that would explain the red, swollen eyes."

"Come on, Gina, let's get to work," said Jan quickly.

Frank flashed Jan a grateful smile. He knew she was trying to protect him from having to endure any more questions that Gina would most surely ask.

"Yesterday was quite a day around here," remarked Sam. "First, we got the news about Howard and then this. We haven't had this much excitement around here in a long time, maybe never. When the Lord closes a door—He always opens a window. I'm happy for you, Frank. So, now what happens with the big, old photo?"

"Haven't thought about that—I guess I'll just leave it. It

sort of keeps up the fifties theme, with the car and all."
He wanted desperately to change the focus of the
conversation. "What do you think about the Reds
dropping three to the Cardinals?" he asked.

"I can't believe they're going to come this close to the
title and then throw it all away," said Sam.

Frank was relieved that Sam took the hint and changed
the conversation to its normal chatter. *Thank goodness.
I'm not sure if I could have handled too much more talk
about the deaths of my brother and my mother.* He felt
cheated and angry when he thought about how he was
never told about them. *How could my father have been
so cruel as to hide the truth about them to m?. It's over.
Let it go,* he told himself.

To distract himself from his anger and resentment, Frank
turned his attention to Mark. He was a handsome, bright
young man. *I'm grateful to Ralph Tyler for his kindness
and sensitivity in sending him to me.* He watched Mark
as he joined the friendly banter between Sam and Gina.
His laugh was easy and unaffected. His sapphire, blue
eyes glistened with mischief when he baited Gina into
an argument about women in the military. Few people
could match Gina's quick wit, but Mark was able to hold
his own with her. *He's a terrific, young man,* he thought
and quickly turned back toward the grill as he felt the
tears welling up in his eyes again.

Around seven thirty, Tom arrived and plopped down on
his stool next to Mark. "You still here?" he asked.

"Yep," answered Mark. "This place kind of grows on you."

64

"I'll explain everything to you, Tom, as soon as Leroy gets here," Sam said, interrupting their conversation. "No sense going through the details more than once."

"What details?" asked Tom.

"Later," said Sam again. "I wonder if Meredith will show up here today. Poor woman, she has to be feeling pretty lonely right about now. I remember those first days; they're rough."

At eight o'clock sharp, Leroy sauntered through the double glass doors and right behind him was Meredith. Sam jumped up from his stool to lead her to her assigned seat.

"Good to see you," he said gently. "How're you doing?"

"The evenings are tough," she said. "But, when you have no choice, you've just got to make yourself go on. I know Howard wouldn't want me to *nurse the hurt* as he used to say. *'Just feel it then move on,'* he'd always remind me when I got upset about something. *'No need wasting a moment of this wonderful world pouting about what you can't change.'* He was quite a positive man." She heaved a deep sigh and plopped down on his stool.

"You still here, kid?" asked Leroy when he noticed Mark sitting at the end of the counter. "Are you from around here or just visiting?"

"Okay, Sam. What details were you talking about earlier?" asked Tom. "We're all here now, let's have it."

Sam cleared his throat and began to tell the details of Mark's arrival, but unlike Mark's straightforward account of the facts, Sam embellished the incident, telling it as a story, complete with his projection about the emotions that Frank and Mark had felt.

Frank caught Mark's eye, and they both smiled at the elaborations to the details. "You sure know how to tell a story," commented Frank when Sam was all through.

"I like to put a human side to the dry facts," responded Sam proud of his rendition of the tale.

"Well, I'll be damned," responded Leroy. "Welcome, young man and congratulations, Frank. It sure is nice when someone gets something he deserves. In the long run, persistence always pays off." He reached across the counter to shake hands with Mark. "Good story, Sam. Now we've got a happy ending to add to the legend of the picture. This place just gets more interesting every day." Then, turning to Meredith, he said, "See, you can't afford to miss a day or you get behind on what's happening around here. This place should be on TV as one of those reality shows or something."

"Hi, sweetie." Gina gave Meredith a quick hug and scurried behind the counter. She carefully lifted Howard's cup down from the shelf and filled it with coffee. She sat the cup down on the counter in front of Meredith. "What would you like, today? We've got to keep you healthy, so you can face all the horrible details of selling a house and all."

"Good morning, Gina. I'll just take a couple of pieces of rye toast and a grapefruit, if you've got it." Meredith glanced at the coffee cup, and she had to swallow hard to fight back the tears.

Frank winced when he noticed that Gina had served Meredith's coffee in Howard's special cup. *What is she thinking, for god's sake?* He watched Meredith look down at the cup and then hesitate before picking it up. *She's probably thinking about how Howard would feel about her using his cup. No doubt she's too polite to say anything that might hurt Gina's feelings.*

"Meredith, I'm sorry," said Gina when she noticed Meredith's hesitation. "I should have asked you if you wanted to use Howard's cup. I just wasn't thinking."

Frank smiled. *Way to go, Gina. Better late than never,* he thought to himself.

"That's okay, Gina," said Meredith. "It was a thoughtful thing for you to do, but to be honest, Howard would never let anyone drink out of his cup, not even me." She smiled and pushed the cup gently toward Gina.

"I hope you don't think I would offer the cup to anyone else but you," replied Gina. "Here, let me get you a good, ol' *Frank's Diner* mug." She carefully washed Howard's cup and placed it back in its spot on the shelf. "My bad," she whispered to Frank as she took Meredith another cup. "Don't you dare say a word. I know I blew it," she threatened.

"I wasn't going to say anything," teased Frank, "but I *am* proud of you for once in your life admitting that you actually made a mistake." He laughed when she glared at him with a look that plainly said *drop* dead.

67

"Hey, Jan. Look what the cat's about to drag in," yelled Gina motioning out the window.

~~~~~

Jan turned around to see Olivia and two other girls pile out of a car. She didn't recognize the car or the girl driving it. The second girl was Olivia's friend, Lisa, who had been arrested several times for drugs and shoplifting. *Oh great, I thought Olivia had agreed that Lisa was a bad influence on her.* She glanced at the clock knowing that Olivia was due at the mall by ten. She was relieved to see her and to know that she was all right, but disappointed that she had been out with Lisa all night and that she wasn't at home getting ready for work. *Don't say anything to upset her,* she reminded herself. *You'll only make things worse. Darn it. Why won't she grow up and take some responsibility? She's just like Robert.*

"Hey, Gina, how's it going?" asked Olivia as she entered the diner. She ignored Jan's presence completely.

"Aren't you going to say good morning to your mom, young lady?" reprimanded Gina. "I swear, Olivia, when are you ever going to show her the respect she deserves?" She sighed and shook her head at Olivia. "Who's your new friend?" she continued. "I don't recall seeing you around here before. I'm Gina," she said offering her hand to Olivia's friend.

"Nice to meet you, Gina. I'm Teresa Thomas," the young woman mumbled coolly.

"Hello, Lisa," Gina muttered icily.

68

Jan smiled as she noticed that Gina didn't even attempt to hide her obvious dislike for Lisa.

"Hi," responded Lisa cheerfully, completely oblivious to Gina's coldness.

Jan watched Gina glare at Olivia as if to remind her that Lisa was bad news. Gina was able to get through to Olivia, when Jan couldn't. *I'm so grateful that she understands what I'm going through with Olivia. Thank god, she's on my side.* From the expression in Gina's eyes, it was obvious that she didn't care much for Teresa either. Jan knew that Gina was remarkably insightful and an excellent judge of character. She could size up a person in the flicker of an eye. *I hope she tells Olivia how she feels about her choice of friends,* thought Jan. *Olivia will take it better from her than she will from me.*

"Hi, Mom," Olivia muttered as Jan gave her an unappreciated hug. "Teresa, this is my mom."

"It's nice to meet you, Teresa," said Jan. As the girls chatted to Gina about their all night events, Jan continued to stare at Teresa. She looked older than her daughter and Lisa. Why would someone her age be hanging out with younger girls? She has to be close to thirty. I don't like *this*, she decided, *but what can I do about it? Nothing; absolutely nothing.* She could feel Olivia watching her. *Put on a happy face*, she reminded herself. She reached around Olivia's waist and gave her another affectionate squeeze. She felt Olivia stiffen, and she quickly twisted away from Jan's embrace.

"What can I get you, ladies?" asked Gina. "Or, are you here just to check out the hunk? That's him sitting next

69

to Tom. Not bad, huh?"

"Well, for once I have to agree with you, Gina. He *is* a real hunk," said Olivia, continuing to stare at Mark.

"Come with me, sweetie. I'll introduce you," offered Jan. "On second thought, wait here. I'll ask him to come back to your table, so he can meet all of you." She hurried off to get Mark, still feeling hurt and angry about Olivia's treatment of her.

~~~~~

Mark laughed good-naturedly when Jan requested that he visit the girls at their table, but he willingly headed over to where they were sitting. "Good morning, ladies," he said. "Which one of you is Olivia? No. Wait. It must be you," he said turning to Olivia. "You look like your mom."

"I do not. I look like my dad," Olivia retorted.

"I don't know your dad, but I have eyes, and you are the spitting image of your mom," he insisted. "And, if I were you, I'd consider that a real compliment. Gina, why don't you let me take this table? I think I can handle it," he said, smiling.

"Be my guest." She shrugged and glanced at Olivia with a smirk of surprise on her face. "Watch it girls, he's new at this—at least, I think he's new at this, but what do I know?"

"So ladies, what's it going to be?" asked Mark. "You

70

name it; we'll fix it." He enjoyed the flirty smile that Olivia flashed at him. *She's gorgeous,* he decided. *Despite her attempt to hide her good looks with unflattering clothes— like that squirrely band around her head and those gargantuan hoop earrings that are resting on her shoulders—she's lovely. She's obviously a rebel,* he concluded. *Why else would someone purposefully create such an unflattering look? She looks so much like Jan though; it's uncanny. Why wouldn't she be proud of that? Must be one of those mother-daughter things that women go through. She'll wise up some day—hopefully, for Jan's sake.*

"We'll all just take some yogurt and trail mix, but go easy on the trail mix," said Olivia sweetly. She smiled up at Mark and stared deeply into his eyes.

He returned her smile with a slight wink and headed back to the grill. Jan was already filling a bowl with trail mix and yogurt. "Make that three bowls of that mix," he said.

"Did they give you a rough time?" she asked.

"Nah. I enjoyed the full body scans that they shamelessly gave me." He chuckled as Jan gave him a disapproving look. "Olivia is a beautiful, young lady, just like her mom."

"Don't tell her that," said Jan. "She'll hate you for life."

"Too late, I already did," Mark replied. "I sense that you two are suffering from the perennial mother-daughter conflict. She'll out grow it eventually, according to my psych courses," he added.

"I hope so. If she doesn't change pretty soon, I'm afraid one of us is going to disappear."

Mark smiled. "Women and their hang-ups," he said as he returned to the table expertly balancing the three bowls of trail mix on his arm and carrying a large pitcher of water in the other hand. "Here you go, ladies." His gaze lingered on Olivia. She smiled at him, and he could see pleasure dancing in her beautiful blue eyes. She obviously enjoyed looking at him as much as he enjoyed looking at her.

"Is that your motorcycle out there?" asked Teresa.

"It is," said Mark. "When you're finished, come on out, and I'll take you a spin around the block." He shifted his gaze from Olivia to Teresa. He really hadn't paid any attention to her before. Now, as he stared more closely at her, he noticed that she seemed older than Olivia and the other girl. There was also something callous or hard about her. Her eyes were cold and unfriendly, especially when compared with the sparkling exuberance of Olivia's deep, blue eyes. *I should ask Jan about her. I can't imagine why she would be hanging out with such younger, less sophisticated girls. Strange,* he thought as he walked away from them and joined the others at the counter.

"Hey, has anyone seen Unabomber 2?" asked Gina. "He's usually here by now."

"Unabomber 2?" repeated Mark. "Don't tell me—he was the guy sitting all alone in the back booth yesterday, right? The one that gave Meredith the candy."

"Right," said Gina. "He's been coming in here for years. He rides up on that old, two-wheeler with all the baskets and junk attached to it. I can't ever get him to talk. He just sits there and writes numbers over and over, but I've noticed that it's a different number every day."

"He might be autistic," said Mark. "I did a case study of a guy like that for my final project in my last psych course."

"That's the second time you've mentioned a psych course," said Jan. "Was psychology your major at The Citadel?"

"Yes. I intend to get my Masters in Psychology while I'm in the Marines. I want to work with marines who suffer from PTSD—Post Trauma Stress Disorders."

"I just hope to God," said Gina, "that you don't end up as one of your own patients. I love my country, but I think that war is nothing more than a male hormone thing," she said, glancing once again out the window.

"Whoa, Gina," said Sam. "Every guy sitting up here spent some time fighting for your freedom."

"That just proves my point—it's a stupid male thing. Why can't you guys work things out peacefully? Think of all the money and lives you waste by going to war."

 Mark watched her as she walked away from the counter and stared through the door at the busy street. *She's obviously genuinely worried about Unabomber 2*, he thought.

"Oh good, here he comes," she said. "Oh no, look at his poor bike. The front wheel is all busted."

Mark glanced out the window. "Forget the bike; look at his head," he responded. "He's got a nasty gash over his eye that looks like it needs some attention."

Teresa glanced out the window, and Mark noticed a look of contempt in her eyes. She quietly laughed and motioned for Lisa and Olivia to look at the bike. Lisa laughed, but he noticed that Olivia refused to look. She dropped her head as if she was embarrassed by the response of her friends. *I definitely do not like Teresa,* Mark decided. *She's hard and cruel. Why would Olivia be friends with someone like her?*

"Poor guy," muttered Meredith. "Someone needs to do something," she said sliding down from her stool and heading toward the door.

"Wait, Meredith, I don't think you should…" started Mark, but Meredith was already out the door before he was able to stop her.

"Wow, that's a mess," Meredith said as she approached Unabomber 2. "You've obviously had an accident."

Unabomber 2 completely ignored her and simply continued to stare sadly at his mangled front wheel.

"I want to thank you for your kindness toward me yesterday," continued Meredith. "Leaving me the candy was a very thoughtful thing to do, and I was hoping that you would allow me to repay your kindness by letting me put some ice on that nasty bump on your head. I would
74

really like to help you the way you helped me yesterday, if you'll let me, that is."

Unabomber 2 stood motionless. He kept his head bowed, but his whole body stiffened. Suddenly, he grabbed up his bike and started to push it toward the street.

"Oh no," groaned Gina as she watched from inside the diner. "I was afraid of this."

"Wait," called Meredith to Unabomber 2. "Please. I didn't mean to upset you. I'll just go back inside, and you can come in and have your breakfast. I'm truly sorry. It's just that you need to put some ice on that bump. I'll just leave some wrapped in a napkin in your booth, just in case you decide you need it," she said.

"I'll get the ice," said Gina as Meredith came back into the diner.

"I'm sorry, Gina," said Meredith looking genuinely apologetic. "I just wanted to help him. He needs to stop the swelling of that bump, but it's obvious he's not going to let anyone do it for him."

"No one should look out the window or look up if he decides to come in," instructed Mark. "It doesn't surprise me that he didn't want anyone to help or touch him."

After several minutes, they were all relieved when Unabomber 2 finally opened the door and came into the diner. Without looking up, he went straight to his booth. He took his yellow pad out of his grubby backpack and laid it on the table, shoving the napkin with the ice to the

75

side. Gina immediately grabbed a cup of coffee and a Danish muffin for him.

Mark carefully watched him from across the room. *He certainly is a study in contrasts,* mused Mark. His fingernails were packed with dirt and his hair was long, but it was neatly trimmed and clean. He was also clean-shaven, and his skin was smooth and tanned. *I don't think he's homeless because his clothes are pressed, even though they are stained at the knees with dirt,* Mark decided. There was a hole in one knee of his jeans, where Mark could see a bloody cut. *He must have cut his knee when he fell from his bike.* He glanced down at feet. He was wearing expensive athletic shoes.

"Good morning," Gina said as she put the coffee and Danish down on the table inside of Unabomber's booth. "I was worried about you. You're a little late. I'm sorry about your bike," she babbled as she started to walk away. Then, she quickly whirled back around and blurted out, "You need to put that ice on your stubborn head or you'll forget how to use all those numbers you're always writing down."

To everyone's surprise, Unabomber grabbed the napkin and pushed it against his head.

"Well, now you're showing some sense," said Gina, walking away. "If you need some help fixing that front wheel, be here at two o'clock this afternoon, and Frank will have it fixed in no time. He can fix anything."

"That Gina's a cat bird I tell you." Sam shook his head. "She can make anyone do what she wants them to do."

76

"She's kind of scary," admitted Mark, but he was impressed with her caring attitude toward Unabomber 2. *Frank is right. She worries about everyone. I wonder who worries about her.*

"Her bark's a whole lot worse than her bite," said Frank. "Remind me to ask Jeff and Colin tomorrow if they know Unabomber 2's real name. They might be able to tell us more about him," he added.

"I think I know it," said Meredith. "There's a plate on the front bar of his bike. It read Property of Kenneth Talbert."

"Kenneth? He doesn't look much like a Kenneth," said Jan. "Nice work, sweetie," she said as Gina plopped down on one of the empty stools. "That knot looked like it was getting bigger by the minute."

"I know. He's got a nasty cut right above his right eye, and one on his knee too, but I don't think he needs stitches." said Gina. "By the way, Frank. I told him you'd fix his bike after you closed at two."

"You what?" said Frank, spinning around from the grill. "I don't know anything about bicycles."

"You're always bragging about being able to fix anything. Now's your chance to prove it."

Sam laughed. "She's got you, Frank. You'd better hope he doesn't show up."

"Why don't we all chip in and buy him a new bike," suggested Meredith.

"Nice idea," commented Mark, "but did you really get a good look at that bike. It's his life. There's no way he would appreciate a new bike. There's a bike shop down the road that we passed this morning on our way here. I'll run down and see if I can pick up a new wheel for his bike."

"It looks like it's a 26" Schwinn," said Tom. "Changing the wheel should be pretty easy, Frank. I wish I could hang around to watch this, but I've got to go. I don't mind chipping in to pay for a new wheel."

"Count me in," said Sam.

"Me too," replied Leroy. "How much do you need?"

"I want to contribute too," said Meredith.

"OK. I'll get the wheel, and we can split the cost tomorrow," said Mark.

~~~~~

Jan glanced up at the clock. It was nine o'clock and clearly time for Olivia to be heading home to freshen up before she was due at the mall. She had hoped that she wouldn't have to be the one to mention the time to her, but it didn't appear that Olivia was going to accept responsibility on her own.

"I saw you look at the clock, Mom," sneered Olivia as Jan approached. "We're just leaving. I have plenty of time to get home and out to the mall in an hour."

78

"I wanted to ask you if we could plan something for tonight," suggested Jan. "Other than our brief lunch yesterday, I haven't seen much of you lately, and I would really like to have a chance for the two of us to talk, or maybe go to a movie."

"Why don't we invite Mark and Frank over? They'd probably appreciate one of your delicious, home-cooked meals." Olivia smiled and kissed Jan's cheek. "Gotta go. See you at home around six."

Jan was speechless. The sweet Olivia was back. *I wonder if she just took her pills.* She immediately felt guilty about thinking such thoughts. *What's wrong with me? That's not being fair. Nevertheless, I'm not stupid. If it wasn't the pills, then it must be the possibility of spending more time with Mark that's the motive behind her willingness to stay home. Oh well, at least she'll be home.* She sighed and began to clear off the girl's table.

"I guess we'll have to take a rain check on the motorcycle ride, Mark," said Teresa. "But I would like to just sit on it for a minute. Can you spare the time, Olivia?"

"Sure, I have plenty of time to get to work," answered Olivia, frowning as Jan glanced up at the clock again.

"Mark, do you mind?" Teresa continued. "My brother and I used to ride. It's been a long time since I felt the thrill of sitting on a motorcycle."

"No, I don't mind," answered Mark. "Be my guest. I'll come out and make sure it doesn't tip over on you,"

Jan stared in amazement at Teresa. *Why in the heck*
79

would she want to try to straddle a motorcycle in that short, tight dress? She certainly doesn't look like the motorcycle type. I can't picture her enjoying the wind messing up her carefully coiffed hairdo. I wonder if she knows that you don't wear Pradas on a motorcycle. She chuckled at her mental image of Teresa on a motorcycle in her stilettos, but Teresa fooled her. Through the window she watched as Teresa hiked up her tight skirt and threw her leg and Pradas easily across the wide seat. *Hmm. Guess I was wrong. She obviously has ridden a motorcycle before, but not recently I bet.*

"There you go, Frank," said Sam, watching the young people out the window. "Just buy yourself a motorcycle. It's obviously a girl magnet."

"That's a good idea, Sam." Gina laughed. "Maybe Mark will let you borrow it for an evening," she said. Her infectious giggle caused Sam and Meredith to burst out laughing too.

"Go wait on the customers, Gina," Frank growled.

Chapter 5

Kenneth pushed his wrecked bike along the curb. He hadn't gone very far from the diner when some young teens passed him, yelling obscenities at him from their car. He never looked up. He was focused on getting to the park located several blocks from the diner.

At last, he reached his favorite tree at the edge of the park entrance where he spent every afternoon. It had taken him longer to get here today because he couldn't ride his bike. Glancing at the broken wheel, he felt angry again. Quickly grabbing his yellow pad, he hurried to his tree. He had learned to control his anger and his anxiety by writing down numbers on his yellow pad. He wrote down all sorts of numbers—addresses, license plates, phone numbers, winning lottery numbers, scores of sporting events—it didn't matter what kind of number. Once he saw or heard a number, it just whirled around in his head until he wrote it down.

He quickly flipped to a new page of the yellow pad and began writing 2:00. Once he started writing down the number, he relaxed and began to think about other things. Today, he had a lot of things to think about. He thought about the big, black car that had gotten so close to him this morning that it caused him to hit the sewer cover. He had been angry and had pounded his head on the curb. He knew that he shouldn't pound his head, but when he lost control, he always did it.

He thought about Meredith at the diner. He realized that she wanted to help him with the bump on his head. He shouldn't have gotten upset with her because her husband had just died, but he didn't want her to touch him or to put the ice on his head. He didn't like to be touched by other people—especially by people he didn't know. He thought about Gina. From the way she yelled at him about the ice, he knew that she was upset with him. He didn't want her to be angry with him again, so he would have to go back to the diner at two o'clock— what he didn't understand was how Frank could fix his bike.

I know that I'm different, that's why people are sometimes frightened of me and sometimes make fun at me and do bad things to me. He thought about the big, black car that had pushed him into the curb. *People think that I don't understand them when they talk to me, but they're wrong. I do understand most of what they say— sometimes I have to think about things for a while and sometimes I realize that I didn't understand correctly, but I do understand most of what I hear.*

There was a lot that Kenneth liked about his life and some things that he didn't. He liked caring for flowers. They were simpler to understand than people were. Flowers simply needed water and sunshine and some pruning and fertilizer, and they would grow. They made the yard look pretty. He had learned a lot about flowers, and in the winter, he grew them in his green house. In the summer, he liked getting up early in the morning and working in the garden before he went to the diner. He glanced down at his mud-stained hands and noticed the dirt on his pants and shirt. He often forgot to clean up before he left for the diner because he didn't want to be late. No one at the diner seemed to care, but his grandmother worried about him when he left the house in his dirty garden clothes.

He liked experimenting with his flowers and working with his friend from the university to learn new things about them. They often grafted a cutting from one type of flower to the stem of another to create a new flower or a different color. He liked color—but he didn't like black. His thoughts jumped to the black car again, and he had to concentrate hard to stop thinking about it. That was one thing that he didn't like about his life—his mind jumped around a lot. He liked to think about lots of things, but often it was hard to think about the same thing very long. His mind would jump from one thing to something different, and he would often forget what he started out thinking about. He didn't like it when his mind jumped. He didn't like it either when he wanted to say something but couldn't get the words to come out the same way he heard them in his mind. He had given up trying to talk with anyone but his grandmother and Dr. Melville, his friend from the university. They were patient with him and could understand what he was talking about, even when the words came out wrong.

~~~~~

Ben, the on-duty park ranger, noticed Kenneth pushing his bike to his usual resting place. He rarely bothered Kenneth, but today he was concerned when he saw the mangled front wheel of his bicycle and the dry trickle of blood on his head. He waited until Kenneth had settled with his yellow pad before he approached him. Then, he pulled an alcohol wipe and a bandage from his first-aid kit and walked to Kenneth's tree.

The park rangers knew all about Kenneth. When he first started showing up at the park, the rangers were bombarded with complaints from concerned parents and others about the strange man sitting under a tree scribbling numbers on a yellow pad. Through the local police, the rangers learned about Kenneth's history and, from then on, they accepted and promoted him as part of the intrigue of the park. They looked for him every day during good weather and tried to make sure that no one harassed him. In inclement weather, he would still come to the park, but shortly after he would appear, his grandmother would show up in her car, load up his bike, and take him home.

"Good morning, Kenneth," said Ben. "It looks like you've had a bit of an accident." He sat down on the ground near Kenneth to get a closer look at the laceration on Kenneth's head and to make sure his eyes were working together. "Did you see that white squirrel in that tree over there?" he asked. "There's a nest up there. White squirrels are rare around here. You shouldn't miss seeing this one."

Kenneth glanced toward the tree where Ben had pointed out the squirrel, and Ben was able to see that his pupils were functioning properly, relieving him of concern that Kenneth might have suffered a head injury. "I've brought a couple of things from the truck that you should use to clean off the blood on your face. There's a wipe for cleaning off the cut and a bandage to keep the germs out of it. You should use them, so you won't get sick. I wouldn't want you to miss coming to the park during this beautiful weather." Ben hesitated before leaving, noting that Kenneth had filled a page on the yellow pad with the number 2:00. "Well, I've got to go check on some fisherman down at the pond. You know

84

where the ranger station is, right?" Kenneth didn't respond, and Ben continued. "If you start to get a bad headache or begin to feel sick to your stomach, make sure you come over there right away, okay?"

Kenneth finally nodded his head, and Ben was satisfied that he had understood his concerns. When he returned to his truck, he pulled out the information on Kenneth that the rangers kept on file. He would feel better if Kenneth's grandmother knew that he had been in an accident. He dialed the number for Edith Talbert.

~~~~~

Edith glanced at the clock on her way to answer the phone. She was worried about Kenneth today. She didn't know why, she just was. She prayed that the call wasn't some bad news. "Hello," she said out of breath from her rush to the phone.

"Mrs. Talbert, this is Ben Carter, from the Metro Park."

"Yes, Ben. I know who you are. Is Kenneth okay?"

"That's why I'm calling you. He's okay, but it appears that he's had some sort of an accident. The front wheel of his bicycle is twisted, and he has a nasty bump and small cut on his forehead. I thought you might want to drive over here to check on him."

"I'll be right there," she said quickly hanging up the phone.

It was a short drive to the park, and Edith spotted her

grandson right away. He was leaning up against his favorite tree and writing on his yellow pad. She slowly walked up to him, keeping an appropriate distance to let him adjust to her being there. "Kenneth, sweetheart, you have a bad bump on your head. Why don't you put your bicycle on the rack of the car, and let me take you home?" she said softly.

Kenneth became extremely agitated, wringing his hands and pounding his head up against the tree. She knew that he was trying to form the words in his head to tell her something. At last, he simply blurted out "two o'clock, diner; two o'clock, diner."

"Okay," she responded. "If you're head isn't bothering you, I'll just go back home, and I'll see you after two o'clock when you get finished at the diner." Noticing the alcohol wipe and bandage on the ground beside him, she added, "You should use the wipe that Ben must have left for you and clean off your head before you go to the diner. The bandage will help keep the dirt out of the cut. I'll fix a special dinner tonight, and we can eat outside on the patio. I love the way you arranged the new garden this morning. It really shows off your latest roses," she said.

She noticed that Kenneth immediately relaxed when she talked about the roses. She was glad she had thought to mention them. Once back in her car, she watched as he reached for the alcohol wipe and bandage. She knew that he didn't like for her to worry about him, but she just couldn't help it. Each time he left the house, she was on edge until he came back. He was capable of handling himself under most circumstances, but his unwillingness to try to communicate with strangers and his obsession

86

with writing numbers often made him the subject of ridicule by uncaring, ignorant people.

Her greatest concern was his tendency to bang his head with his fists or against something when he became angry or highly agitated. She wondered if that was how he got the cut on his head. He tried very hard to control those behaviors, but when something interfered with his daily routine or made him angry, he lost his battle for self-control. Writing down numbers that were somehow meaningful to him was his way of coping with anger and tension. He only wrote the numbers when he was away from home. He never used his yellow pads when he was with her or with Dr. Melville.

He was such a sensitive and talented person, but only she and Dr. Melville knew about his incredible creativity and his brilliant knowledge of plants. He was particularly knowledgeable about flowers of all kinds—but roses were his favorite. *If only the world could see his creations, they would certainly see him in a different way.* She and Dr. Melville had both tried to get him to pursue a degree in horticulture, but he resisted their attempts. He was convinced that he would never be able to prove what he knew without the language skills required in a classroom. His unfortunate experiences in high school had confirmed that to him.

Before leaving the park, she drove around to the ranger station. She wanted to thank Ben for his call. The rangers had always been so good about calling her whenever there was a concern about Kenneth. She spotted Ben's truck parked near the fishing pond and waited until he came toward her. "Thank you very much, Ben, for calling me. I know that watching after Kenneth isn't part of your job description, but I certainly appreciate your interest and concern for him."

"It's my pleasure, Mrs. Talbert. Do you think he's okay? I was sort of worried that he might have a concussion, but his pupils responded to the change in light okay."

"I think he's okay. I take it you left him the antiseptic wipe and the bandage. I saw him open them. You may know that, with his disorder, he has a very high tolerance of pain and doesn't even realize sometimes that he's been hurt."

"Yes, I know," responded Ben. "I noticed that he was writing 2:00 on his notepad today. Does he have to be somewhere at two o'clock?"

"I think he wants to be at the diner down the street at two. At least, that's what I got from our conversation."

"I'll stop by around one, and let him know the time."

"Oh, that won't be necessary," replied Edith. "Unlike some people with autism, Kenneth has a keen sense about time. I'm sure if he has somewhere to be, he'll leave in order to arrive on time. Thanks again for your help. I think he's okay. I plan to drive by the diner at two o'clock to see if I am right about his wanting to be there. I think they close at two, so it seems a little strange that he wants to be there at that time. It's unusual for him to change his daily routine."

"Just let us know if you need anything. Kenneth has become an important part of the park. There are all sorts of urban legends floating around about him. You would
88

laugh at some of the wild stories I've heard people tell."

"He's just a wonderful grandson, trapped in a world of his own that no matter how hard he tries, he can't escape from. I love him very much, and the ignorance and intolerance that others display toward him breaks my heart—even his own parents have essentially abandoned him. They were going to put him in an institution when he was diagnosed with autism. His idiosyncrasies interfered with their social life. I intervened, and they finally agreed to establish a trust fund for him and let him come to live with me. I wouldn't have missed the wonderful moments I've had with him for anything in the world. He truly is special, but not just in the way that others see him," she added.

"He's lucky to have you, and please know that we'll do everything we can to keep others from mistreating him while he's in the park."

"I know you will. I'm grateful more than you'll ever know. His visits to the park are an important part of his daily regimen. He has a hard time when his routine is changed, even when the weather interferes."

"I know. I'm glad you come to get him during bad weather. I always worry about him, especially when it is so cold."

"Well, I won't take any more of your time. Thanks, again."

"You're welcome—anytime," replied Ben.

Back in her car, Edith glanced at her watch. It was only

89

eleven o'clock. She would have time to go to the grocery and be back in time to run by the diner at two.

~~~~~

At the diner, Gina examined the wheel that Mark had gotten for Unabomber's bike. She was glad that Mark was so thoughtful. He was a welcome addition to the *Frank's Diner* family. "Thanks, Mark. This looks like the right size wheel. I appreciate your willingness to help with this."

Mark smiled. "I hope we can carry this off. Uncle Frank, I'm assuming you have some tools around here," he said. "The guy at the shop told me how to replace the wheel. Since the bike isn't one of those complex road bikes with all of the gears, changing the wheel seems to be pretty straight forward."

"Well, well, well. The cavalry has arrived. You're one lucky dog, Frank, ol' boy," said Gina, pointing out the window. She was surprised to see Sam once again pulling into the diner parking lot. He typically left every morning right after breakfast because of the work he had to do at the farm. He never came back for lunch. "Sam, you are an angel," she said as he came through the door.

"I came back just in case Frank needed some help with the bike," he said. "I brought my tool box with me. It should have everything that we need."

"Good," said Frank. "I have some tools in the back, but most of my stuff is at home."

"Likely story," teased Gina. "I bet you've never fixed

anything in your life except these wobbly tables. I've watched you try to tighten the screws under the table tops. You fumble around worse than any woman. You're just lucky that Sam here was kind of enough to come back to bail you out." She gave Sam a quick pat on the back and walked away laughing at the thought of Frank trying to fix the bike himself.

"Gina, you're merciless," said Jan.

"She is," agreed Frank. "I always look forward to Tuesdays because Kelley's back, and it's her day off," he said gruffly.

"Oh, you miss me when I'm not here. I know you do," Gina replied.

"The only one who misses you is Unabomber 2. He's a nervous mess when you aren't here. Poor guy, why anyone could miss your presence is a mystery to me," growled Frank.

"If I thought you weren't teasing, Frank, I'd fly over that counter and relieve you of some that wavy brown hair!"

"OK—time out, you two," said Jan. "Come on, Gina, let's start filling up the salts and peppers, so we can get out of here on time. By the way, Olivia suggested that we have you all over for dinner tonight. I think she wants to have a closer look at our resident hunk," she added, smiling at Mark. "What about you Sam; you want to join us for some lasagna?"

"I'd love to, but I'll have to take a rain check on that. I told Meredith that I would stop by this evening to be with her when she met with the realtor who was going to list her house —and none of your snide remarks, Gina," he quickly added.

"What?" screeched Gina, feigning wounded pride. "I wasn't going to say anything. I think it's nice that you're willing to help Meredith—so there! And, about dinner, Jan. I'd love to come, but I already have a hot date tonight. I promised Kelley that I'd take her kids to the mall for a while, so she could have some peace and quiet when Carl calls her tonight. But, I'd better have some lasagna waiting for me when I get back on Wednesday— and some garlic bread too," she added.

Jan took off just before two o'clock, but Gina waited around just in case Unabomber 2 did show up. She knew that he would probably feel more comfortable if she was there. At two o'clock sharp, Kenneth pushed his bicycle on to the sidewalk in front of the diner and stood silently beside it. Gina spotted him and realized that he wasn't sure what to do next. She immediately went out to meet him, carrying the new bicycle wheel with her. "I'm glad you came back." She smiled at him, hoping to help him relax. "I see you have a bandage over that cut. That's a good thing. The guys are coming out to fix your bicycle. Here's the new wheel they got for you. See, it's just like your other one, only it isn't all smashed."

When he started rocking back and forth and wringing his hands, she realized that she needed to tell him what to do. "It's okay," she said soothingly. "Why don't you come on into the diner and bring your notepad? You can wait in here until they're finished." She put the new wheel down and headed back inside. "I'm not sure this is all going to happen," she said softly to the others as she came back into the diner.

"Just give him some time," said Mark.

After several minutes of pacing back and forth, Gina saw Unabomber reach for his notepad and head toward the diner. He came through the door and went straight to his booth. She grabbed the coffee pot and a Danish she had held back. She served it to him just like she did every morning. "I saved this for you," she said. "The guys are going to go out now and work on your bike. It'll take them a little while because they aren't too good with tools, but they'll figure it out pretty quick. Sam is the expert; he'll have it fixed in no time," she chattered.

"She never misses a chance for a good jab." Frank shook his head and laughed as the three of them headed outside to work on the bicycle.

~~~~~

From her car, in the parking lot across the street from the diner, Edith watched in amazement at the scene that was unfolding in front of her. The folks at the diner had obviously made arrangements to fix Kenneth's bike. *Why*? she wondered. She couldn't believe that strangers could be so much more compassionate and caring than his own family, but she had witnessed it twice today. She wondered how she could repay them for their trouble and the new wheel. She knew Kenneth carried just enough money with him to pay for his breakfast and a tip. He never ate lunch other than what she packed him in his backpack every day. Since she didn't want to upset him by going near the diner, she wrote down the address, intending to send them a card and some money as soon as she got home.

~~~~~

With Mark's assistance, it only took Sam a few minutes to remove the busted wheel from the bike and put on the new one. As Gina pretended to be busy wiping off tables, she smiled as she watched Frank observing the entire process. *At least he has enough sense to stay out of the way,* she thought. She had actually believed he would be able to fix the bike on his own. That was why she had suggested it in the first place. She laughed at the predicament she had put him in. *Thank goodness for Sam.*

Kenneth never looked up to watch what was going on outside but continued to write 2:00 on his yellow pad. After Mark had ridden the bike around in the parking lot a couple of times to make sure that the wheel and brakes were working, Sam got in his truck and left, and the other two came back into the diner.

"Your bike's all fixed," said Gina filling up Kenneth's coffee cup. "When you're ready, you can go out and see it for yourself," she encouraged.

Kenneth grabbed his notepad and immediately headed out the door. When Gina started to clear the cup and dishes from his booth, she noticed that he had left four pieces of candy on the table. "Would you look at this," she said, "he left us each a piece of candy."

"Man, how would you like to be in his shoes?" Mark sighed. "Autism often makes it hard to relate to anyone, even when you want to."

94

"You think that's what's wrong with him?" asked Gina. "Just how much psychology do you know anyway?"

"Right now, I know just enough to be dangerous to myself and others, but that's why I want to continue my studies. It's fascinating how the brain controls how we respond to others and our environment."

"Whatever that means," smirked Gina. "Well, I'm out of here. This is my day for good deeds. I hate it when I'm so nice." she muttered as she left the diner.

Chapter 6

Gina was glad to get out of the house for the evening. Greg was beginning to bore her with his jealousy and possessiveness. He resented her relationships with Jan and Frank and thought that Kelley depended on her to babysit more than she should. When she explained why she had been late getting home from the diner, he accused her of having an affair with Unabomber. *Why do my relationships with the opposite sex always end this way,* she wondered. *It's such a blasted mess getting rid of them. How many black eyes am I going to have before I finally find someone I can truly love, and who will love me back? One thing is for sure, it isn't Greg. He definitely has to go. Why am I always attracted to losers?*

Gina had been on her own since she was seventeen. She left home because she could no longer stand to be around her mother's lecherous boyfriends who often found Gina more attractive than her mom. Now at twenty-two, she found herself living her mother's life—a different boyfriend every six weeks that sponged off her until she got tired of supporting them. Then, there was always the physical brawl to get them out of the house, which typically left her with either a black eye or a sore jaw. At least, she hadn't given in to drugs and alcohol as her solace. Her mom died two years ago of an overdose. Gina hadn't seen her since she moved out of the house, even though she lived just on the other side of town. There were no other relatives in her life. She

96

never knew who her dad was, and neither she nor her mother had any siblings. Her grandparents had died before she was born, so she was alone in the world except for her friends at the diner and the male strays she kept dragging into her life.

She had such grand plans at seventeen when she left home. She had done well in high school and graduated early by taking additional courses each semester. Even though her high school counselors had managed to get her an academic scholarship to OSU, she wanted nothing more to do with education. She just wanted to get away from home. She intended to go to Nashville and make a career out of singing. She loved country music and had a decent voice.

She took the job at the diner with the purpose of saving her money and moving to Nashville within two years. Of course, that still hadn't happened. The cost of maintaining her own apartment and her junk car payments soaked up almost everything she earned at the diner, leaving very little for other expenses and nothing for savings.

She sang with a couple of local bands in area bars and lodges, but she did that mostly for the experience and the pleasure she got out of singing. She was a favorite at many karaoke competitions and frequently won, resulting in a slew of T-shirts, some trophies, and a few extra bucks, which she typically turned over to some bum she had met in the bar and had dragged home with her.

It was five o'clock when she pulled into the apartment parking lot at Kelley's. Carl was expected to call Kelley at 5:30. Gina had offered to take the little ones to the shopping mall and let them play on the indoor playground. Afterward, they would go to Red Robin's for corn dogs and balloons—more of her Nashville money spent on someone else. She actually didn't care about the money because she had given up on Nashville. It was just good to have an excuse to get out of the house and away from Greg's constant badgering.

Being with Kelley's kids always cheered her up. They were beautiful children and were full of spunk and energy. They behaved perfectly for her—not so well for Kelley—but for her, they were always good. When she knocked on the door, she could hear the chaos inside as Kelley was trying to get four little ones corralled and properly dressed for their outing. The kids were obviously excited about going with Gina as evidenced by the shrill squeals and giggles coming from behind the door.

"Anybody home?" Gina called as she poked her head in the door.

"Gina, Gina," squealed the two older ones as they ran down the hall to greet her. They grabbed her around the legs and practically bowled her over.

"Hello, there, my little urchins. Where's your mother?" she asked.

"What's an urchin?" asked Carl junior.

"I'm in Sara's bedroom," yelled Kelley. "We're almost ready. You might want to start getting those two into their booster seats, while I finish getting the other two ready.
98

Keys are on the table."

"On it," yelled Gina. "Let's go, my little angels. You two are the first to be strapped into your little car cocoons."

"I hate my car seat," pouted Carl. "It's too small for me, and I can't move at all."

"That's the purpose of those crazy things." Gina laughed. "I actually think they're a wonderful control device, most certainly invented by Nanny McPhee."

"You talk funny," said Thomas.

"I do?" said Gina laughing and giving him a hug.

Gina was still struggling with the buckle on Carl's booster seat when Kelley came out carrying the other two kids. "Why in the heck don't they make all of the buckles alike on these contraptions?" Gina muttered. "I always have trouble with this one. It's like some weird Chinese puzzle."

"I know," said Kelley. "That one is hard. I always have trouble with it, too. Here, you take these two little squirming worms, and I'll load the stroller in the back. Are you sure you want to do this?"

"Sure, piece of cake, huh kids?" said Gina. "Getting them in and out of the stupid van is the hardest part."

"Now you know why I never want to go any place that we can't walk to." As Gina turned around, Kelley grabbed her and gave her a hug. "You'll never know how much I appreciate this. It'll be so much easier to have a coherent conversation with Carl without the four of them yelling in the background."

"Maybe you can even have a little phone sex," Gina teased.

"Gina, you are terrible," said Kelley laughing. "But, I'll appreciate the peace and quiet. By the time the kids all get a chance to talk when he calls, he barely has time to say anything but *'I love you'* to me."

"Still, that must be nice to hear." Gina sighed. "Well, I'd better go before the kids start helping one another escape from their car seats."

Kelley leaned her head in the back door of the van, "Bye, sweeties. Have fun and make sure that Gina has fun, too. Be good! I love you!" Then, turning to Gina, she added, "There's a CD in the front that the kids like to listen to. The music is calming, and it helps keep them occupied so you can concentrate on driving. Carl can usually only talk for about twenty minutes, so I'll try to have myself back together by the time you get home. I can't help but cry after every call. You'd think I'd be used to it by now."

"I don't how you have managed all this by yourself for so long. You're shouldering a pretty hefty load by yourself, Kelley. You deserve a good cry. We won't be back until around seven o'clock any way," said Gina hugging her.

~~~~~

When they got to the mall, Gina found a parking spot
100

near the front entrance and began unloading the kids from their car seats.

"Look, Gina, is that Olivia?" asked Carl Junior as Gina was putting Sara into the stroller.

Gina turned around and saw Olivia and her new friend Teresa walking toward the black car that they had been driving this morning. While she watched, two men got out of the car. That's weird, she thought. From a distance, it looked like Teresa was actually holding Olivia up.

"Look, Gina," called Edward from inside the van. "I got the top buckle un-fastened all by myself."

"Good for you," said Gina glancing up at him. "I'm coming to get you in just one second, so just sit tight. You're next. Just let me get Sara settled here." When she turned back around to look for Olivia, the sedan was pulling away.

"Is Olivia sick?" asked Carl.

"What made you ask that?" asked Gina.

"Well, it sort of looked like those men and that other girl had to help her get into the car."

"Really? Did the other girl get into the car too?"

"Yes. But she didn't need any help," he added.

Gina quickly loaded Edward into the stroller. "Carl, you

get on this side of the stroller and Thomas you get on the other. Grab hold of the handle with me. Here we go. I want to check on something before we go to the playground."

Gina pushed the stroller with Thomas and Carl running beside her, holding on to its side bars. When they got inside the mall, she headed to the shop where Olivia worked.

"Cool, look at those lights," said Carl, pointing to the lava lamps.

"Excuse me," Gina said to the male clerk. "I'm a friend of Olivia's. I just saw her leaving the mall, and she looked like she wasn't feeling well. Was she all right when she left here?"

"She complained of a headache because she was up all night. Her friend Teresa gave her a couple of aspirins and brought her a smoothie. They just left here a few minutes ago."

"Did you happen to hear where they were going?"

"Ummm, Olivia talked about going to her mom's for dinner. Teresa was sort of in a hurry, and they left right after Olivia finished the smoothie."

"Okay. Thanks," Gina said. As she pushed the stroller out of the shop, she continued to think about what she had seen out in front of the mall. Finally, she admonished herself for thinking something was wrong. She was always borrowing trouble. *Maybe Olivia hadn't driven to the mall today, and they were just giving her a ride home.*

She knew that Olivia sometimes had severe migraines that made her sick, so Teresa was probably just helping her get into the car. "Okay, Kiddos, it's off to the playground! Grab hold boys, it's blast off time again."

~~~~~

At seven thirty, Gina rolled back into the parking lot at Kelley's. Two of the kids were asleep in their car seats, and the other two were close to dropping off. Gina hoped that they would stay asleep, so Kelley could have some more time to herself.

From the front window, Kelley saw them pull in and hurried out to help Gina unload the kids. Gina took one look at her and knew something was wrong. "What happened, Kelley? You look like you might bleed to death through your eyes?"

"He didn't call. That's what happened. I know something is terribly wrong. He has never missed calling. Let's not talk about it in front of the kids. Can you stay for a little while?"

"Sure, I don't want to go home anyway. I called Greg while I was watching the kids at the playground, and he started going off on me about being gone all the time. I've had it with him, so I told him to get his stuff and get out. I hung up on him before he could say anything and ignored all of his returned calls. I finally turned my cell phone off to keep from hearing it ring."

"Let's get the kids inside to bed, so we can talk. I hope we weren't the reason Greg was so mad," said Kelley.

103

"Nah. It was time for him to go anyway. I sure know how to pick 'em."

"Hi, baby," said Kelley, turning her attention to half-sleeping Carl Junior. "Let mommy carry you into bed." She reached in the van to lift him from his car seat. "My goodness, sweetheart, you're getting almost too big for me to carry."

While Kelley put her kids to bed, Gina decided to call Jan to see if Olivia actually showed up at the dinner party. She was surprised when Frank answered Jan's phone. "Frank? It's Gina."

"Do you actually think I wouldn't recognize your voice, Gina? Where are you? We still have some lasagna left."

"Thanks, but Carl didn't call Kelley tonight, and she's pretty bummed out, so I'm going to spend the night with her."

"That should go over well with Greg."

"I kicked him out. I'm hoping he'll be gone tomorrow, so I won't have to go through another bad scene. Anyway, that's not really why I called. Did Olivia show up over there tonight?"

"No, she didn't. Jan is pretty upset about it."

"Shit. I was afraid of that. I am really worried about her." Gina told him what she had witnessed at the mall.

"Come on, Gina. You watch too many of those crazy

crime shows on TV. I'm sure she simply got to feeling better and decided a dinner party would be too boring for her, so don't you go adding any more worries to Jan. She worries enough about that ungrateful little brat as it is."

"Fine," said Gina, "but you promise me that if Olivia doesn't show up tonight or by tomorrow morning that you'll call me. Things just didn't look right at the mall."

"OK, I promise. I'll see you Wednesday."

 Gina spent the night trying to console Kelley, who was certain that Carl was lying dead somewhere in the desert. Gina tried to convince her that he was probably out on some surprise night patrol and couldn't get back to call her. Kelley wasn't easily convinced, but she finally gave up and went to sleep around two in the morning with the phone on her pillow. In the back of her mind while she was trying to console Kelley, Gina continued to worry about Olivia.

Chapter 7

The next morning, Gina left Kelley's apartment before Kelly and the kids got up. She wrote them a note saying she would come by to check on them later this morning. When she pulled into her parking spot in front of her apartment, she could see that her front door was standing wide open. "Oh, great," she muttered aloud. "The idiot is still here." She grabbed her purse and some other things from the car and headed for the apartment. When she walked in the front door, she couldn't believe her eyes. "Shit, shit, shit," she screamed dropping her handbag and jumping up and down like a wild woman. "He took everything!" she screeched.

Her living room was empty—no TV, no couch, no computer, no CD or DVD players—in fact, there were no CDs or DVDs left—everything that was worth carrying off was gone. She ran from room to room cursing and crying hysterically. Finally, she fell in a heap on the kitchen floor, screaming and pounding against it like a child having a major melt down.

Why didn't I see this coming? When am I going to learn? After sobbing uncontrollably for several minutes, she finally pulled herself up from the floor and headed to the phone to call the police. "Oh, of course," she screeched. "The SOB took the portable phone." She went back into the living room and dug through her purse trying to find her cell phone. She finally just turned her purse upside down and emptied its contents on the floor. She picked up the phone and dialed 911. She realized that this wasn't an emergency, but she didn't know the number

106

for the police. She made a mental note to find out what it was—given her luck, she would no doubt need to call them again.

Twenty minutes later a cruiser pulled up in front of her apartment. In the meantime, Gina had started a list of everything that was missing and had dragged out her receipts and warranties looking for serial numbers. Colin and Jeff got out of the cruiser and knocked on her door.

"Hi, Jeff, Colin," she said. "I thought you two always got off at seven."

"We do," said Colin. "But I heard the call on the way home and recognized your name. I called the station and told them that Jeff and I would take the call. We figured you'd rather see us than someone you didn't know."

"Wow, you've really been cleaned out," said Jeff. "What the heck happened? At least you're not banged up yourself this time," he consoled. "I take it that it was Greg who did this."

"Right," said Gina. "He'll probably head for the nearest pawnshop." She sighed. "Here's the list of things that he took that I can remember right now. I hope you can find the jerk, and I will definitely press as many charges as you can lay on him," she promised. "I have some serial numbers of the bigger items, but some of the other things, I don't have anything for. I must have had over a hundred Karaoke CDs and fifty or more DVDs."

"This is good, Gina, that you have the serial numbers, I mean. It'll make it easier to track stuff down," said Colin. "What can you tell us about Greg? He had to have help

107

getting the couch and chairs out of here."

Gina racked her brain trying to recall the names and locations of Greg's friends and relatives. She was surprised at how little she did actually know about him.

When they were ready to leave, Jeff told her that she should probably have her locks changed. "Are you sure you will be okay? Do you think he might try to come back?" he asked.

"I hope the SOB does come back, and then you can pick me up for castrating him!" she screeched.

"Don't tell us that." Jeff laughed. "If something ever happens to the jerk, that threat will most certainly make you a person of interest."

"Speaking of a person of interest," Gina remembered. "Have you got a couple more seconds? I want to ask you about something I saw at the mall last night that involved Olivia, Jan's daughter."

"Sure, we've got time. We could tell that Jan was upset this morning when we had breakfast at the diner. Mrs. O'Connor told us that Jan's daughter didn't come home again last night," said Jeff.

Gina instantly felt sick to her stomach. "Oh, my god. I was so afraid of that." She proceeded to tell them about what she had seen at the mall and described how Olivia had to be helped into the car. She watched as Jeff exchanged a strange look with Colin when she told them that Teresa had given Olivia aspirins and a fruit smoothie.

108

"What?" she said. "I saw that look between you two. Tell me. Do you think Olivia might be in trouble?"

"Tell me more about the two men, and the car," said Jeff. "Can you describe the men? Did you happen to get the license number on the car?"

"No, the men had their backs to me, and I never saw the license plate. I'm sure that it was the same car that Teresa was driving yesterday morning when she came to the diner with Olivia. It was a big, black sedan with dark tinted windows. Why? Please tell me what you're worried about," she begged.

"Look, Gina. I'm going to level with you," said Colin. "There's been a report out about a human trafficking ring that might be targeting some young girls around here. We've been checking on leads about two girls who disappeared from the campus area. Some of the details match what you've been telling us. The two missing girls had just befriended another young lady, who also seems to have disappeared."

Gina thought she was going to faint. She sank to the floor, pulling her knees tightly against her chest trying to keep herself together. "What did the girl who befriended the missing girls look like," she asked rocking back and forth.

"We have a composite drawing of her at the station. Do you think you could come with us to take a look at it?" asked Jeff sitting down next to her on the floor and putting his arm around her.

Gina leaned against his shoulder trying to gather enough

109

strength to answer him. She felt like she was in a fog and was sinking deeper and deeper into a pit of sand.

"Are you okay, Gina?" asked Jeff, turning her toward him so he could see her face. "You're not going to pass out on us, are you?"

His voice finally cut through her fog. "No, I'm okay, I think. It's just that I knew something was not right last night. I should've called the police right away. If something happens to Olivia, it'll all be my fault," she cried.

"No, it isn't your fault, but to be honest with you. We shouldn't sit here on the floor any longer. If you think you can get up, we need to have you take a look at the picture and send a missing person bulletin out on Olivia as soon as possible. Of course, we're going to need Jan to report her missing."

"Oh, my god. This will kill Jan." She forced herself to get up from the floor. "I'm fine," she said, steadying herself with Jeff's help. "I don't want to waste another second. I'll follow you in my clunker because I want to get over to the diner to be with Jan before someone else tells her about this."

"Jeff can drive your car to the station," said Colin. "You don't look like you should be driving just yet. We're actually off duty, so it won't matter if he drives you over there in your car."

On the way to the police station, Gina begged Jeff to tell her what he knew about the human trafficking ring. He explained that most of the information couldn't be shared with her, but he did tell her how such groups generally
110

operate.

"Essentially, someone in the ring befriends the targeted girl," he said. "Once they've gained the girl's trust, then they have someone slip her something like Rohypnol or GHB."

"The date rape drugs?" interrupted Gina.

"Yeah, that's right. Rohypnol is tasteless, colorless, and odorless and is usually dissolved in a drink. GHB has a salty taste, but the saltiness can be masked by mixing it with a sweet fruit drink. Didn't you say that Teresa brought Olivia some sort of fruit drink before they left the shop?"

"Yes. The clerk told me that Teresa brought Olivia a fruit smoothie, but what about the aspirins she gave her?"

"They probably were just sugar pills or something to make Olivia think that Teresa wanted to help her. Unfortunately, it was too bad that Olivia had a history of headaches because that's what threw you off and might even have made Olivia think it was the headache that was making her weak and dizzy. These extremely powerful, fast-acting drugs leave you dazed and confused. Depending on the dosage, you might even pass out."

"I remember that the clerk at the shop said that Teresa seemed to be in a hurry. Would the drugs take effect immediately?"

"Like I said, the drugs are really powerful. They can affect you very quickly and without your realizing it. Typically,

111

you can be totally out of it within thirty minutes or less depending on the dosage consumed. The length of their effect also varies according to the dosage. These trafficking rings know how much of the drug to give. If they give the girl too much, she could go into seizures and even die," Jeff explained.

"Oh, my god," moaned Gina.

"You'd be surprised how many women OD on these club drugs."

"No, I wouldn't," said Gina. "My mom died of an overdose of cherry meth—isn't that a form of GHB?"

"I remember," said Jeff. "Yeah, cherry meth is one of the street names for a GHB type drug."

"What happens to these kidnapped girls when they start to wake up," asked Gina not sure that she truly wanted to know all the sordid details.

"They keep the girls pretty doped up until they get them where they have a brothel set up. Most of them never realize until it's too late what happened to them or where they are. Some of these human trafficking thugs ship the girls out of the country fairly fast."

"Out of the country?" Gina began sobbing and covered her face with her hands. "Oh, please, dear God, don't let that happen to Olivia," she prayed. "I promise I'll never miss another day at church; I'll gladly tithe; I promise, I promise, I promise," she cried hysterically.

112

Jeff parked the car and gently pulled her hands away from her face. "We're here," he told her softly. "Are you sure you want to do this? We can go get someone else who saw the girl at the diner," he whispered.

"No. I can do this," said Gina, now more determined than ever.

Colin met them inside and led them into a detective's office. "Gina Meyers, this is Detective Baxter," he said.

"Thanks for coming in. I understand that you've had some problems of your own this morning," said the Detective.

Gina stifled the urge to scream '*cut the small talk and find Olivia,*' but instead she simply nodded and plopped down in the closest chair. "Can I see the picture, Detective? I don't want to waste a minute. You have to find my friend's daughter."

Detective Baxter opened a file that was laying on the desk. He shuffled through some papers at the speed of the flow of extra thick molasses on a winter day but eventually produced the picture.

"Oh, my god," gasped Gina. "It's her. It's Teresa."

"The name is probably an alias. One of the friends of the other two missing coeds called her Danielle," reported Detective Baxter.

"I don't care what you want to call her. That's the girl who was with Olivia yesterday morning in the diner. She's the

113

same girl I saw helping Olivia into the black sedan. Please, let me know what to do next. I have to help you find her before it's too late."

"The next step is to file the missing persons report. Her mother will need to come down here to do that," he said.

"I'll go and get her right now," said Gina jumping up from her chair a little too fast, causing her to wobble a little.

"Do you want me to come with you?" asked Jeff. "You still look a little unsteady on your feet."

"No, thanks. You two have been great. I need to do this by myself. This is not going to be easy, but it'll be less difficult for her coming from me. At least, I hope it will. Do I just bring her back here to you Detective?" she asked.

"Yes. I'll have the papers all filled out based upon Jeff and Colin's report."

Chapter 8

Olivia tried to roll over on the bed, but she couldn't move. Her hands seemed to be held by something above her head. She struggled to open her eyes, but the room was spinning, and she felt sick to her stomach. She was trapped halfway between being awake and still being asleep. Everything was all mixed up in her mind. She tried hard to wake up and to focus, but she couldn't.

"Well, well, Sleeping Beauty is finally returning to the real world," said Teresa, sneering at her.

"Teresa?" moaned Olivia, trying once again to open her eyes. "Where are we? And, why can't I move my hands. They feel like they're tied above my head."

"That's because they are," Teresa responded with a nasty, menacing laugh.

"What? Why? What's going on? Where am I?" moaned Olivia yanking her arms again. She frantically blinked her eyes in an attempt to make them focus. Finally, she could make out a silhouette of Teresa standing beside her next to the bed. "Come on, Teresa, this isn't funny."

"It isn't meant to be funny. You really have no clue about what's happening here, do you?" said Teresa. "You young girls are all alike—naive and stupid," she snarled. "Well, let me enlighten you, my dear Olivia. You have been snatched from your smug, little existence, and you will soon find yourself living a whole new life far, far away."

As Teresa's words began to sink in, panic swept through Olivia. She frantically yanked her arms and tried to kick her feet, but they were also bound together. "Please, Teresa, let me get up. You're not making any sense at all. Let me go for god's sake," she demanded. She could see more clearly now and stared at Teresa in horror. The menacing look on Teresa's face was terrifying. "Teresa, please. Tell me what's going on. You're scaring me. Untie my hands and feet and let me up," she begged.

"I just told you all you need to know. And frankly, your chatter is getting on my nerves." Teresa grabbed the roll of gray tape laying on the nightstand. She tore off a piece, and leaning close to Olivia, she slapped it across her mouth.

Olivia tried to scream, but her muffled sounds caught in her throat. She lashed around on the bed, pulling and tugging at her hands with all her might. *This has to be a horrible nightmare. This can't be happening to me*, she thought. *In a minute, I'm going to wake up, and I'm going to be okay.*

"Stop lashing around. You're only going to hurt your wrists. There is no way you can escape, so you just better learn to cooperate. If you don't, you're going to find yourself lying on the bottom of the ocean chained to a very large rock!" threatened Teresa. "This shot of heroin will make you feel a little better about all of this," she said.

116

Pinning Olivia's left arm to the bed, she expertly inserted the needle into the cephalic vein in Olivia's arm and injected her with her first dose of heroin.

Olivia felt the jab of the needle and struggled hopelessly to get free from Teresa's firm grip. A warm flush spread across her skin as the heroin was injected into her arm. Her arms and legs became heavier and heavier, and she could feel herself slipping into an abyss of confused thoughts. Tears rolled down her cheeks as she realized that she wasn't trapped in a dream. This was real.

~~~~~

Teresa watched as Olivia stopped struggling and slowly faded into a comatose state of euphoria. She actually envied the effects that Olivia would soon feel from the drug. She considered injecting herself, but she knew it would be her end. She had been drug free for years, but she still remembered the first euphoric rush and the later numbness about life that heroin provided.

Teresa truly hated life, especially hers. She was bored and was terribly afraid of Hastings. She knew that any moment he could snuff out her existence, and he would if he ever thought she was using again. A sudden pounding on the door startled her, causing her to drop the needle.

"Teresa, it's Antonio," he whispered loudly.

Teresa unlocked the dead bolt on the door of their cheesy motel. "Are we ready to take off so early," she asked as her brother shoved past her. She stared at Antonio, who seemed highly agitated. He had obviously

117

not had much sleep. His eyes were bloodshot, and his typically clean-shaven face showed the re-growth of his heavy, black beard. His clothes were wrinkled. He wore the same thing he had worn the day before and his dark wavy hair was uncombed.

"Of course, we're ready," he snarled as he glanced at Olivia lying motionless on the bed. "How much did you give her?"

"Enough to keep her confused and quiet for the flight to Miami," Teresa replied.

"Good. Get the ropes off and take that stupid tape off her mouth. I hate it when you do that. It'll leave a mark on her face that's too easy to spot if someone looks too closely," said Antonio.

"Oh, I'm sorry," said Teresa sarcastically. "I suppose you'd rather explain her screams for help."

"Don't be an idiot," said Antonio, obviously disgusted with her smart remark. "You're supposed to keep them doped up so that they don't scream. What's wrong with you anyway? You've been acting sort of strange with this one."

"I'm tired of all this. Hastings told me that, after the last one, I could stay in Miami. Remember? He promised me. I'm getting too old to fit in with these little princesses. Come on, you have to notice that I don't exactly look like a young twenty something any more. This had better be my last one."

"Don't talk to me; talk to Hastings. You know he's the one
118

calling the shots. But, I'd be careful if I were you," he cautioned, tossing her a glance that registered a loud warning of her own vulnerability.

"Where is he, anyway?" asked Teresa. "We're going to need his help getting her out of here." She knew that her brother was trying to warn her that he would never be able to protect her if Hastings ever turned on her. It startled her as she suddenly realized that Antonio was as afraid of Hastings as she was.

"Here he comes with the car. My god, Teresa. It still has Florida plates on it. Didn't you change them before you drove it around in Ohio?"

Teresa stared back at him in terror. "Oh, shit. I forgot. I'm just not thinking clearly any more. Please, if Hastings asks about them, tell him you changed them back to the Florida plates this morning."

"Dammit, Teresa. You'd better hope that he didn't notice them yesterday. Come on, let's get this stuff off of her. He's in a hurry to get going because his pilot is going to pick us up at H-J International."

"We must be close to the airport. I felt like I was sleeping on the runway last night," complained Teresa. "There must have been a hundred planes taking off every hour. It sounded like they were right on top of us."

"Yeah, I know. I couldn't get to sleep at all, and I have to take the car on to Miami. At least you get to fly with Hastings in the jet," said Antonio.

"Didn't I hear Hastings tell you that you were to stay here
119

one more day before heading back to Miami? Why? What are you supposed to do here?" asked Teresa. "I'd feel better if I knew you were coming to Miami today. It's only about a ten hour drive from here. By the time you drop us off, you could be on the road by eight this morning. That would put you into Miami tonight around nine or ten, allowing some time for stops for food and fuel."

"Why does it matter to you if I get to Miami tonight or tomorrow, Teresa? I'm beat. I drove the whole way here last night. I need some rest. I think even Hastings realizes that," replied Antonio. "I intend to sleep the rest of the day today. I'll leave here in time to get to Miami around noon tomorrow or a little after. Hastings said he wanted me back in Miami by one o'clock on Wednesday for some major meeting or something."

"Are you two ready?" asked Hastings, bursting into the room. "We've got to get out of here before we hit the morning commute traffic."

Unlike Antonio, Hastings looked as impeccable as ever. Sharply dressed in a blue double-breasted suit with a touch of gray pinstripes, and a highly-starched, white shirt and paisley tie, he looked like he had just stepped off the cover of *GQ*. Teresa admired the way he dressed, but she knew that beneath the well-appointed, outward appearance was a heart as cold as ice—if, in fact, there was a heart at all. His eyes were cold, and penetrating— dark abysmal pools of suspicion and contempt.

"You look like a bum," he said to Antonio. "Go in there and get yourself presentable," he demanded, pointing to the bathroom.

120

Antonio quickly whipped out a comb and turned toward the mirror over the vanity. "I'm sorry, Hastings. I didn't sleep at all, and since I wasn't going on the plane, I didn't think my appearance would matter this morning."

"Appearance always matters," yelled Hastings. "Don't forget that."

"Why did you decide to fly out of H-J International instead of Fulton County, like we always have," asked Teresa, trying to draw Hastings' attention away from her brother, who was frantically trying to tuck in his shirt and smooth the frizzy natural curls of his thick, black hair.

"There's more activity around H-J, so we're less important," answered Hastings. "Besides, I don't want to arouse too many suspicions. I didn't like the way that flight dispatcher at Fulton was asking so many questions the last time we flew out of there with those other two girls. I'm not sure he completely bought my story about them being runaways on drugs and that I had been hired by their parents to bring them back to Miami. Anyway, let's get her into the car, so we can get out of here. Go out and check to make sure there's no one out there," he commanded. Then, turning to Antonio, he said, "I'm glad to see you put the Florida plates back on the car. When did you manage to do that?" he asked.

"I, uh, I did it early this morning," he stammered. "I didn't relish driving it all the way to Florida with the Ohio plates on the car, in case someone got the numbers," he said. He avoided looking at Teresa.

Teresa grabbed her bags and headed out the door. *Thank god Antonio had noticed the plates earlier.* She

121

knew she owed her brother big time. She glanced around the parking lot of the Atlanta motel. No one was outside at that hour of the morning, so she quickly opened the back door of the car and returned to the room to help with Olivia.

Olivia moaned as Hastings yanked the tape off her mouth and dragged her from the bed. Teresa smiled as she watched Olivia try desperately to speak. She knew what Olivia was most likely experiencing right about now. Her tongue was no doubt plastered to the top of her parched mouth. Strange, disconnected thoughts would be swirling through her head. Theresa had experienced those feelings many times in her years of addiction. The nausea and parched mouth were the worst part of the sensations. The weird thoughts were sometimes fun.

Olivia could barely keep her head up as they began lugging her across the room. When they finally tossed her into the car, waves of nausea and retching dry heaves racked her body. Then, she was quiet again. Teresa climbed into the back seat with her and looked over at her slumped body with utter disgust.

The girls she helped to abduct were essentially all alike—spoiled, belligerent, arrogant, and vain. Teresa easily won their confidence with a few expensive gifts and lots of fake flattery. Olivia had been an easy target. She was mad at the world because of her father's death, and she liked nice things, which her mother could no longer afford to give her. In less than a week, Teresa easily won her trust with feigned compassion and a pair of expensive shoes.

After Teresa arranged for her victim's abduction,

122

Hastings' took over from there. He relied on two weapons to break the girls' resistance—violence and drugs. He used them both without mercy. He threatened to kill or maim the girls or members of their family if they didn't cooperate, and he injected them immediately with highly addictive, mind-altering drugs. He used heroin because addiction to it was fast, and it had horrible side effects during withdrawal. The girls would quickly agree to his demands to get injections to stop their vomiting, muscle aches, and cold sweats. With heroin, symptoms of withdrawal typically began within several hours of a dose, so the girls lived in a constant state of need. Once he was sure they were addicted, he would begin to withhold the drug unless they agreed to perform the lewd acts he demanded. The less intelligent girls buckled easily; the smarter ones resisted, but eventually, they either caved in to his demands or simply disappeared.

Although she was easily abducted, Olivia would be difficult to break. Teresa felt sure of that. Hastings never wasted much time on difficult ones like her. He depended on a quick turn-around for the girls by selling them to owners of dance and strip clubs in the United States, Asia, and in the Middle East. The clubs he dealt with were fronts for prostitution and drugs. They appeared legitimate to the police because their principal dancers were not part of the prostitution ring. Dancers were hired and paid only to dance and entertain. The captured girls were used as sex slaves and were never brought to the club. They were housed in brothels commonly accessed through bogus massage parlors or some other legitimate business. They were prisoners, who were carefully guarded and rarely escaped alive.

Club clients, seeking sex and drugs, were carefully screened by club owners to avoid infiltration by undercover police operations. Access to these 'special services' was handled by club managers and was kept hidden from most of the club employees and other unsuspecting patrons.

Hastings himself didn't run the sex brothels. He served more or less as the broker for the club owners. His job was to find the girls and 'train' them. Then he would sell them to the highest bidders. Within a couple of weeks, if the girls weren't 'trainable,' as Hastings described his method of beating or drugging them into submission, girls like Olivia were typically sold to foreign traffickers and shipped out of the country. She would bring a good price on the foreign slave-trade market because she was young and attractive.

As they pulled away from the hotel, Teresa glanced toward the front seat at Hastings. She had known him from childhood, but she was still afraid of him. They grew up together in the slums of New York. Hastings started dealing in drugs in high school, and Teresa quickly got hooked on them. She would do anything for him to get money for drugs. By fifteen, she was deep into prostitution and theft. At sixteen, she was arrested, and she spent two years in a juvenile detention center. When she was finally released, she discovered that her brother and Hastings had moved to Miami. She begged Antonio to let her come to live with him. Hastings agreed that she could come to Miami provided that she stayed free of drugs and did what he told her.

She never even bothered to ask what he meant by '*doing what he told her.*' She simply assumed that she would once again be sold by the hour. At that point in her life, she didn't care what she had to do. She just wanted out of New York. When she arrived in Miami, she was surprised when he told her about his plan to have her work for him in a human-trafficking ring. '*No more prostitution and no more poverty,*' he had promised her. All she had to do was travel once or twice a month to befriend and entrap some naïve young girl. He would do the rest.

 She was paid handsomely for her part in the abductions and earned enough to purchase an expensive condo in a high rise on the ocean. She loved living in Miami, but she was nearing thirty, and she was bored with playing babysitter to a bunch of young girls. She had asked Hastings about the possibility of finding someone younger to set up his abductions and letting her manage his accounts for several of the clubs in Miami. To her surprise, he had told her that he already had found someone younger to replace her, and he had promised to think about her offer.

Several weeks had passed since their conversation, and she still hadn't heard any more about when he planned to switch her to an accounts manager. Now, she was afraid to bring it up a second time. She knew that she was a potential threat to him if she ever decided to go to the police, but instead of making her more confident that he would keep his promise, her position scared her. She wasn't stupid—she could easily become one of his victims that he shipped out of the country.

As Hastings stared hatefully back at her through the rear-view mirror, cold chills ran down her spine. She feared that, like Olivia, time was running out for her. She knew this would be her last abduction and she had better plan her exit now. From his vile glare in the mirror, it was obvious that Hastings had already planned something for her, and there was no doubt in her mind that she wouldn't be managing his accounts.

Chapter 9

"What in the heck is Gina doing here, today?" said Frank as he watched her wheel her car into the parking lot. "I was just going to call you," he said as she burst through the door.

"Were you, Frank?" snarled Gina. "Well, now you won't have to. Where's Jan?"

"She's in the back. You'd better not upset her with your cockamamie story about a human-trafficking ring because Olivia still hasn't come home."

"Shut up, Frank," said Gina whirling around to face him. "For once in your life, just shut up!" she repeated as the tears started flowing down her cheeks. "For your information, I just came from the police station, and that's exactly what has happened to Olivia. It was that stupid Teresa," she sobbed.

Everyone seated at the counter stared at her with gaping mouths and stunned expressions. Mark rushed toward her, embracing her and leading her to the nearest stool. "My god, Gina. Are you okay? I thought you were going to faint. Are you telling us that Olivia has actually been abducted?"

"Yes, yes, yes," sobbed Gina. "And, I have to get Jan to the police station right now to sign some stupid missing person papers before they can even start looking for her." As she turned around to head for the back room, she saw Jan frozen in the doorway. By the look of horror on her face, Gina realized that Jan had heard every word she had said. "Jan, honey, I'm so sorry. I didn't mean for you to hear it that way," said Gina rushing to help Jan to a stool.

"No. I don't want to sit down. Get me to the police station. NOW!" she screamed.

"I'm coming with you," said Mark. "Neither of you is in any condition to drive."

Frank stood motionless, unable to utter a word. He could only stare as Mark ushered Gina and Jan out the door and into the car. He flinched when the tires squealed on the hot pavement as they sped out of the driveway.

"My god," moaned Sam. "How can I help, Frank?" Then, noticing that Frank was in some sort of stupor, he yelled, "Frank! Snap out of it buddy."

"This is all my fault," whispered Frank. "Gina told me that she thought Olivia had been abducted from the mall yesterday. Only, I told her it was non-sense. They could have taken her miles away by now."

"It isn't your fault," replied Meredith. "It isn't any one's fault. Blaming yourself is not going to solve anything. We have to use our heads. Come on you guys, think. We were all here yesterday when Olivia came in with those girls. What did we see?" she asked, whipping out a pad and pencil from her purse.

"They were driving a black Mercedes sedan, looked like a S600 Hybrid," said Tom.

The others stared at him in amazement. "What makes you so sure of the model," asked Leroy. "Do you have one?"

"Are you kidding?" replied Tom. "Those cars cost $90,000 plus. I used to sell Mercedes, so believe me, I know what I'm talking about. It was an S600 Hybrid Sedan with extra dark tint on the side windows in the front and rear. There was a scratch on the right front fender near the bumper," he repeated. "Write it down, Meredith."

"How'd you see the scratch on the front? You have your back to the window," asked Leroy.

"I left early yesterday, on foot, remember?"

"Let's not argue about *how's* and *why's*," reminded Meredith. "Let's just concentrate on the *what*."

"Honestly, I don't recall even seeing them," said Frank. "I always have my back turned, watching this stupid grill. I don't pay much attention to what goes on beyond the counter."

"I remember that Teresa was wearing an expensive white sundress, and she was carrying a Coach purse," said Meredith, adding that to her list.

"Did any of you notice the license plate?" asked Sam. "What about you, Tom? Did you notice the plate while you were looking at the scratch?"

"I must have seen it, but nothing registers," Tom admitted. "I do think I remember it being an Ohio license, or was it out of state? Nope, I can't remember."

"That's too bad. That could have helped the police. Well, anyway," said Meredith, "can anyone remember anything else?"

"When they left, Teresa climbed on to Mark's motorcycle," mentioned Sam. "I remember teasing Frank about that."

"Right, she did," responded Leroy. "Hey, maybe her finger prints are on the handle bars. I saw her grab hold of them when Mark sat the bike up. Write that down, Meredith. And, Frank, make sure you don't let Mark wash his bike until the police have a chance to go over it."

"This is ridiculous," said Frank. "Who do we think we are? We're acting like we're a bunch of private investigators or something. None of this will help Olivia," he yelled as he rushed toward the back room.

Sam slid down from his stool and headed into the back. "Can I come in, buddy?" he asked, laying his hand on Frank's shaking shoulder. "This has been a tough week for you, but you've got to get yourself together. Jan is going to need someone, and, right now, all she has is us. Is there something more to all of this that you'd like to talk about?"

Frank fought to gain control of his emotions. "Thanks, Sam. I know you're right. Jan really is going to need us
130

to be strong for her. All of this has just opened a floodgate of emotions that I kept buried for years. I know what it's like to have someone just disappear out of your life and never come back. It hurts like hell. But, Jan's situation is even worse, and I don't know what to do or say to help her."

"There isn't much we can do or say that's going to make this any easier for her. This human-trafficking thing is horrible."

"It's the knowing that they're out there someplace, but you can't find them—no matter how hard you try," said Frank. "Every day you keep looking, hoping. You're never at peace, ever."

"Losing someone, yet knowing they're out there someplace has to be worse than having someone you love die the way Judith did," said Sam. "I thought I would just fade away when she was killed. I wanted to murder that man who broadsided her car. She was my whole life. If I hadn't stumbled in here years ago when I did, I think I would have killed myself."

Frank turned around to face Sam. "Yea, you were in pretty bad shape," he said. "I remember, at first, we thought you were just some mean, old grump who hated the world and everyone in it." He sighed. "We couldn't have been more wrong."

"No, you were right. I did hate the world. I blamed everyone for killing Judith," admitted Sam. "But Gina kept at me—teasing me, and tormenting me. She even bought me that coffee cup with the picture of Grumpy from *Snow White*, remember? She was also the one who went with me to that first meeting of Victims of Drunk Drivers. I would never have gone, but she showed up at my house and made me go with her. "

Frank heaved a deep sigh. He knew Gina was terribly angry at him for not taking her seriously last night. "She's something, that kid," he said. "She doesn't have two nickels to rub together, but she just keeps plugging away. I really hate that I let her down last night. I don't think she's going to ever forgive me for that."

"She'll bounce back," soothed Sam. "She's got a lot of spunk and staying power, but I have to admit that she was really wiped out today. I've never seen her so drained."

"Olivia is like a younger sister to Gina. She really loves Olivia even though she gets upset with how she treats Jan. She has a lot more patience with Olivia than I do. I'd like to wring her neck half the time."

"Hey, Frank," said Leroy poking his head in the door. "I hate to interrupt, but you two had better get out here. Meredith has taken over the grill and Tom's waiting on tables." He laughed. "It looks like they're doing okay, but I'm not one to judge that."

"Meredith is one amazing woman," said Sam. He turned around to peer through the door at Meredith, who was expertly flipping some pancakes. "Almost as amazing as my Judith." Turning back to Frank, he said, "Come on, you'd better rescue your customers, and I'm going to take off for the police station. I think they would like to hear what we came up with on Meredith's list. Are you going to be okay?"

132

"Yeah, I'm fine. Thanks, Sam." Frank gently patted his trusted friend on the shoulder as he headed back into the diner. He smiled as Meredith, came rushing toward him. She had tied a dishtowel around her waist and had a napkin tucked into the neck of her pale, pink silk dress in an attempt to protect it from the splatters bouncing off the grill.

"I hope I haven't messed up the orders, but I think I've got them right," said Meredith as the two men came into the diner. "I kind of like cooking like this, on the grill and all."

Tom hurried past them carrying a tub of dirty dishes. He had a cleaning cloth tucked into the elastic band of his jogging pants and a pencil stuffed behind his ear. "I'll hang out through lunch, Frank. I like waiting tables again," called Tom, over his shoulder as he headed into the backroom with the dishes. "It reminds me of my college days."

"Are you sure?" asked Frank. "I could use the help with all my waitresses gone. I could call Kelley, but Jan said she was an emotional mess when she came in this morning, so she sent her back home. I don't want you to feel like you have to do this."

"No problem," said Tom, coming back into the diner. "Honestly, I'm enjoying it. Those ladies actually left me a tip." He held his hand out showing the two quarters he had collected and laughed. "Do you have a tip jar some place? I'd rather leave the tips for the gals."

"No, we don't have a tip jar. They just keep their own tips, but I can get you an envelope. They'll appreciate the

133

extra money, I'm sure."

"Meredith," said Sam, smiling at the smudge of pancake batter on the side of her face. "How'd you like to ride over to the police station with me?"

"I'd love to," she responded as she pulled off her makeshift apron. "I think they need to get over here right away and check out the fingerprints on the motorcycle. Come on, let's go. What about you Leroy, are you coming with us?"

"I can't," said Leroy. "Sam knows how to reach me if you or the police need anything from me. Good luck."

~~~~~

Sam helped Meredith into the cab of his truck. He had a strange feeling when he held her hand to steady her as she climbed up onto the high step. He hadn't held a woman's hand in more than five years. He had forgotten how soft their skin was.

"Sam, I'm really worried about all this," Meredith said as they drove out of the parking lot. "I certainly hope they can find Olivia before it's too late."

"Me too, but honestly, I don't hold out much hope. There were two girls missing from the campus area a month or so ago, and there's been no report of their return yet."

"Do you ever listen to that Nancy Grace on TV?" asked Meredith.

134

Sam laughed. "Judith used to listen to her. She would get so upset about the cases that they talked about that she would worry for days."

"I know that some men don't like to listen to her whiney voice, but I think she really provides a service—just like that other guy who does the ten most wanted or whatever that program is called."

"You mean Tom Walsh on *America's Most Wanted?*" asked Sam.

"Yes. That's the one. I think we should contact people like that and get as much publicity out there about Olivia as possible, so people can see her face."

"I wonder if Jan would want to expose Olivia like that?" he cautioned.

"We should ask her," agreed Meredith. "But if we don't find Olivia pretty quick, her whole life will be changed forever, and Jan may never be able to really have her back, even if they eventually find her."

Sam was impressed with Meredith's compassion and concern for others, especially since she had just lost Howard. She wasn't one to engage in self pity, not like he had done. He had wallowed around in self deprecation, anger, and sadness for months after Judith's death. *Women must be emotionally tougher than men*, he decided. *But Howard didn't die the way Judith did—he hadn't died because of the stupidity of some drunken bastard.*

"What's wrong?" asked Meredith. "You look sad and
135

angry at the same time. Don't worry. I think we'll find Olivia, I just sort of have a hunch that we'll find her."

"It wasn't Olivia I was thinking about," he said. "But I hope you're right. I hope we do find her."

"Sam, I don't mean to pry. Howard told me about Judith's accident."

"It wasn't an accident," he shouted. "It was stupidity."

"I know," responded Meredith. "But, it wasn't your stupidity, or Judith's."

They rode the rest of the way to the police station in silence. When they pulled into the parking lot, Sam turned to Meredith. "I'm sorry," he said. "I didn't mean to snap at you."

"I know you didn't," she soothed. "It's okay. Losing Howard was hard, but loosing Judith the way you did would be a lot harder to accept. You have a right to be angry. Now, let's go in here and protect Jan from ever having to experience that same anger," she said patting his hand.

Chapter 10

After he closed the diner, Frank shuffled through the pile of mail left on the counter. Most of it was junk that he tossed aside, but there was one small envelope addressed to *Frank's Diner* that caught his attention. There was also an envelope from the leasing company— probably a reminder that his lease was up for renewal next year. He picked up the small envelope. The handwriting on it looked like a woman addressed it. He tore it open and took out the small card. A check fell on to the counter.

This is interesting, he thought examining the check. *Fifty dollars made out to Frank's Diner from an Edith Talbert. I don't know anyone by that name. Why would she be sending me $50.00?* He opened up the card and began reading.

> *Dear Friends,*
>
> *I want to thank you for your kindness in helping to fix Kenneth's bicycle. He is my grandson. I hope that the amount of the check is sufficient to cover the expense of the wheel. Kenneth looks forward to coming to the diner every day. He tells me about all of you, so I feel I already know you.*
>
> *Please don't mention the card to him. I*

137

wouldn't want him to think I was interfering.

Thanks again for your kindness,

Edith Talbert

"Gina will get a kick out of this. So, Meredith was right." He chuckled aloud. "Unabomber's name is Kenneth Talbert." He was glad to know his name. He'd never felt right about calling him Unabomber 2.

He reached for the other envelope from the leasing company just as Sam's truck pulled into the parking lot. Behind him was Mark with Gina and Jan. He tossed the envelope back on the counter without opening it and hurried to the door to unlock it. "What's going on?" he asked as Sam came through the door.

"The police will be here in a few minutes. They want to ask us all some more questions and to dust the cycle for prints," said Sam. "I called Leroy, and he's on his way back, but I don't know how to get hold of Tom, do you?"

"Yeah." answered Frank. "Luckily he left his phone number with me in case I need for him to come in earlier tomorrow."

As Jan came in the door, Frank reached out and put his arm around her. "How are you holding up?" he whispered.

"I'm numb," she mumbled. "It's like a horrible, horrible

138

nightmare. I don't believe it's real."

"I'm sure," he soothed. "I'm sorry you have to go through all this. I'll make sure the police don't question you about personal things concerning Olivia in front of the rest of us," he assured her.

"It's okay. I don't really want to be alone, and you guys are all like family anyway."

Frank glanced over at Gina who was getting coffee for everyone. After he got Jan settled on the nearest stool, he walked over to Gina and put his arms around her shoulders, gently squeezing her. "Will you ever forgive me?" he asked. "I should know by now that I should never doubt you. I am so sorry."

"Forget it," she said, leaning in to him. "You take care of Jan. I can take care of Gina."

"Here, this might cheer you up a bit," he said handing her the note from Edith Talbert. "She sent us $50.00."

Gina took the card and began silently reading the note. "Oh, my god. Did you read this?" she asked excitedly.

"Yes," answered Frank. "Meredith was right about his name."

"No. Not that," she interrupted. "Right here. His grandmother wrote, *'he tells me about all of you'*. Don't you get it? He must be able to talk."

"So?" asked Frank.

"Never mind. I'm just glad he can talk, that's all. Hey everyone," she said. "I think we could all use a little good news today. Frank got a letter from Unabomber 2's grandmother, she sent us a check for the wheel, but that's not all. She referred to him as "Kenneth," so kudos to Meredith. But, the best part is that she said that he *tells* her about us—you get it—he *tells* her," she repeated.

"A lot of people with autism can speak, it's just that they have a difficult time forming the sentences and initiating social conversation," supplied Mark.

"Well, maybe if he felt more comfortable around us, he would talk in here," said Gina.

"I wouldn't count on it," replied Mark. "He's pretty comfortable with you, but he hasn't ever spoken to you, has he?"

"Nobody can get a word in around Gina." Sam chuckled, releasing some of the tension in the room.

"Very funny," snapped Gina. "I'm just going to try harder to get him to relax more when he's in here, then maybe he could stop writing down all those numbers," she said. She hesitated for a moment and then snapped her fingers as she continued, "Just maybe," she said with a gleam in her eye. "Frank, where's the envelope that card came in?"

"I pitched it, why?"

"I want to see if there is an address on it, genius," she responded. "I should have thought about this sooner."
140

She scanned the address on the envelope. "Good, it's not too far from here."

"Don't tell me you intend to go to his house to drag him to some support group for autism?" said Sam, winking at her.

"I am going to his house, but not for the reason you think," she said. "I'll be back as soon as I can," she said hugging Jan. "Don't let the detectives leave until I get back. Mark, did you leave the keys in the car?"

"No, here they are," he said tossing them across the counter to her. "Do you want me to go with you?"

"Nope. I need to go by myself. I'll be right back," she said running out the door, grabbing the check that was lying on the counter as she ran out.

"That girl is like tornado." Meredith smiled as she watched Gina sprint across the parking lot to her car. "Let's get going on our list again before the police get here. What else should we put down here?"

~~~~~

Gina drove up the long driveway leading to the sprawling ranch home of Kenneth and his grandmother. She marveled at the beautiful gardens that lined the driveway and bordered the front entrance. She hoped that she was doing the right thing in coming here and prayed that Kenneth might hold the key to the missing piece of evidence that the detectives needed. She jumped out of the car and rang the doorbell.

Edith glanced through the window in the door before opening it. "Hello," she said, opening the door. "You're Gina from the diner, right?"

"Yes, I am. How did you know my name?" she asked.

"Oh, I know all about you," she said. "Kenneth talks about you all of the time. I hope you're not here to return the check."

"I did bring the check," she said handing it back to Edith. "We all wanted to do this for Unabom... Kenneth," she said, "but that's not really why I came."

"Would you like to come in?" asked Edith opening up the screen door.

"Is Kenneth here?" asked Gina.

"No, he isn't. He hasn't come home from the park yet. I don't expect him for another hour or so."

"The park?" said Gina. "Do you mean the Metro Park around the corner from the diner?"

"Yes, he goes there every day after he leaves the diner. May I ask why you need to see him?"

"This is going to sound crazy, I know," said Gina, "but would you please come with me to the park. I'll explain everything on the way."

"Sure, I'll come," said Edith. "Just let me grab my purse, and lock up the house."

142

On the way to the park, Gina told Edith the story about Olivia's abduction and that she was hoping that Kenneth might have noticed the license plate on the car. Edith told her that he wrote down every number that he heard or saw. She explained that he used the process of writing the numbers to calm himself, so he could think about other things. She knew he threw away his notepads when they were filled up, and she really didn't know if he remembered the numbers after he wrote them.

"There he is," said Edith. "Under that tree over there. You'd better let me go first and explain everything to him. I wouldn't want to upset him by having him see you out of your normal context before he knows why you are here."

Gina watched as Edith talked to Kenneth. He immediately began flipping the pages of his note pad. He finally tore off a sheet and handed it to his grandmother, then he began gathering up his things. He headed toward his bicycle as Edith hurried back to the car.

"He wants to go to the diner. Here's the number he gave me." she said, showing the sheet to Gina. "Do you mind if I come with you?" she asked as she climbed into the car.

"Of course, you can come," replied Gina. "Hop in, so we can get to the diner before the police leave. Did you tell Kenneth the police might be at the diner?"

"Yes, he understands the whole situation. He wants to help. You know, he isn't mentally retarded."

"I never thought he was," said Gina. "I was just never sure what he understood and what he didn't? I don't know much about autism."

"He understands a lot more than people give him credit for. You recognized that he was autistic?" Edith asked.

"No, not really. Mark told me that was what kept Kenneth from talking to us."

They passed Kenneth on his bicycle on their way to the diner. When they pulled into the parking lot, everyone was outside watching the detectives as they were examining the motorcycle. Gina hopped out of the car and ran up to them waving the yellow sheet of paper. Edith waited by the car watching for Kenneth. She could see him coming down the street, but she couldn't help but wonder why he wanted to come here and what would happen when he did.

"Look, look," shouted Gina. "Kenneth wrote down a number that he thinks is the license plate of the car."

Detective Baxter took the sheet of paper from her. He glanced over where Mrs. Talbert was waiting by Gina's car and waved to her. "I take it you got this from Kenneth Talbert," he said.

"Yes, how did you know?" asked Gina.

"Let's just say that my wife loves roses and that I know Kenneth very well." He smiled as he watched Kenneth park his bike next to his grandmother. "This will save us a lot of time," he said heading toward Edith and Kenneth. "You should wait here," he called over his shoulder to
144

Gina.

"Kenneth," said Detective Baxter, "I am going to need to ask you some questions about the numbers on this sheet. This number could be very important to us in helping to find the missing girl."

"Olivia," said Kenneth.

"Yes, Olivia. It seems that maybe the black car that was at the diner was the one used to take her away. Did you see the car here at the diner yesterday?"

Kenneth struggled to get the words in the order he wanted them to come out. He had practiced them repeatedly in his mind as he pedaled to the diner. Finally, he said, "The black car broke my wheel. I saw the license plate."

"I'm not sure what you mean about your wheel," said Detective Baxter.

"Let me explain," interrupted Edith. "Yesterday, Kenneth had an accident with his bike. His wheel was smashed. I think that what he's trying to tell you is that the car was responsible for his accident with the bike. Is that right, Kenneth?"

Kenneth nodded enthusiastically.

"Are you sure, Kenneth, that these are the numbers on the plate of the car that was parked in front of the diner? There is usually a letter on the plate too."

"No letter," replied Kenneth, starting to wring his hands.

"Okay, that probably means it was an out of state license. I'll call this in right away."

"Kenneth, do you want to go into the diner?" asked Edith.

Kenneth shook his head and got on his bike.

"Wait, Kenneth," called Gina. "I want to thank you. You did a wonderful thing by coming here. I am glad you wrote down the number. It will really help us find Olivia."

"Okay," he called as he rode away, leaving Gina thrilled to hear his voice.

"Edith, I'll take you back home. I just need to tell the others that I will be right back."

"Do you mind if I come in with you?" asked Edith. "I would like to be able to put names and faces together when Kenneth talks about all of you."

"Sure, come on in," said Gina. "The diner's not much to look at, but it's the people in it that make it special."

Chapter 11

Gina was exhausted as she headed to Kelley's after dropping Edith Talbert off at her house. Edith had invited her to stay for dinner, but Gina explained that she needed to stop by and check on another friend. She agreed that she would come for dinner on Friday. She was fascinated when Edith told her about Kenneth's love for flowers and about the work he was doing with his friend from the university. She marveled at the beautiful gardens that surrounded the front of the house, which, according to Edith, were nothing compared to those in the back.

So much had happened today that it was difficult to believe that it could have occurred within a single day. She wasn't sure what to do about her own mess at the apartment. She would check with Jeff and Colin later when they came back on duty, but there was actually nothing she could do at the present. She certainly didn't have enough money to replace all that Greg had taken. She did have some sort of renter's insurance, but she wasn't sure how much would be covered since he was actually a resident of the apartment. *Frankly, right now, I am far more concerned with bigger things than about missing computers and CDs*, she thought.

She was worried about Jan and couldn't imagine how she was going to get through this. Olivia was her life. Right now, Jan seemed to be numb, but when she faced the horror that her only daughter might be in the hands of people who intended to make a sex slave and drug addict out of her, Gina wasn't sure she could handle it.

147

She shuddered at what might be happening to Olivia at this very moment. *Poor baby*, she thought. *She must know by now that she's been abducted. She has to be frightened to death.* "Please, dear God, help her. Give them both the strength to get through this," she prayed aloud.

Her cell phone rang and she jumped, bumping her knee against the column of the steering wheel. "Shit," she yelled as she fumbled in her purse to find her phone before it stopped ringing. "Hello," she moaned as she tried to manipulate the turn into Kelley's apartment with one hand.

"Gina, it's Mark."

"Where are you?" she asked. "It sounds like you're standing in the middle of a freeway."

"I'm at a gas station."

"What? Where?"

" I'm headed to Miami," said Mark.

"So, you're just taking off for the surf and sand, and you're leaving us up here with this mess?" she shouted.

"No, of course, not," said Mark impatiently. "I'm heading to Miami because of that mess up there. Will you just listen and let me explain?"

"This better be good."

148

"I overheard the call that Jim Baxter got on his radio about the license plate. It was a Florida plate from Dade County. It came back to some guy named Hastings Gutierrez. He supposedly runs some private investigation company that locates missing persons. I'm betting that his business is a front for something else."

"My good god, Mark," interrupted Gina. "You actually believe that you can find this guy and his car faster than the police can. Come on Mark, that doesn't make sense."

"No, the reason I want to get down there is because I know what Olivia and Teresa look like, and I think Teresa must work for this Gutierrez. If I can find Teresa, then I hope she will lead me to Olivia. I can expedite the search faster than the police will. They must have hundreds of missing girls that they're trying to track. I'm only looking for one."

"Mark, this is ludicrous! You certainly shouldn't be taking this on by yourself. These people won't take lightly to some college boy spying on their business. People like that don't mess around."

"I'm aware of that. I'm not naïve about the danger involved in what I'm trying to do, but I think this is the surest way for us to help Olivia before she gets beyond being helped."

"Good god, Mark, does Frank know that you're doing this?" asked Gina, already knowing that he probably he didn't.

"No, that's why I'm calling you. I want you to tell him in the morning. He's spending the night at Jan's, so he won't miss me until then."

"This is not smart, Mark. Have you forgotten that Teresa knows what you look like, too? What if she spots you before you find her? I'm warning you again, these people won't mess around. You might end up floating around with Howard if you're not careful." Then, realizing what she had just said, she quickly responded, "Ooh, that wasn't very respectful, was it? Anyway, I think you should just turn your little motorcycle around and head back up here."

"I want to do this. I know I can expedite the search for Olivia from down there. I have a place to stay, and I promise to call the diner every morning. I've got to go. Don't forget to explain all this to Uncle Frank."

"Explain what, that you're an idiot? For god's sake, be careful. We don't need to be searching for two missing people," she shouted.

"Thanks for worrying, Gina," said Mark sarcastically. "I'll call tomorrow."

"Jeez Louise, what next?" said Gina as she snapped her cell phone closed. She headed toward Kelley's apartment, limping and rubbing her injured knee. Kelley was in the back yard with her kids when Gina arrived. "Hey, everybody, what's up?" greeted Gina.

A chorus of little voices called her name and four sets of tiny arms grabbed her around the legs. She hugged each of them in turn. She reached down and picked up Sarah, then turned her attention to Kelley. "I take it there's no news?"

150

"No," said Kelley, waving the portable phone in the air. "I haven't been two inches away from this thing all day. I must have checked it a hundred times to make sure it was working. I'm just about at my wits end."

"Sarah, my love," said Gina, "I've got to put you down. You're getting too big for me to hold anymore. Why don't you show me how you slide down your big slide," she said.

"You're so good with my kids," said Kelley. "They absolutely adore you. By the way, Carl Jr. told me that you saw Olivia at the mall last night. He said she was sick."

Gina took in a deep breath as she tried to decide how to tell Kelley about Olivia. She wasn't sure Kelley needed anything else to worry about right now.

"Is something wrong, Gina?" asked Kelley. "You look like you're about ready to cry. What is it? Tell me. What's going on? Come on, let's go inside, the kids will be okay out here."

"No, don't leave them alone, Kelley. Never take your eyes off them," cried Gina.

"Gina, tell me what's going on. I've never seen you like this."

Overwhelmed with anger, fear, and extreme sadness, Gina turned around so that the kids couldn't see or hear her as she spewed out the story of Olivia's abduction. The tears she had stifled all day gushed like water surging from a broken dam. As she listened to herself
151

telling Kelley that Teresa was apparently part of a human-trafficking ring, she felt like she was describing one of the dozens of crime shows she watched on TV.

Before today, she had watched those shows with complete detachment, oblivious of the fact that there were actually evil people like that in the world. It never occurred to her that such crimes would ever reach into her own little, insignificant life and destroy someone she cared about.

"Oh, my god, Gina. What can we do? Oh, my god," Kelley repeated.

"There's nothing we can do but pray," Gina muttered.

"I've been praying all day that Carl would call me," replied Kelley. "I'm not sure anyone is listening anymore."

"Don't say that, Kelley. If we don't have faith, then we will never get through this."

"I'm sorry, Gina. I know you have a strong faith and believe in the power of prayer. It's just that right now, I can't share your convictions. There must be something we can do besides pray, isn't there?" Kelley lamented.

"Mark has taken off for Miami to see if he can find Teresa. He thinks that if he can find her, she will lead him to Olivia."

"What?" screeched Kelley. "Miami is a huge city. That can't be a good idea. And, even if he does find her, people like her and her associates won't think twice of getting rid of someone like him. Surely, Frank didn't suggest that he should go down there."

"Of course, not," said Gina. "I have to tell him tomorrow morning that Mark has left. Lucky me. I know he'll go berserk. In just the few days Mark has been here, Frank has really gotten attached to him."

"What about Jan? How is she coping with all of this?" Kelley couldn't fathom dealing with the loss of a child in such a horrific way. She glanced over at her four little ones suddenly frightened for their safety.

"I don't think it's sunk in, yet. She's still in shock and denial. At first, she said she was just numb, but after the police left, she told us that we were all wrong and that Olivia had just made another stupid choice that was going to get her in more trouble with her parole officer. She's actually angry with Olivia, right now."

"I hope to goodness she's right, and all of you are wrong," said Kelley.

"It's just easier for her to avoid facing the truth," said Gina. "The police have a composite drawing of Teresa created by their own artist based on the descriptions of the friends of two other missing girls. They showed the drawing to all of us, and everyone agreed it was Teresa. Even Olivia's friend, who was with her and Teresa in the diner, and the sales clerk where Olivia worked identified the picture as Teresa."

"But you don't know for sure that Teresa is actually linked to any human-trafficking ring, right? Kelley knew she was

153

grasping at straws, but she just wanted Olivia to be safe and all of this to be a big mistake.

"That's right," sighed Gina. "But, we do know that she was with the other missing girls who have never been found and that she was later with Olivia, who is now also missing. That just can't be coincidental. Even if she isn't involved in human-trafficking, she obviously is involved in kidnapping or maybe something even worse."

"What could be worse than forced into being a sex slave?"

"Murder?" suggested Gina.

"Don't say that; don't even think it," screeched Kelley. "There must be something that we can do," she repeated.

"That's what's so terrible about all of this. There's nothing we can do." Gina looked up to the sky, trying to get control of the surge of emotions that threatened to undo her.

"What about putting up posters with Olivia's picture? Carl has army buddies all over the place. Come on, help me get the kids inside, and I'll fix their dinner. Then, I'm going to email the wives I know and send them a picture of Olivia. I have digital pictures of Carl's last going away party we had at the diner. I know there must be a picture of Olivia among them. I can also put her picture on my *Facebook* page. I have gobs of friends on *Facebook* and *Twitter*. That will at least get people to start looking for her."

154

"Kelley, I think we'd better ask the detective working on Olivia's case about this and also Jan. What if we tip Teresa and her thugs off, and they decide to dump Olivia because too many people might recognize her?"

"Do you have the detective's number? Let's call him first. Only, use your cell phone; I don't want to tie up the line on my home phone."

Once again, Gina fumbled through her purse looking for her phone while Kelley rounded up the kids and began fixing dinner. She agreed that Kelly's idea was a good way to get Olivia's picture scattered everywhere, but she wasn't sure that the timing was right. She was certain that Jim Baxter would agree with her.

"Gina, get on my computer, and look up the pictures of the going away party," called Kelley from the kitchen. "They're in a folder called My Pictures. I think I downloaded them into a subfolder labeled Going Away #3. I'm sure that I took some pictures of Olivia that night."

"OK, just let me get Jim on the phone first." The number she had entered into her phone contacts was supposedly a direct line to Jim's Office, but her call went straight to his voice mail. Gina left a message for him to call her, and then sat down at the desk to begin to look for the pictures that Kelley wanted her to find. A few seconds later, Kelley's home phone rang.

"Here, that was quick," said Kelley as she handed Gina the portable phone. "Don't talk too long and listen for the beep that signals another call is coming in."

"I left Jim my cell number to call, not your home phone
155

number," said Gina.

Kelley just stood there staring at the phone.

"Answer it for heaven's sake," shouted Gina.

"I can't," said Kelley, shoving the phone to Gina. "I'm afraid to."

Gina grabbed the phone. "Hello, Johnson's residence," she said.

"Mrs. Johnson?" answered the voice on the other end.

"No, just a moment, I'll get her," said Gina. "It's for you, Kelley."

Kelley turned pale and reached for the phone with trembling hands. "Hello. This is Kelley Johnson," she said softly. She motioned for Gina to come closer, so she could listen to the conversation.

Gina leaned in close to Kelley. She heard a formal sounding, male voice saying, "Mrs. Johnson. This is Captain Roger Stafford. I am with the Department of Defense."

Gina grabbed Kelley's hand. The color had totally drained from Kelley's face as she sank to the floor. Gina sat down beside her and leaned in close to listen to the conversation.

"How bad is it? Is Carl going to be okay? I know that since you aren't here in person that he's not dead,"

Kelley gasped. "How bad is he hurt?"

Gina heard Roger Stafford draw in a deep breath. "Carl received some serious injuries to his right shoulder and leg from sniper gunfire during a routine inspection yesterday. He's still under care at the base hospital in Afghanistan but will be transported to Germany or stateside as soon as he can be moved—probably within a day or two."

Gina felt Kelley fall toward her, and she quickly reached around Kelley's waist to steady her. She listened as Captain Stafford asked. "Are you still there, Mrs. Johnson?"

"Y..yes," stammered Kelley. "I'm listening."

"I'll let you know," he continued, "where and when he will be transferred, as soon as I know something. I'll also have him call you as soon as he's able. Right now, he's pretty heavily sedated. I wish I knew more to tell you, but I don't know any more than that right now. Would you like for me to send one of our Care-Team members to help you and your family with any questions you have about the notification process or to help you to prepare for visitation as soon as he is moved?"

"No, that won't be necessary," said Kelley regaining her composure as she noticed her children staring at her from the kitchen. "I just need to know who to contact to get updates on his condition."

Carl Jr. ran to the desk and grabbed a pen and paper from the middle drawer. He handed it to his mother as tears streamed down his cheeks. Gina reached up and

157

pulled him on to her lap. Kelley quickly jotted down the numbers as the Captain repeated them.

"Is there anything more that I can do to help?" asked the Captain.

"We'll be fine, Captain Stafford," said Kelley. "Thanks for asking, but we're a military family," she continued as she reached over to squeeze Carl's little, trembling hand and motioned for her other children to join them on the floor. "We're fine, but we'll be much better once Carl is home with us," she said opening her arms and gathering her kids close to her. "Thank you for calling. I'm sure these calls aren't easy for you. I'll call in the morning for any more information that you might have on Carl's status. Please call me if there's any change in his condition," she said as she hung up the phone.

"What is it, Mommy? Is Daddy hurt?" asked Carl Jr. immediately after she put down the phone.

"Daddy is coming home soon," answered Kelley. "He has a couple of booboos on his shoulder and leg, but he's going to be okay," she said reaching out to touch each of the kids gently on the head. "Right now, though, Mommy needs to make some phone calls to some of Daddy's friends, and Gina is going to help you all finish your dinner, okay?" she asked. She glanced at Gina with pleading eyes.

Gina jumped up from the floor and offered Kelley a hand to help her up. One, by one the kids quietly got up and headed to the kitchen, all except for Carl Jr.

"Don't worry, Mommy. Daddy's going to be all right. He
158

promised me that he would come home for good this time," he said hugging her around the waist. "Do you want me to sleep with you tonight?" he asked.

Kelley knelt down and hugged him tightly. "You *are* my little man," she said kissing him on the cheeks and wiping the tears from his face. "You know what? I'm sure our dinner is cold and yucky by now. I think we should all just climb into our van and go to McDonalds. What do you say? We can celebrate that daddy will be coming back to us soon, and I can make those phone calls when we get back. How about it, Gina? Are you up for a Big Mac?"

"My favorite sandwich." Gina smiled, impressed with Kelley's plucky response in front of her kids.

Chapter 12

Teresa glanced out the window of the luxurious, private jet as they landed on the runway of the small public airport located about twenty-five miles south of Miami. As the pilot taxied toward their private hangar, Hastings grabbed Olivia and shook her so hard that Teresa was afraid that her neck would snap. Olivia moaned but didn't open her eyes.

"I'll get her ready," said Teresa. "The drug should be wearing off pretty soon."

"It looks like you've overdosed her. She hasn't even moved since we left Atlanta. You'd better not have screwed this up."

"I didn't overdose her, Hastings. Just give me a few minutes, and she'll be ready to be moved to the car."

"I don't intend to hang around here and wait for you to wake her up. I'll send someone back to get you. Make sure she's awake and able to walk down the gangway on her own, and don't give her any more heroin. It's time for her to learn that she has to work for it," he snarled. He shot a look of utter hatred at Teresa as he left the airplane.

Teresa quickly looked away so that he couldn't see the fear in her eyes. All the way from Atlanta, she had tried to plan her escape from his grasp, but nothing she came up with would put her out of reach of his vast network of thugs. From his contemptuous treatment of her, she
160

knew that she had been right about her time running out. If she was to have any chance to escape, she had to do it now, before he sent someone to pick them up.

Trying to calm herself, a strange thought streaked through her mind. "He has never left me here alone before," she said aloud. Her mind was reeling as she considered that, perhaps, he was intentionally giving her a chance to get away. Maybe he wanted her to leave on her own. Could it possibly be? *My god,* she thought, *is he just going to let me get away?*

She got up and moved over to the other side of the plane, so she could look out of the window and see which of Hastings' drivers was waiting for him. She saw two of the staff members of the airport leaving the hangar in the golf cart with the pilot and recognized Lance, leaning up against Hastings' car. He was one of the few bodyguards that she actually liked. Lance had gone with her on several of their abductions when her brother Antonio was busy on some other assignment. He was tough, but he had a gentle side too. He didn't get emotionally attached to his victims, but she could sense that he was particularly protective of her—even more so than Antonio.

She stared down at his neatly dressed, statuesque body, casually leaning against the side of the black SUV. His shoulders were broad, and his waist was slim. His suit obviously was tailored to fit him perfectly. He looked the part of a wealthy, business man. His dark hair was slicked back on the sides and was cut in a short wave in the front.

Lance had been a Marine, but some indictment for his

part in the torture of a prisoner had resulted in a dishonorable discharge. She wasn't sure how he got messed up with Hastings, but she knew Lance was dedicated to him. Hastings trusted him—more than he trusted some of his other thugs. She trusted him too.

After the others had left the hangar, she watched as Hastings' walked up to Lance and said something to him. Lance raised himself up from the car and seemed to be disagreeing with Hastings over something. Hastings suddenly grabbed Lance by the lapel of his jacket and shook him. When Hastings let loose of him, Lance dropped his head and slowly shook it back and forth. He glanced up at her window with a look of sadness and regret as he headed toward the plane. When their eyes met, she quickly ducked away.

She realized her assumption that Hastings was actually going to allow her to slip away was only wishful thinking and stupid. She was just grasping at straws. Hastings would never let her go. The argument between the two men had obviously had something to do with her. She knew that Lance liked her, but she was also aware that he had committed more than one assassination for Hastings.

"Oh, my god," she wailed. "He's going to force Lance to do his dirty work." She sat frozen in the seat as she listened to the sound of Lance's footsteps on the portable metal gangway. *Was this how it was really going to end for her? No. They wouldn't risk shooting her here.* She jumped as she heard the loud thud as the door of the cabin slammed shut. She stared toward the galley of the plane, expecting Lance to appear any moment out of the darkness.

When she heard him going back down the gangway, she was stunned. He wasn't coming inside to get her after all. What was going on? She quickly looked out the window again. She couldn't believe her eyes—Lance was rolling the gangway away from the plane, leaving an eight foot drop to the concrete floor below.

As she watched, Hastings climbed into the rear seat of the car and never looked back toward the plane. Lance glanced up at the window once more before he climbed into the driver's seat. Teresa stared back at him and was certain that she saw him mouth the word, '*run*.' Then, he climbed into the car and peeled out onto the tarmac. She watched as the gigantic, automatic door of the hangar slowly lowered, shutting out any light as it reached the ground.

Obviously, Hastings intended to make it difficult for her to get out of the plane. He was probably buying time to allow her captors to come for her. How much time did she have? Minutes? Hours?

As she moved away from the window, she was aware of the stifling heat inside the plane. There was no circulation of air through the cabin, and she knew that the prediction for the outside temperature was over a hundred degrees. It would soon be much hotter than that inside the plane. There was no remaining doubt in her mind that Hastings planned to do away with her.

Surely, he doesn't think I will just sit here and wait for his henchmen to find me passed out from the heat. How stupid does he think I am, she mused. Frantically, she fumbled in the darkness around the floor of the plane trying to locate her purse and cell phone. The backlight

163

of the phone would give her enough light to guide her to the door of the plane and allow her to manipulate the locks. After that, she would have to drop from the door onto the concrete floor—a feat that she wasn't sure she could manage without breaking a leg or an ankle.

Olivia moaned when Teresa shoved her legs to the side as she continued to search for her purse. "I don't feel so good," Olivia stammered before leaning over and retching loudly as violent dry-heaves once again consumed her. "Someone, help me," she pleaded in between the gagging and vomiting.

"You're on your own, Olivia. I'm out of here," snarled Teresa as she headed to the galley of the plane. She finally reached the door and struggled to move the heavy bar that locked it from the inside. After several attempts, she lifted the bar and pushed open the heavy door. A rush of air swept through the plane. "Thank, god," she said. "Air!"

She shined the light from her cell phone toward the ground and stared down at the concrete floor below. "Oh, my god, that looks farther down than I thought it would be," she muttered aloud. After several moments of just standing there looking around for other options, she decided that there was no choice. She would have to go out backwards, easing her way out the door while she clung to the bottom edge of the opening. She would then have to drop the remaining way to the ground. "At least it will reduce the distance to the ground," she consoled herself.

She turned around and got down on the floor in the galley of the plane, putting the phone back into her purse and wrapping the purse strap over her head, so her hands were free. On her knees, she started cautiously backing toward the door. When she felt her feet reach the edge of the plane, she quickly glanced around for something to hold onto to keep her from sliding past the edge and careening toward the ground. Feeling around in the darkness, her hands touched a strap dangling from something above her. She yanked on it to make sure it would not come loose from whatever it was attached to. Satisfied that it would hold her, she grabbed it and wrapped it around her hand.

"This is not going to be easy," she moaned aloud. She continued to back out of the plane, until her knees reached the ridge at the edge of the door. Holding on to the strap with her left hand, she pushed herself out the door with her other hand. She screamed as she felt her body drop, and she was left dangling from the airplane by her left hand. She felt an excruciating pain in her left wrist as she swung back and forth like a pendulum, and she realized that she was losing her grip on the strap. Closing her eyes and preparing herself for the final fall, she let loose of the strap and fell with a crash on to the concrete below. The heel on her left shoe snapped and her foot twisted as the weight of her body crushed it beneath her. She managed to keep from falling over backwards and hitting her head on the concrete, but the jolt of the fall sent sharp shooting pains from her foot to the top of her head. For a moment, she just sat on the floor —unable to breathe or move.

"Oh, my god," she moaned. "I feel like I've broken every bone in my body." Slowly she began to take inventory of her injuries. Her left wrist hurt terribly, but she could bend it. She gathered her legs beneath her and tried to stand up, but she quickly discovered that she couldn't put any pressure on her left leg without pains shooting out the top of her head. "Oh, this is wonderful," she moaned. She reached for her cell phone and shined the light around the hangar. She hoped she could find something to help her keep the weight off of her left foot, but the beam of light from the phone didn't reach very far into the darkness, and there was nothing within easy access to where she had landed. *If I can just get outside, I can flag someone down who will help me get out of here before Hastings' henchmen arrive*, she thought.

She took off her shoes to make it easier for her to hop on one foot toward the control that would open the hangar's automatic door. She pushed against the floor to get some leverage to lift herself up onto her right leg. She tried to hop but screamed as she attempted to use her left leg to steady herself. The pain was so severe that she thought she might pass out, and she dropped once more to the ground, bending her head between her knees to try to keep from fainting.

She took in deep breaths to rid her stomach of its queasiness. She refused to cry—*what good would that do anyway*, she asked herself. After several minutes, she finally decided that it would be easier simply to scoot toward the door. *How much time have I wasted? How much time do I have left*, she wondered.

Scooting across the floor, she finally managed to reach the door. Clinging to the door frame to steady herself, she managed to get up from the floor and press the button of the door opener. She sighed in relief as the massive door slowly began to rise.

The bright Florida sunlight was blinding after being in

166

semi-darkness, and she raised her injured wrist to shade her eyes to try to determine her options for help. In the distance, she could see the grass thatched hospitality hut and the building that housed the service center. She quickly took out her cell phone again and searched through her contacts, remembering that she had entered the phone number of the service center when she called there once to make arrangements for a late arrival for Hastings. She located the number and pushed the "Send" button. The friendly voice at the other end was a welcomed relief. She briefly explained that she had accidently slipped on the ground and twisted her ankle.

"Oh, my," said the friendly woman. "I'll send someone out right away to get you."

Teresa hopped outside and reached around the doorframe to put down the door. She didn't want anyone to see inside of the hangar. Within minutes, she saw the approaching golf cart speeding toward her and noticed a pair of crutches sticking up over the top of the windshield. She had forgotten how friendly and accommodating the people were at this small airport.

Once inside the service center, she glanced outside toward the security gate entrance just as a black Lincoln Navigator pulled into the drive. "I'm sorry, but I need to lease one of your rental cars right away," she said to the clerk who came rushing to help her toward a chair. She held out her driver's license and credit card to the woman. "I'm really in a big hurry, can you just have them bring me a rental car, right away?"

"Certainly," said the clerk. "But are you sure you'll be able to drive? We can have someone take you to the Urgent

Care Center just down the road a bit."

"I'll be fine," said Teresa, trying not to expose the urgency she was feeling. "If you'll just take my information and let me sign for the car, I'd appreciate it. As I said, I'm rather in a hurry." She glanced at the security gate where the black SUV was still waiting for clearance.

The clerk brought the rental agreement on a clip board. Teresa scribbled her name and initials next to all of the X's, and tried to get up on her own. She winced as she accidentally transferred weight onto her injured leg, and the young clerk reached out to help her.

"Here, let me help you through the door. It'll take some time getting used to those crutches—believe me I know. I broke my ankle a year ago." The clerk continued her friendly chatter while Teresa kept her eyes fixed on the security gate that was slowly swinging open to allow the SUV to enter.

She pretended that she needed to rest for a moment before going out the front door to allow time for the SUV to pass through the gate and onto the road leading back to the hangars. She didn't want to risk them spotting her before she could get away from the airport.

Once inside the car, with the crutches that the young woman insisted that she keep along with directions to the nearest Urgent Care Center, Teresa peeled out of the driveway toward the road leading to the main highway. Where was she going to go? Where could she go? Certainly, she couldn't go back to her apartment. The sign for the Miami International Airport caught her attention, and she quickly maneuvered the car toward

168

the exit.

She reached for her cell phone thinking maybe she could reach Antonio before he left Atlanta, and they could find a way out of this mess together. She knew that he would be in danger too as soon as Hastings discovered she was missing. She quickly pushed the speed dial number for Antonio. The call went directly into his voice mail. "Shit," she yelled. "He must have his damned phone turned off." *Now what*, she wondered? In her rearview mirror, she stared in horror at a large, black SUV weaving in and out of the traffic behind her.

Chapter 13

When he pulled in to the parking lot at five o'clock Wednesday morning, Frank was surprised to see Gina sitting on a patio chair outside of the diner. "What dragged you out of bed at this hour?" he grumbled.

"Well, let's just say that I felt a twinge of pity for you. I know that's out of character for me, but I did. How'd things go last night with Jan?" she asked.

"When Olivia didn't come home again last night and didn't answer her cell phone, Jan finally realized that we might be right. She was hysterical, pacing back and forth and repeating '*oh my god; oh my god,*' over and over. I couldn't snap her out of it. I finally found some tranquilizers in her medicine cabinet and made her take one. She fell asleep about three this morning. I hated to leave her alone, so I tried to call you, but you didn't answer at home or on your cell. Then, I tried to call Mark at my apartment, and he didn't answer either. Luckily, I had Sam's number on my cell phone, and I finally got hold of him. He called Meredith, and she came right over."

"I spent the night at Kelley's, and my cell phone ran out of battery. I didn't have my charger with me. In fact, I probably no longer have a charger," she said.

"What's that supposed to mean?" asked Frank as he unlocked the front door to the diner. "Did you drop it in the toilet again?"

170

"No, I didn't drop it in the toilet again," she mocked. "It's a long story of very little significance considering what else I have to tell you." She heaved a big sigh as she flipped over the *Closed* sign. "Just remember that you should never kill the messenger," she added.

"Okay—out with it. What are you talking about?" called Frank over his shoulder as he headed to the back to get the meat from the freezer. "I wonder where Mark is? I don't think he knows anyone around here, but he didn't answer at the apartment."

"Funny you should mention Mark," said Gina. "It's his message that I have to deliver."

"Dear, god," shouted Frank, stopping in his tracks and whirling around to face Gina. "Please don't tell me that strong-headed kid has taken off for Miami? I heard him talking to Jim Baxter yesterday about the license plate on the car."

"Well," muttered Gina, "that was easier than I thought it would be."

"Oh, my god. He did head for Miami, didn't he?"

"Yep, he sure did. What an idiot!" she said, shaking her head. "I don't think he learned too much about life while he was studying psychology. He should have studied more about the minds of criminals. I warned him that this was stupid and dangerous, but he's convinced that he can find Olivia faster than the police can."

"He's probably right on that account. He'll have more time to devote to finding Olivia than the police will. She's

171

probably just one of a thousand missing people they're looking for. But I agree with you, he's putting himself in a lot of danger."

"You're taking this a lot better than I thought you would," said Gina. "I fully expected fists pounding the wall and a string of expletives that would highlight the diner in blue."

"I'm just sorry that I couldn't have gone with him," said Frank. "If you'd have seen Jan last night and had heard Jim Baxter talking to Mark and me about how those thugs work, you'd understand why we couldn't just sit back and wait for the police to find Olivia."

"Well, anyway, he promised to call you this morning. He said he had a place to stay in Miami and would call you every day. Don't you have the number of his cell phone?" she asked. She headed for the backroom to grab an apron.

"No, I don't. Things have been happening so fast around here that we haven't really had much of a chance to talk since Sunday. We never got around to exchanging contact information yet."

Gina headed in to the dining room and started pulling the chairs down from the table. "Well, I have it on my phone, but, of course, I can't get it until I get the stupid thing charged up. I hate things that run on batteries." she said. "If those technology gurus are all so smart, why don't they build the darn charger right into the phone, and while they're at it—why don't they make the chargers all alike?"

"Are we really going to have a conversation about phone
172

chargers?" asked Frank.

"Well, you have to admit, I have a point. Anyway," she continued. "Mark's isn't the only message I have to deliver."

Franks's shoulders dropped, and his entire body uncontrollably slumped, showing his utter despair. *What else*, he thought. *I'm not sure I can handle one more piece of bad news.* From the look that Gina gave him, he knew she hated to add to his worries. "Go ahead, Gina. What else?" he said, trying to conjure up a smile of encouragement.

Gina stared at him for a minute, then finally went on. "Why do I always have to be the messenger? Well, it doesn't matter," she continued. "Kelley won't be in for a while. I'm not sure how long, but she got a call from the Defense Department last night."

"Oh, no," interrupted Frank. "How bad is it?"

"Carl has been injured, and they'll be shipping him out of Afghanistan today or tomorrow," reported Gina. "She doesn't want to leave her kids alone now because they're all a little confused and scared for their daddy. I guess the military will pay her expenses to visit him when he gets transferred out of Afghanistan. So, she'll be taking off as soon as arrangements can be made for her and the kids."

"I was afraid of this. Poor kid, he was due out of there next week. What rotten luck! How serious are his injuries? Did they elaborate about the potential for full recovery or did they know that yet."

"I really don't know. They told her he was shot in the shoulder and leg by some sniper. Anyway, it looks like it's just you and me in the diner today," she said as she started putting the small, wire condiment trays on the tables.

For the next half hour, they were both quiet—lost in their own thoughts. They were simply operating on automatic pilot as they silently completed the necessary prep work to get the diner ready to open.

Frank couldn't help but worry about what was happening to Olivia. His anger swelled as he thought about the abuse she must be going through. A hot flush seared his face and neck, and his heart pounded as he opened and slammed the doors of cupboards and coolers while trying to do the work that had to be done. He glanced up at the clock—almost time to open. *Funny*, he thought, *somehow life just goes on, even when something has managed to change it drastically. I shouldn't be here, but here I am getting ready to serve my customers the same way I do every day. I should be with Jan or in Miami searching everywhere for Olivia. But what could I do that Mark can't do?*

He recognized the anger and utter helplessness that he was feeling now. He had felt that same vulnerability and rage when his mom and brother suddenly disappeared. Back then, when he finally realized that no amount of wailing, wishing, or praying would ever bring them back, he'd promised never again to care too deeply about anyone. He thought he had kept that promise, until last night.

Watching Jan go through the same feelings that he had

174

felt as a boy, made him realize that he did care for her—very deeply. He wanted to hold her and reassure her that things would be okay, but he couldn't do either one. For years, he'd denied the strange feelings he had whenever she brushed past him in the close quarters behind the counter. At first, she'd been married, but now she wasn't. *So, why hadn't he tried to tell her how he felt?* He didn't know. *That wasn't true. He did know. He was afraid. But what was he afraid of—rejection? No, he was quite certain that Jan had feelings for him too. Then, why hadn't he told her he loved her? Why hadn't he been able to hold her last night? Why was he afraid?*

"What's Tom doing here so early?" asked Gina, interrupting Frank's thoughts. "He just jogged into the parking lot right behind Sam."

"He's going to help out with waiting tables," said Frank. "He offered yesterday, and I called him on my way here this morning. You don't mind sharing your tips, do you?"

"Are you kidding? I'm running on half of my cylinders today. I didn't get any more sleep than you did last night. Does he know what he's doing?" she asked.

"Seems to. He said he used to wait tables, and he did fine yesterday."

"Morning folks," said Sam. "Heard from Mark, yet?"

"How'd you know Mark wasn't here?" asked Frank.

"What do you mean? Didn't he talk to you before he left?" asked Sam. "After you and Jan left yesterday, he told me that he was going to leave right away for Miami to see if

175

he could expedite the search for Olivia. Meredith and I agreed that somebody needed to do something. She gave him the key to her condo, and he took off from here yesterday afternoon. He should already be in Atlanta or farther by now."

"My good god," shrieked Gina. "You're all nuts. Do you even have a clue about what kind of people snatched Olivia? They aren't like any of you, for god's sake. They're mentally deficient, horribly mean animals who would just as soon run a knife though your gizzard as to look at you. How could you encourage Mark to put himself in that position?"

"Look, Gina," said Sam, "we're not stupid. We're just not willing to sit by and leave this in the hands of overworked and overwhelmed police. Mark is a smart young man. He's not going to try to do anything foolish, but he can do some of the grunt work for the police. We made him promise that as soon as he got any information about Teresa's whereabouts, he would contact the police."

"This is amazing—simply amazing," said Gina. "I'm off work one day, and *Frank's* somehow has transformed itself from a diner into the headquarters of a group of unlicensed, uninformed private eyes. I love you all, but I hope you haven't gotten Mark into something he can't handle."

As she went to get Sam his coffee and toast, she noticed another car pulling into the parking lot. "Good grief, here come Jan and Meredith."

Frank rushed to the door to meet them. "What are you doing here, Jan? You should have stayed at home."

176

"I can't just sit at home. It was driving me crazy. I need to do something," said Jan. "Has Mark called yet?"

"Oh, my god," moaned Gina. "I can't believe this. You're all in on it."

"What, Gina?" snapped Jan. "I know that Mark is taking a big chance, but I feel like at least someone is doing something to help Olivia. I'm grateful, very grateful to him."

Gina reached out and hugged her. "I know, sweetie. I'm glad he's willing to help. I just think this is too dangerous for any of us to mess around in. What if he tips Teresa and her thugs off, and they decide to…" she stopped. "Oh well, maybe I've just watched too many crime shows. If I can't beat you guys, I guess I'd better join you! Okay let's figure this out. What time did Mark leave yesterday?"

"He left about four o'clock yesterday afternoon," said Sam. "It's about an 18 hour drive to Miami."

"He's had to have stopped several times along the way for gas and stuff, so it's possible that he could get into Miami by around noon, right?" asked Meredith.

"Yea, I'd guess pretty close to that, depending on whether he stopped to sleep. When he left here, he said he intended to keep going straight through to Miami. But he might have felt the need to pull over for a couple of hours. We'll just have to wait until he calls in," answered Sam.

"We should give him a definite time to call every day,"

177

said Gina, catching the spirit of the others. "That way we'll know that if he doesn't call us on time, we should notify someone down there to start looking for him."

"That's not a bad idea," said Sam. "I'm glad to see you're finally on board with us."

"Hey, I'm just as frightened for Olivia and as frustrated with having to wait around here for something to happen as the rest of you. I just didn't want us to have two people to worry about," said Gina, defending her earlier feelings about their involvement in helping to find Olivia.

~~~~~

For the next hour, the diner operated as usual except that Frank kept checking the phone to make sure it was working. The same customers arrived, sat in their same seats or booths, and ordered the same breakfasts. Jan tried to wait on tables, but the well-intentioned inquiries about how Olivia was doing in her new job from customers who had no clue about what had happened to her were more than she could handle. She finally decided to stay in the back and let Gina and Tom handle the customers. At seven-thirty Jeff and Colin came in.

"Hey, Gina," said Jeff. "How are you holding up? I stopped by your place to check on you last night, but you obviously weren't home. I was worried about you."

"That's nice, Jeff. Thanks. I stayed at Kelley's last night. Have you heard anything about Olivia?" asked Gina.

"No, not yet. As soon as we hear anything, I'll let you know. I do have some good news and some bad news
178

about Greg, though."

"Hopefully, the good news is that you found him at the bottom of Hoover Dam."

Jeff laughed. "Gina, you have to stop making such menacing threats against him. Someone might think you were plotting to dispose of him yourself."

"Believe me, I've considered it." retorted Gina. "Anyway, what's your news?"

"Well, what I thought would be good news is that we found him alive and well, and we are holding him for grand theft."

"That is good news, actually. Hopefully, you can keep him locked up without bail and then throw him in jail forever."

"I'm afraid we can't hold him much longer."

"What?" shrieked Gina. "Why can't you hold him?"

"Well, the bad news is that he claims he didn't take anything," explained Jeff. "He says he left right after he talked to you on the phone. According to him, he was so hurt and angry that he stormed out of the apartment, and he must have forgotten to lock the door. He claims that he was on his way back to the apartment to try to make things right with you when we picked him up. He maintains that you either moved the stuff yourself and are lying about him to get even, or someone else robbed you both."

179

"That lying bastard," screeched Gina, causing everyone in the diner to glance her way.

"What's wrong with you?" stormed Frank. "Keep your voice down, for god's sake, Gina. What's going on anyway?"

"Never mind, Frank. This doesn't concern you," snapped Gina.

"Of course it concerns me. When you're upset, everyone in the diner feels it. Now, tell me what in the heck is going on?"

"You mean you haven't told anyone about this?" asked Jeff.

"Look, Jeff. They have other, more important things to worry about. My problem is small in comparison."

"But these people care about you, Gina. I care about you too. It isn't right that you feel you have to handle this alone."

"I appreciate your concern, Jeff, but I've had to take care of myself for years. I've learned that life throws you lots of curves and that you have two choices—either deal with them and move on or cave and give up on life. I don't intend to cave, and I've learned that when push comes to shove, I'm the only one I can depend on. I don't need anyone's help," she said, dropping her head to hide the tears that she desperately didn't want to shed.

"Gina, for heaven's sake. What is it?" asked Frank.

180

Without answering him, Gina whirled around and headed for the restroom in the back of the diner. She didn't want them to see her cry, and she always cried when she was mad. She hated it when she cried; it made her seem weak, and she was tougher than that.

Self-deprecating thoughts streamed through her mind. *How many times was she going to be ripped off by some jerk who never seriously cared for her in the first place? Why did she consistently open herself up to such disappointment? There has never been anyone in my life that I could trust,* she thought—*well, except for some of the folks at the diner,* she corrected. *But, at least, they all have someone else in their life to care about and to care for them—even Frank, since Mark arrived on the scene. Maybe not Sam or Meredith any more, but at least they have a memory of someone who cared for them. Yep, I'm truly the only one without someone to care for or someone I belong to. That's okay*, she decided, staring at herself in the mirror. *If that's the way it was going to be, so be it. At least, I don't have to answer to anyone or be responsible for anyone but me,* she decided—*sole control of the remote does have its advantages.* "Get a grip," she said talking aloud to herself in the mirror. "You're it—the only one who really cares just for you. Get use to it!" She turned the faucet on and splashed cold water on her face.

"Hey, baby," whispered Jan, tapping lightly on the restroom door before coming in. She took hold of Gina's shoulders and turned her around. She pulled her close to her and held her tightly. "You don't have to go it alone anymore, sweetheart," she whispered. "You have us. We want to help you, but you have to meet us halfway. We aren't ever going to let you down—I promise. Now, tell me. What the heck is going on between you and Greg?"

Fighting to control her tears, Gina poured out the details of Greg's theft and her frustration about his lies.

"What a jerk!" said Jan. "Surely, there's a way to find out where he's holding your stuff."

"Well, let's just put Meredith and Sam on his trail." Gina smiled.

"Now you sound more like the Gina we all love." Jan hugged her.

"Jan, you don't need to worry about this. It's so minor in comparison with what has happened to Olivia. I'm sure that the jerk will perjure himself and land in more trouble than he's already in. And then, maybe he'll get a longer sentence."

"Jeff seems mighty concerned about you, did you notice? I think he's more interested in you than in your situation. What do you think?"

"Are you kidding? He's just doing his job."

"Didn't I overhear him say that he went by your apartment last night to check on you? That's going way beyond the expectations of his job."

Gina just stared at Jan in amazement. "How could someone like Jeff ever be interested in someone like me? Do you realize how many times he's been called to my apartment on domestic disputes? I can't believe that he sees me as anything other than a stupid bimbo, who makes the same mistakes repeatedly."

182

"Well, Gina, for what it's worth, I think you've misread him. I think he genuinely cares for you."

"I find that hard to believe," Gina insisted. "And anyway, I'm not looking for another man in my life, not now—maybe not ever!"

Jeff knocked lightly on the door of the restroom. "Everything all right in there," he called.

Gina and Jan exchanged glances. "Told you," whispered Jan.

"I'm fine," answered Gina, opening up the door and starring into Jeff's worried grey eyes. "I'm sorry about that. I just lost it, that's all. Thanks, for worrying. I'm okay."

Gina stared at him as if she was seeing him for the first time. She didn't realize how tall he was and how broad and muscular his shoulders were. His posture was straight and reeked of authority, but the look in his eyes was gentle. She had seen the same look yesterday in the car when he was trying to comfort her, but today it seemed particularly special.

"I just want you to know that I'm going to do everything I can to find your stuff. I don't believe for a minute that Greg is innocent. I promise I'll find it," he said.

"Thanks, Jeff. You're doing more than expected. I really appreciate it." She dropped her head, afraid to look again directly into his eyes. She was obviously reading more into his concern than he intended. She quickly tried to bring herself back into the real world and shrug off the obviously false romantic notion she was allowing herself to get sucked into. *Get a grip, for gods sake, Gina,* she warned. *Here you go again. Always looking for romance in all the wrong places.* She backed away from Jeff and tried to appear nonchalant. "Now, what do you want for breakfast, or have I managed to kill your appetite?"

As she started to walk back into the diner, Jeff grabbed her by the hand. He gently took hold of her shoulders and turned her around. He lifted her chin, so she had to look directly into his eyes. "You do know that breakfast is not the only reason I come in here every day, don't you?" he asked softly.

"I'm not sure what you mean by that," answered Gina. She tried to sound light-hearted, even though she was feeling anything but jovial. Her heart was pounding so hard that she was sure that everyone in the diner could hear it.

"Well, maybe I could explain it to you over dinner. What about having dinner with me Friday night?"

"Are you serious?" she asked. "Why would you want to have dinner with me? Anyway, I can't on Friday night. I promised Kenneth Talbert's grandmother to have dinner with her on Friday."

"Well then, how about Saturday? I'm not going to give up. I'm tired of watching you get messed up with losers."

"Jeff, you don't have to worry about me. I'm able to take care of myself. I don't really need a big brother to bale me out of my messes."

184

"I'm not interested in being your big brother." Jeff smiled and took hold of her hand. "I already have six sisters to watch over, and I know you are able to take care of yourself."

Gina stared at him in amazement. She didn't know what to say—something she rarely experienced. Finally, she muttered, "Well then, Saturday night it is."

"I'm off on Saturday. Why don't I pick you up after work on Saturday afternoon, and we can make a day of it?" he said looking deeply into her eyes.

"Sounds great." She smiled, scarcely able to pull her eyes from his. As she walked away, she felt a warm, tingling sensation in her hand where Jeff had gently squeezed it. *That's strange*, she thought as she stretched and wiggled her fingers. *Oh, my god, here I go again,* she moaned. *What was it I just proclaimed in the bathroom about not letting a man in my life? My god, that didn't even last 60 seconds. I am weak, dammit,* she admitted.

~~~~~

Promptly at eight, Leroy entered the diner. "What's going on? Have you heard from Mark yet?"

"No. Nothing yet?" answered Meredith.

"What time is he supposed to call in?" asked Leroy.

"We don't know. Gina suggested that from now on, we ask him to call every day at the same time, so we can

185

keep track of him too."

"Good idea," replied Leroy. "How's Jan doing?"

"She's in the back." Sam sighed shaking his head. "She's doing okay under the circumstances. Wait 'till you hear about Gina. Poor kid, that jerk she's been living with took off with all of her stuff yesterday. She didn't tell us anything because she didn't think her problem compared to Jan's." He looked over at Leroy and shook his head. "I worry about her. She thinks she's so tough, but I know she's hurting deep down. She tries to take care of everyone else and ignores her own problems."

"Good grief," responded Leroy. "They say that bad news comes in threes. What else is going to happen around here?"

"I think we've already had our three pieces of bad news," said Sam. "Actually, we've had four awful things happen this week."

"Four? What else have I missed?" asked Leroy.

"Kelley's husband was injured and is being shipped to a military hospital somewhere today," reported Sam.

"Jeez. How could one day have been so full of bad things? asked Leroy. "That's terrible. Will he be all right? How badly was he injured?"

"No one knows. Gina said they told Kelley that he was hit in the shoulder and leg by sniper fire," said Frank, joining their conversation.

186

"My good grief." Leroy sighed. "How are they going to make it if he has to be laid up for a while? What in the heck can we do to help them out?"

"I'm going over to Kelley's as soon as Mark calls," answered Meredith. "I'll tell her that we all want to help. I'm sure there must be something we can do. That poor little boy of Kelley's. I wonder how he's handling all of this. As the oldest child, he's certainly going to bear the brunt of this—much more than his younger siblings. He's old enough to realize what's actually going on."

"Here comes Kenneth," interrupted Leroy. "Thank goodness he had the number of that license plate."

"Hey, Kenneth," greeted Sam. "Thanks for your help yesterday."

Kenneth nodded without looking up. He headed for his booth and opened his backpack. As Gina brought him his Danish and coffee, she was surprised that instead of reaching for his yellow pad, he carefully took out something wrapped in white tissue. Gently he removed the wrapping and uncovered a magnificent, white rose. Although the beauty of every rose is a delight to see, this rose surpassed the grandeur of any flower that Gina had ever seen. The center of the large rose and the tip of each petal had a delicate touch of pink, and the blossom was enormous, rivaling that of a large peony.

"Wow, Kenneth," said Gina. "That is the most beautiful rose I've ever seen. Did you grow it yourself?"

Kenneth nodded and muttered, "Jan."

"That's very thoughtful of you," said Gina. "'She's in the backroom. If you'd like, I can take it to her, or I can have her come out here, so you can give it to her yourself. We still haven't heard anything about Olivia, but the rose will help to remind us all that there is beauty and delicacy in the world even when life seems cruel and ugly. A white rose represents innocence, doesn't it?"

Kenneth nodded in agreement and gently pushed the rose to Gina. She gently picked up the delicate flower. "It really is lovely, Kenneth. I can't wait to see your gardens on Friday. Your grandmother invited me to have dinner there. I hope you don't mind if I come."

"Come," replied Kenneth without looking up.

"Good, I'll be there. Enjoy your Danish. I'll come back and check on your coffee. It's a beautiful day. You should definitely enjoy your afternoon in the park."

Chapter 14

Mark pulled into the truck stop off of route I-75. He was approaching the Florida border and would be merging onto the Florida turnpike. He was glad to be getting close to the end of the trip. He was extremely tired and was having trouble staying awake. It was eight in the morning, and he knew that everyone at the diner would be waiting for his call. He also needed to get some coffee if he was going to be able to continue to Miami without stopping for a rest. He was determined to get there by noon. The sooner he got to Miami, the better. Every minute he wasted would put Olivia in more jeopardy. *God only knows what she's been going through during the past thirty-six hours,* he thought angrily. *Dammit, she must be scared out of her wits. Surely, she'd know that Jan and the gang at the diner would try to find her.*

Detective Jim Baxter had warned them that her captors would start injecting Olivia with drugs immediately. *'Once Olivia loses her sense of self and becomes addicted to the drugs,'* he had warned, *'there's little hope for her.'* He'd also told them that many of the women trapped in these conditions resort to suicide as their only way out. According to Baxter, the suicide and murder rate among young women ensnared in a life of drugs and prostitution was high, especially in cities like Miami and L.A. Many of them also die of diseases such as HIV and other sexually transmitted infections. If they do somehow escape, they typically are afraid to talk to police because they fear that their captors will retaliate by killing them or

189

members of their family.

 Mark realized that the drugs would be Olivia's greatest enemy. If he didn't find her soon, they would take control of her mind, and she would become trapped in a haze of confusion and dependence. *Eventually*, as Detective Baxter had explained, *she'll probably have to submit to any demands to get more of the drug.* Mark shook his head, trying to clear his mind of such horrible thoughts.

Before going into the restaurant, he took out his cell phone and dialed the diner. Frank answered on the first ring. "Hi, Uncle Frank. It's Mark."

"Thank god, we've all been hovering around the phone for the past two hours. Where are you? How are you doing? Have you seen anything yet?"

"Whoa," answered Mark. "One question at a time. First, I'm sorry I didn't connect with you yesterday before I left, but I wanted to get on the road, and I didn't know how to reach you at Jan's. I want to get your cell number, so I can reach you someplace other than at the diner."

"Got a pencil?" asked Frank.

"I don't need one, I'll just put it in my cell phone. Go ahead," he said, keying in the phone number that Frank gave him.

"Now—where are you?" impatiently pursued Frank. "Are you all right?"

"I'm on I-75 about to hop onto the Florida Turnpike. I

190

should be in Miami this afternoon. I just stopped to call you and to get some coffee to help me stay awake," answered Mark.

"Don't overdo it. If you need to rest, stop. Don't risk... What, Gina?" Frank yelled. "Hang on a minute, Mark. As always, Gina wants to say something."

"Mark," said Gina taking the phone. "We think you should call us a couple of times a day at the same time every day. What do you think?"

"That's fine. I'll call the diner in the morning at eight and either you or Frank, around eight at night. Will that work?"

"That sounds great." Turning to the others, she shouted, "Hey, does anyone else want to say anything to Mark before I give the phone back to Frank?"

"I'd like to say something to him," said Jan.

"Hang on, Mark. Jan wants to talk with you. Take care of yourself and don't try to be a hero," said Gina handing the phone to Jan.

"Mark, I really appreciate what you're trying to do," said Jan. Her voice wavered and cracked. "It helps to know that someone is in Florida looking for Olivia. I can't thank you enough," she murmured.

"How are you holding up?" he asked. "I'm so sorry. It has to be hard—not knowing, I mean."

"It's terrifying. I just don't know what to do or where to be. It's a desperate feeling. I feel like I'm suspended in time and space. I'm not satisfied anywhere, and I can't focus on anything. I just want to scream and pace back and forth. I'm just so glad that someone is down there. I know the police will do everything they can, but they don't have the personal investment that we have."

"I agree. Don't worry. I intend to sleep very little and to spend every waking moment looking for Olivia."

"Thank you—I know you will, but please be careful," she sobbed.

"I will. I will call you the minute I hear anything," he promised. He felt desperately sorry for her and more anxious than ever to get back on the road. In the background, he could hear the others asking Jan about what he had said to her. He smiled as he imagined the scene at the diner with Sam, Leroy, Tom, and Meredith leaning over the counter straining to hear every word of the conversations.

"Hey, Mark," said Gina, taking the phone again. "Meredith wants to tell you something about the condo. Can you hang on a minute more?"

"Sure, put her on," he said glancing at his watch.

"Mark, Meredith here," she said in an officious tone. "I want to know if you would have any objection to me calling my neighbor and asking him to look out for you. We're all worried up here that you may find yourself in a mess, and we'd feel better if someone down there knew what you were doing so that, if you didn't show up at the

192

condo some night, he could notify the police right away. He's a retired policeman, so he might be able to help you in some way. What do you think?"

"That's fine by me, Meredith. What's his name? I'll introduce myself to him as soon as I get there."

"Bill Fleming. He lives in the first condo to the east of mine. He's a great guy. I'm sure you'll enjoy meeting him. I'll call him right away."

"Okay. Thanks. Is Uncle Frank, nearby?"

"Yes, I'll get him. Take care of yourself," she added.

"Wait," yelled Sam grabbing the phone. "I want to tell him something. Hey, Mark, I spent some time on the Internet last night searching for information on this Gutierrez. On the county appraiser's site down there, I found an office building in his name located at 1100 S. Biscayne Blvd. There was also a commercial building listed and a private home. Call me as soon as you get to Meredith's condo, and I'll give you all of the details."

"Nice work, Sam. You guys are impressive," said Mark.

"Hey, buddy, don't mess with these people. We don't need to have you come up missing too," warned Sam. "Here's your Uncle. Take care."

Mark knew that they were all worried about him. *Strange*, he thought, *I've only known them a couple of days, and they already feel like family that I've known for years. His grandfather did a wonderful thing by sending him there*, he decided.

"Mark, take care of yourself, son," said Frank.

"I'll be fine," he said turning to glance at a car that had pulled in just a few parking spaces away from where he'd stopped. "Holy shit," he whispered in the phone. "You are not going to believe what just pulled into this parking lot. My god, it's the black sedan. Holy shit! I can't believe it," he whispered again.

"What?' shouted Frank. "Are you sure?"

"Positive. I have the license plate memorized. Damn. It looks like there's only one guy in the car. I've gotta go. I'm going to pull to the other end of the truck stop and wait till he leaves, so I can follow him."

"No," shouted Frank. "Call the police. Now! Don't do anything stupid... Dammit," he sputtered as the phone went dead.

Mark pulled out of the restaurant parking lot and headed to the other end of the truck stop next to a small mini-mart. From there, he watched as a burly, sour looking man with dark hair got out of the black sedan and headed into the restaurant. He watched as the man slid into a booth next to the large, front window. He was obviously ordering something to eat, so Mark knew that he would have time to get some coffee for himself. He got off his bike and headed into the mini mart. He hated vending machine coffee and stale donuts, but he was afraid to go into the restaurant and possibly attract the driver's attention. After forcing himself to swallow two cups of the most disgusting coffee he'd ever tasted, he

194

noticed that the sedan driver was sliding out of the booth and heading toward the cashier. "I bet his coffee was better than mine," Mark muttered.

Mark waited until the black sedan had pulled out of the parking lot before leaving the truck stop. The sedan turned south onto I-75, and Mark followed, keeping a safe distance behind. It was obvious that the driver was headed for Miami, *but where was Olivia*, Mark wondered. *Maybe she is still in Ohio. God, she could be anywhere between here and Ohio. Perhaps, Frank was right. I should just call the police and let them arrest the driver now, but what good would that really do? He would probably not confess to anything, and then they would be left without any clues about where Olivia was.*

As he sped down the highway, Mark argued with himself about whether or not to call the police. He finally convinced himself that he was right to follow the car into Miami and not to call the police right away. He shook his head as the buzz from the coffee started to wear off, and the monotony of the long, boring highway allowed the drowsiness to seep back into his mind. *Stay awake, dammit*, he told himself.

A huge truck sped past him, causing his bike to swerve as the air turbulence from the truck practically swept him off the road. A huge jolt of adrenalin flooded his mind as he struggled to keep his cycle upright. The earlier drowsiness immediately vanished. He was completely awake now. The truck suddenly cut back into his lane, and Mark slammed on his brakes to avoid smashing into its tailgate. His bike skidded sideways and for a moment, he thought he was going to lose control of it.

"What in the hell?" he shouted, struggling to keep the bike upright. Furious, he pulled into the passing lane, intending to pull up even with the trucker and give him a piece of his mind. But just as he started to change lanes, the truck pulled into the passing lane in front of him. Again, Mark slammed on his brakes and his bike wobbled. He struggled to keep his cycle from veering into the median and realized that the trucker was intentionally playing games with him.

Luckily, the years of road travel across country on a motorcycle had taught him the skills needed to handle such stupid situations. Although he was worried that he would lose sight of the sedan, he slowed down and let several cars pass him. Finally, he maneuvered his bike between two cars, and, using them as a shield from the trucker, he sped past him. In the huge mirrors on the side of the truck, he could see the trucker laughing at him. "What an asshole," Mark muttered.

In the distance ahead of him, he could see the black sedan. The driver wasn't wasting any time. He was flying down the road, obviously in a hurry to arrive in Miami. Mark glanced at the large green highway sign on the side of the road—120 more miles to Miami. Just two more hours, he thought as he tried to close the gap between the sedan and him. He knew that there would be multiple exits coming up as they got closer to Miami, and he didn't want to lose sight of the car.

In his rear mirror, Mark could see the big truck barreling down on him, and he quickly changed lanes to pass the car in front of him. He darted back into the right lane in between two cars, cutting in too close to the car behind him as the truck pursued him. The driver of the car blasted his horn at Mark as the truck sped past both of them. Mark was getting tired of the road games and was falling farther behind the black sedan.

He was relieved when he saw a truck weigh station sign and hoped that it would be open, so the truck would have to exit. The trucker obviously either missed the sign or had no intentions of turning in as he sped past the entrance to the weigh station. Mark laughed aloud as he watched the highway patrol car speed out of the weigh station with its lights flashing. The patrolman chased the speeding truck until he caught up with it and forced the driver to pull off to the side of the road. Mark tapped his horn and blew the truck driver a kiss as he slowly passed the truck.

The sedan was out of sight by now, and Mark had to speed to try to catch up. The exit signs were beginning to appear more frequently, and he knew that if he didn't catch up soon, he could easily lose track of the black car. Keeping one eye on his rear view mirror to watch for patrol cars and the other on the road in front of him, he pushed the cycle forward at a speed he knew was dangerous, not to mention illegal.

It was several miles before he could see the black sedan in the distance. He slowed his motorcycle to a more comfortable speed as he began to close the gap between them. He didn't want to be directly behind the sedan, but he wanted to be close enough to be able to turn off the highway should the driver make a sudden exit.

The traffic became heavier as they got closer to the city, and the demands on his ability to watch the sedan at the same time he kept his eyes on the stop and go of the noonday traffic began to wear on him. He was feeling the effects of the long ride without any rest and hoped that the sedan would leave the highway soon.

In the distance, he could see the skyline of the city. Under different circumstances, he would leave the busy highway and head for US Route 1 and 1-A to enjoy the view of the ocean and to inhale its salty air. *Surely, the sedan would be exiting soon.* Instead, the driver headed right into the heart of the city, finally exiting on Biscayne Boulevard.

"Hmm," Mark muttered. "Thank you, Sam," he shouted aloud, as he realized that Sam obviously had identified the correct location of Gutierrez' office. As he watched the sedan head for the exit ramp onto south Biscayne Boulrvard, Mark hesitated, not sure whether he should follow the sedan down the exit ramp. He was fairly certain that the driver was headed for Gutierrez's office on Biscayne, and at this point, he didn't want to tip him off that he was being followed. He finally decided to pass the south Biscayne exit and get off going north. He could then turn around and head back down Biscayne the opposite way. All he wanted to do was to locate the office and make sure that the sedan was there. Then, he knew he had to head for the condo. He was really feeling the effects of no sleep. Maybe he could connect with Meredith's neighbor and get some ideas about how to proceed with looking for Olivia after he had a couple of hours of rest.

~~~~~

Bill Fleming spotted the sedan as it pulled into Gutierrez'

office. There was no sign of the motorcycle that Meredith had told him would probably be following it. Maybe the young man had been smart enough not to follow the sedan to the office, or maybe he just lost him somewhere on the highway.

Bill watched as a muscular, sour looking man got out of the sedan. The man stretched his arms and rotated his upper torso back and forth before reaching into the front seat to grab a black suit coat and slip it on. Bill noted the holster clipped to the belt of the man's pants and the handle of a gun sticking slightly above his belt. *These people obviously don't mess around*, he thought.

He continued to watch as the driver of the sedan slowly mounted the white marble steps and entered the huge glass doors of the office building. The two guards seated at the front desk in the lobby apparently knew him and made no attempt to detain him as he got onto the elevator behind them and disappeared. He was the fifth male who had entered the building in the past half-hour. *There must be a major meeting of some sort going on*, Bill decided.

The office was a two-story, white stucco building with attractive arches across the glass-front entrance. Large concrete planters filled with colorful flowers and tall, impressive plants decorated the entrance at the base of each arch. The overall appearance of the structure was very much in keeping with the architecture in the area and was attractive without being pretentious. Bill knew that leasing and ownership costs for office space in this area of Biscayne were high, indicating that Mr. Gutierrez was not hurting for money. The entire front of the building was glass and Bill could see large, colorful abstract paintings hanging on the back walls. In the center of the lobby was a huge, black marble desk where two guards monitored surveillance screens and greeted entering patrons. A cluster of modern, black leather couches and chrome and glass tables provided seating for would-be entrants to the sanctum of the offices, which seemed to be accessed through the stainless steel doors of a private elevator. Bill had only seen two clients waiting for someone in the lobby. He had watched them leaf through magazines until some man exited the elevator, shook their hand, and then ushered them back onto the waiting elevator.

There were security cameras mounted along the three sides of the building that Bill could see from his position down the street and from his earlier drive past the building. The muscle-bound men arriving for the suspected meeting were driving a fleet of black Lincoln Navigators. The Mercedes sedan was dwarfed by the larger SUVs in the row of cars. Bill had recorded all of the license plates on the vehicles, noting that there was no easily recognized number among them. They were all random numbers from different Florida counties, so there was no common, recognizable pattern of numbers or letters—no doubt strategically planned.

He glanced in his rear view mirror as the roar of a motorcycle engine attracted his attention. He observed the single rider as he slowed slightly and stared at the row of cars in the parking lot of the office. The West Virginia plate on the motorcycle supported his assumption that the rider was the young man that Meredith had called him about. "Don't stop," whispered Bill under his breath and was relieved when Mark went on down the street. He watched as Mark stopped at the intersection just north of the office building and hesitated
200

as if he was going to make a U-turn and come back past the office. "Don't go back by the office," Bill again muttered aloud. "They'll pick you up on the security cameras. One pass would go un-noticed; a second slow pass by the building would attract their attention." He was relieved when Mark continued through the intersection and hoped that he was heading to Meredith's condo.

Bill reached over and opened the brown-bag lunch that his wife had fixed him. *Just like the old days.* He smiled. *Cold turkey sandwiches, chocolate chip cookies, and hot coffee—it feels good to be back on a stakeout and being useful again.* He owed Meredith for this opportunity to get involved in police work again.

After an hour of huddling down in his car and watching the parking lot of Gutierrez' office, Bill was starting to feel drowsy, so he reached for some more of his coffee. He jumped when his phone vibrated against his hip, and he quickly reached for it. He recognized Meredith's phone number at her condo. "Bill Fleming, here," he answered in hushed tones.

"Bill, this is Mark Tyler. I got your number from your wife. I don't know how to thank you for helping me."

"I'm glad to have something to do besides fishing," answered Bill, "especially now that my fishing buddy, Howard, is gone. I saw you pass by the office a few minutes ago. You were smart not to go by twice on that cycle of yours. It attracts too much attention. Meredith told me that the keys for her car are in the refrigerator in a mayonnaise jar—like that wouldn't be the first place that criminals look for valuables." He laughed. "I think you should drive her car if you do any surveillance."

"Right. How'd you know where to find Gutierrez' office?" asked Mark.

"Meredith and someone named Sam Weston called me and gave me the addresses. I also checked out the old warehouse that this guy owns. If the girl you're looking for is in Florida, my bet is that's where she's being held before she's shipped out or whatever," said Bill.

"What do you think I should do next?" asked Mark.

"For starters, you need to grab you a couple hours of sleep. Then, give me a call. I'm going to stay here for awhile and see what's going on. I think there's some big meeting happening because I've seen so many muscle-bound thugs in nice looking clothes going into the building. Give me you cell phone number. I assume you have one since all you young kids spend most of your life texting or talking on one."

"I do have one." Mark laughed good-naturedly, repeating the number to Bill. "Again, I really can't thank you enough. I'm beat, but I'll only need a couple hours. If I don't hear from you before I wake up, I'll call you as soon as I do."

"Sounds like a plan," said Bill. "Now, get some rest. I've got you covered here."

Chapter 15

Olivia curled up in a tight ball on the cot in her small wooden cell, hugging her knees and rocking back and forth to get relief from the horrible pains in her stomach and legs. She was shivering even though the heat in her cell was stifling, and sweat was dripping from her forehead. She was scared, and she was sick. Her hair was matted, and her dress was dirty. She had a horrible taste in her mouth, and her tongue felt thick and swollen. Her throat was raw, making any attempt to swallow extremely painful.

She tried to remember what had happened to her, but everything was hazy and confused. The only clear memory she had was of her lying on a bed with her hands and feet tied and of Teresa sticking a needle in her arm. Everything else was a blur of people dragging her from one place to another and finally, roughly tossing her into this cell. *How long had she been gone, she wondered. It seemed like forever. When would someone come to bring her some water and food?* The thought of eating made her gag again. *What was going to happen to her?* "I want to go home. I want my mother," she cried softly. "Please, please help me," she begged.

A rustling outside her door, caused her to draw herself up even more tightly into a tiny, shivering ball. *Was someone out there? Were they coming in? Who were they? What would they do to her?*

Her door suddenly swung open, and she stared in fear at the silhouette of a large man.

"Hello, Olivia," said Hastings. "I'm Hastings Gutierrez. Your host," he said menacingly. "I am here to help you; that is, if you choose to help yourself."

"I, I don't know what you mean," said Olivia her voice weak and husky from her thickened tongue and parched throat.

"First, Olivia, you're never going to escape. You have a new life now—one that can be either pleasant, or very painful. The choice is yours."

"Please give me some water and something to stop my pain, please," she begged.

"Sure. We can give you anything you want, but you have to do exactly what I say," snarled Hastings. He reached down and grabbed her by the hair, yanking her from the cot. "Do you understand me?"

"Let go of me. You're hurting me," yelled Olivia, feeling suddenly strong and defiant. "Someone will come for me, I know it. You might break my body, but you will never break me," she screamed turning her head to stare defiantly into his eyes.

Hastings slapped her hard across the face and shoved her back onto the cot. "Grow up, Olivia. No one is coming for you. Not now, not ever. Your days as a little princess are over. You belong to me now, and I will do anything I want with you. You got that? You'd better get that through your head if you don't want to be swimming with the
204

sharks in the ocean." He grabbed her by the arm and squeezed it so tightly that she thought it was going to snap in two. "Now, let's try this again. Either you do what you are expected to do, starting right this minute, or I'll make your life so painful and so miserable that you'll be begging me to kill you. I am not a patient man, Olivia."

Olivia tried to free her arm, but he only squeezed it tighter, causing her to cry out in pain. How much of this could she stand? Would someone find her before it was too late? *Maybe it will be smarter to pretend to go along with whatever he wants—just until someone comes to take me home.* She was sick. She didn't want to die. She was young, and she could be strong. She'd live inside of her mind. She'd block out everything that was happening to her and think about things she wanted to think about. *They can never take my mind away from me, unless I let them, and I don't intend to do that. Someone will find me. They will.* "Okay, okay," she said defiantly. "Just let go of my arm and bring me something to drink," she demanded.

"Now you're making sense," he said releasing his steely grasp on her arm.

The rush of blood to her upper arm caused an excruciating pain, which Olivia tried to ignore as she clutched tightly to the spot that he had just released. "Bring me a drink of water," she demanded again.

"Watch your tone, Olivia," Hastings cautioned her. "Don't forget that I give the orders. You only obey them." He leaned in close to her face and yanked her hair again, snapping her neck back.

He's not human. He's some sort of wild animal, she thought, staring back into his dark, threatening eyes. *How could any human be so full of hate and anger? When they come for me, they'll put him in a cage forever. He should be in a cage.* "Please, master, may I have a drink of water," she mocked causing him to tug even tighter on her hair.

"Don't play games with me, Olivia. You'll lose. Your brave act is betrayed by the fear in your eyes," he snarled, shoving her down on the cot and storming from her cell.

"Give her something to eat and drink," she heard him shout to someone in the hallway. "And, give her another dose of drugs."

Chapter 16

Mark jumped up from the couch in Meredith's darkened living room. For a brief moment, he was confused by his surroundings. Then, remembering where he was and why he was there, he grabbed his watch from the coffee table. How long had he been asleep? It was pitch black outside. *Oh, my god, it was midnight—too late to call Bill. Why did he let me sleep so long*, Mark wondered. Dammit, a half of a day wasted. He grabbed his cell phone—two voice messages and three texts. "Uncle Frank must be worried crazy," he moaned.

He dialed his voice mail. The first one was from Bill at six o'clock telling him that he had followed Gutierrez and one of his body guards from his office to the warehouse and then, to his private residence. He reported that there were no signs of any women at either place. *'You obviously need your sleep, buddy,'* Bill said on the phone. *'Call me when you wake up. The time won't matter. I think we need to check out that warehouse together. Don't try to do it on your own,'* he warned. *'Meredith told me earlier that you had a check-in time with them back in Ohio. I called her and told her that you were tucked into bed and that you would call them when you got up. Call me,"* he said.

The second call was from Frank. *'Meredith told us that you were okay, but call me as soon as you wake up.'* The texts were all from Gina with the same message, *'just checking.'*

207

He dialed his Uncle Frank first. The phone rang only once before Frank answered, "Mark?" he asked, keeping his voice low to avoid waking Jan. "You, okay?" he asked.

"Yeah, I'm fine. Jeez, I can't believe I slept so long. I never do that."

"Well, you haven't had much sleep the past couple of days. What's going on down there?"

"Nothing, yet. That neighbor of Meredith's is something else. He's going to be a great help. He seems to think that they may be holding Olivia in that old warehouse that Sam found out about. I think he's right. As soon as we hang up, I'm going to give him a call, so we can check it out."

"At this hour? You shouldn't be roaming around in Miami at this time of the night, for god's sake, especially with some seventy-year old man as your back up. Use your head. Wait until it gets daylight, at least."

"Every minute counts, Uncle Frank. I'm just damned glad that Bill followed those creeps while I was asleep. I haven't met him yet, but if he is seventy, I'm willing to bet he's a fit seventy. Look, I've got to go. I'll call you at eight this morning at the diner. Tell everyone hello for me. I hope to have some good news by then."

"Don't forget! The suspense on our end is killing us."

"I realize that," said Mark. "I'm sure it's harder for all of you up there to have to wait to hear from me than it is for me down here checking things out. I'll do better about
208

calling from now on," he promised.

After he hung up, he sent Gina a brief text, and had no sooner sent the message than his phone rang.

"Well, sleepy head. Are you finally awake?" mocked Gina.

"My god, Gina, do you sleep with your phone on your pillow?" he asked.

"Yes. When I'm expecting a call, I do sleep with my phone. Maybe you should too," she teased.

"What do you hear from the police up there? I just talked to Frank, and I forgot to ask him. I take it not much, or he would've told me," said Mark.

"I'm staying over at Kelley's for now, and Jeff stopped by tonight to tell us that the Miami police had someone watching the office of this Gutierrez character. Hastings is Gutierrez' first name. Sounds autocratic, doesn't it? It's not the anticipated name of a low-down, sleazy criminal, don't you agree?"

Before Mark could answer, Gina rattled on. "Jeff said that the sedan arrived there about 1:00 this afternoon, or I guess it's yesterday afternoon by now. Anyway, they saw you cycle by just a short time later. There's not been any sign of Teresa or Olivia, although they found out that Teresa left by herself in a rental car from the small airport where Hastings keeps his private jet. Must be nice, huh? I guess he has a big yacht too. Anyway, according to the people working at the airport, she had some sort of accident and had injured her leg or foot. What do you
209

think about that?"

"So, they think they flew Olivia here by jet? Did they find any trace of Olivia having been on the jet?" he asked.

"They're going back tomorrow, I mean today, with a search warrant. You'd have thought they would've had one with them, but I guess that's not how the system works. If they can prove that Olivia was on the plane, they can call in the FBI since they transported her across the state lines. It should help to have the 'big guns' in on the case. So, that's all I know, what about you? What did you dream about?"

Mark ignored the jab. "Look, Gina, I've got to go. I'm going to call Meredith's neighbor, Bill Fleming. I haven't met him yet, but he seems like an all right guy with lots of police experience. I'll call you as soon as I learn something, and let me know if you hear anything more up there. It sounds like you have an intimate link with the police department up there."

"Jealous?" Gina laughed.

"Good bye, Gina." He chuckled as he closed his phone. *She's incredible,* he thought as he dialed Bill Fleming's number. *I don't think I've ever met anyone quite like her in my life. I pity the poor guy who ever tries to tame her.*

"You ready?" asked Bill. "I'll be right over," he said before Mark could utter a word into the phone. Within seconds, there was a light knock at the door.

"Now, that was quick," said Mark still staring at his phone. He hurried to the door and found a tall, lithe, and
210

slightly graying man, towering above him. He'd been right, Bill Fleming was as fit or more so than any of his drill sergeants at The Citadel. "Bill?" he asked.

"You'd better hope so, or you're in deep trouble. Lesson number one—never open a door before you check out who's behind it," he admonished. "Bill Fleming," he said sticking out his giant hand. "Mark Tyler, I presume," he said shaking Mark's dwarfed hand.

"Sorry about that," muttered Mark, rightly chagrined. "I'm new at this detective thing."

"That's all right. You won't be green by the time this is all over. I'll make sure of that. I've trained more greenhorns than I can count. Are you ready? We'll stop and grab you something to eat on the way."

They stopped at a 24-hour drive through, and Mark ordered a hamburger, fries, and a large drink, which he practically inhaled. He was starving. Bill didn't order anything. As they drove through the dark streets of Miami, Mark was impressed at the people and things that Bill pointed out that he never even noticed. He told Mark to study how people were walking or standing. "The way someone walks and their posture are your first clues as to whether they were looking for trouble or just scared to death to be where they were," he said. "Meredith tells me that you studied psychology in school and are headed for the Marines. Good choice," he said, "The Marines, I mean. I was a Marine before I joined the NYC police force."

Mark already suspected that Bill had been a Marine, but he was surprised to learn that he had been a policeman in New York City. "How'd you end up down here in Miami?" asked Mark. "This is quite a distance from New York City."

"Why do any of us snow birds fly south—the weather. I love the heat down here."

"Do you have family down here?" Mark asked.

"Just my wife. I have a son on the force in New York. I was damned proud of him during that 911 attack. Unlike a lot of his fellow police officers, he was lucky. He came out of it a decorated hero—went in and out of the twin towers for two days straight, dragging injured folks to safety. He's a good, god-fearing young man—got three kids and a sweet wife."

"Don't you miss them?" asked Mark.

"Sure. But they fly down here in the winter and spring for all of the holidays, and we go north for a month in the summer—works out best for everyone. I think you need a little distance from your kids once they're married— makes them grow up faster, and you appreciate each other more. I can't say that my wife agrees with me, though. She'd be living with them, if she had her way."

As they turned onto a long street that was lined with huge warehouses located just north of the Port of Miami, Bill turned off the lights of the car and found a parking spot away from the streetlights, between a truck and another car. "There's our warehouse," he said pointing to a tall, rectangular stucco building. He turned off the car's engine and reached around in the back seat. He pulled out a brown paper bag and a huge thermos.

212

"Looks like you came prepared."

"Yep, I brought enough cookies and coffee for both of us. I love a good stake-out," he said. "I can honestly say that's what I miss the most—laying back and just watching and waiting for something to happen. Blood's always pumping, expecting everything to come down any second—god, I love that adrenalin rush when it's all about to happen."

"You're not, by chance, having that adrenalin rush right now, are you?" asked Mark.

Bill laughed. "No, not yet, but I do have a suspicion that we'll see something of interest before too long. If these jerks are going to move anything or anyone in and out of that warehouse, they'll do it about three o'clock in the morning. They mistakenly think the police are all busy rounding up the drunks and shutting down the bars that are violating their liquor licenses, so they always try to conduct their dirty business about that time of the night. They couldn't be more wrong, but it happens all of the time. You'd think the poor, dumb bastards would wise up, but they don't ever seem to."

Mark glanced at his watch. It was two o'clock. He shifted uneasily in his seat. Neither of them said anything for a while. Each was lost in his own thoughts, while keeping his eyes glued on the door of the warehouse. Occasionally, Bill looked in his rear view mirror, and Mark would immediately glance behind him through the side mirror.

Mark wondered about what was happening behind those doors to Olivia. He felt certain that she was in

213

there, and he wanted to get her out, right now. But how? The place looked as solid as an old fort. The huge wooden doors looked impenetrable, and there were no windows. He could see the red beam from the light of security cameras on each end of the building and above the door. He wondered if their car was far enough away to avoid showing up on their monitors inside. They must have monitors inside, he thought, and someone was probably watching them.

"Want a cookie?" asked Bill. "I baked them myself."

"You are a stack of surprises," said Mark his voice cracking from nervousness.

"I love to cook and bake. My wife hates to cook, so it works out just fine. Tell me a little about yourself. What are you expecting out of life?" asked Bill.

"Wow, now that's a good question. I don't think I've ever been asked about my life in that way before?"

"Well, save the answer," Bill interrupted. "Duck down. We're about to have some intruders," he said watching his rear view mirror as an approaching SUV flipped off its lights and headed their way.

Mark sank as far down in his seat as humanly possible, holding his breath until the car passed. He avoided glancing out of his window, afraid he would see someone staring back at him.

"That's interesting," remarked Bill. "They aren't pulling inside. I wonder what that's all about?"

214

Mark raised up enough to see out the front window. The SUV that had passed them was just sitting in front of the big-overhead doors. No one was getting out.

"Do you think they saw us?" he whispered.

"I don't think so. Look, someone is coming out of the small door. For god's sake, I think they're just having trouble opening the big door. Humph, technology fails again." He chuckled.

Mark stared at the SUV as the front and rear doors on the driver's side swung open, and two men got out, guns pulled. "Oh, my god. They have guns," he moaned.

"Here," said Bill, handing him a pistol. "Ever fired one of these before?"

"Not really, but I've fired something a lot bigger," said Mark, as he grabbed the gun with cold, clammy hands. He was amazed as Bill reached under his seat again and pulled out two more hand guns. "Jeez, I've been sitting on top of an arsenal."

"Someone is getting out of the back seat and dragging someone out with him," whispered Bill.

Mark stared at the woman being dragged out of the back of the car. He squinted trying to get a better look. He noticed that she was hardly able to stand up, but he couldn't get a good look at her since she was facing the other way. Suddenly, the man holding on to her spun her around, and he could see her face. "Oh, my god," he said. "I think that's Teresa, the girl that helped entrap Olivia," he blurted out.

"Here," said Bill thrusting a pair of binoculars at him. "Look through these."

Mark quickly adjusted the lenses to get a clearer view of the woman being yanked around by her captor. "That's her. I'm sure of it. She looks like she's been roughed up—her face is swollen, and her lip is busted, but that's her. Look! She's trying not to put any weight on her left foot. Gina told me tonight on the phone that Teresa had hurt her leg in some sort of an accident. I'm sure of it— it's definitely her."

"Give me the binoculars. It looks like the other guy in the handcuffs is your sedan driver." Bill readjusted the binoculars and zeroed in on the man he suspected as being the same one he saw getting out of the sedan earlier at Gutierrez' office. "Yep, it sure is, and the guy who is just getting out of the front seat is your Mr. Gutierrez," Bill muttered. "Okay, it's time to call in the troops," he announced reaching for his cell phone.

"What do you mean?" asked Mark.

Bill held up his index finger signaling for him to be quiet. "Jim, it's Bill. You've got them all in one place. I would say it's now or never." There was a pause and Mark could barely hear the voice of the person on the other end of the phone, and then Bill continued, "We'll stay out of the way," he said snapping his phone shut.

"Who was that? What did you mean about us staying out of the way?" asked Mark glancing over at Bill.

Bill didn't answer. His eyes were focused on the activity around the van.

216

"Oh, my god, they're dragging Theresa and the other guy inside," whispered Mark. "Are we just going to sit here and watch two murders happen in front of our eyes," he asked impatiently. "You saw their guns. I bet they intend to kill both Teresa and the sedan driver."

"I bet you're right," he said. "But, there are at least four of them and only two of us. Lesson number two—don't move in until you outnumber the enemy unless you are sure you can out maneuver them or have more powerful weapons than they have," he said glancing in his rear view mirror. "Here comes our back-up," he whispered.

Mark looked in his side mirror in time to see a parade of Miami police cars headed their way. Gutierrez and his body guards also saw the cruisers and ran back toward the SUV. As they peeled away from the warehouse, Mark saw one of them lean out of the back window of the car and fire two shots at the two prisoners who were trying to help one another get behind the warehouse. Mark watched in disbelief as Teresa and the sedan driver dropped to the ground.

"My god," he shrieked. "He shot both of them." The first two cruisers in the parade continued to pursue the SUV, the others surrounded the warehouse. Mark opened his door to get out, but Bill leaned over and yanked him back inside.

"Not yet," he yelled. "Let them do their job. I promised we would stay out of their way. If you go out there now, you'll just distract them and give them someone else to have to protect."

"But, Olivia is in there," argued Mark. "What if whoever

217

is left in there has orders to shoot her?"

"You don't know that. Sit still," ordered Bill. "I'll let you know when it's time to get out."

Mark's military training kept him from disobeying an order. He yanked the door shut and watched as the action in front of him seemed to take place in slow motion. In the distance, he could see the two police cars chasing the SUV up the ramp and onto the freeway. He saw the flashes of light flying out the windows of the SUV as shots were fired at the police. Suddenly, the SUV careened out of control, hitting the median and rolling over and over down the highway, finally coming to rest on its top as the officers leaped from their cruisers with guns drawn. There appeared to be no one crawling out of the SUV.

"Got the tires. Great shooting. Three down, who knows how many more to go," mumbled Bill.

Mark shifted his attention back to the warehouse. The police had completely surrounded it, and one of the officers was leaning over Teresa and the driver of the sedan. In the distance, he heard the sirens from what he assumed would be emergency vehicles and more police cruisers. Their flashing lights lit up the dark sky, creating streams of color streaking along the highway.

In front of the warehouse, he could see one of the police sergeants holding up a microphone and talking into it, but he couldn't hear what he was saying as the piercing sounds from the approaching emergency vehicles sped past him.

218

After what seemed like hours but was actually only minutes, he watched three tough looking men walk slowly out of the warehouse with their hands up, fingers locked behind their heads. When the sergeant again raised the microphone to his lips, the men dropped quickly to the ground, face down. What looked like an entire army of police rushed forward—some of them leaped on top of the three men, pinning them to the ground as they expertly slipped the hand cuffs around their wrists. Other officers were leaning up against the building and slipping one-by-one through the door. The three men were yanked up from the ground and led to the waiting police vans by officers who were talking to them as they walked. *They are probably reciting them their Miranda rights*, Mark thought. He had watched the scene hundreds of time on TV and in the movies. It seemed surreal that now he was living it.

 Bill finally let go of his arm. "Okay, now we can get out," he said.

Mark darted across the street toward the warehouse. A police officer, using a loud speaker, yelled at him to stop, and bright spotlights blinded him. "It's okay, Sergeant. He's with me," yelled Bill.

Then turning to Mark, Bill calmly said, "Lesson number three—don't ever go running through the dark with a pistol in your hand toward a bunch of armed and revved up police officers without identifying yourself first. You're just lucky they're disciplined enough to not shoot first and ask questions later."

"Sorry, Bill. I wasn't thinking. Thanks," Mark replied, embarrassed by the fact that his emotions had gotten in

219

the way of his thinking. "I've got a lot to learn before I head into combat, that's for sure," he admitted.

Bill introduced him to the Sergeant in charge of the operation, and Mark learned that Bill had actually been working with the police all along. He was the one that Gina had referred to as watching the office and reporting on Mark's arrival there.

Bill had gone to the police as soon as Meredith had called him, and they agreed to let him participate in the investigation. It turned out that they had been investigating Gutierrez and his thugs for several months but had never had any real evidence to book him.

"Was there anyone else inside?" Mark asked. "Did you find the girl that we're looking for?"

"No, not yet," replied the Sergeant. The warehouse appears only to be full of stuff that Gutierrez exported. You can go in and look around yourself if you'd like. Here, put this on," he said offering him a clip-on tag with the words *Official Observer* typed on it. Mark immediately headed for the warehouse.

When he walked into the open space of the building, although it was spacious, he was immediately struck with the impression that it seemed smaller than he had anticipated from its appearance outside. He stood for a moment just inside the room and glanced around. Metal shelves lined the walls of the open space. They were stacked full of what appeared to be used auto and machine parts. Down the center of the room, was a row of five or six late model cars, out of which the police were now lifting large sacks of a white powder from false floors

220

in the trunks—probably cocaine he guessed. Next to the cars, there was a mixed row of used farm and highway equipment. Off to the right was a spiraling, metal stair case leading to a glass enclosed office that looked out over the space below.

He watched as police carried computers and files down the stairs and outside to the awaiting police van. There was a constant hum from the fans and lighting hanging high overhead and a dominant odor of oil and grease mixed with the smell of salt water as a breeze blew through the doors from the Port of Miami. The building seemed to have just a single story, except for the small office space.

Mark moved around trying to stay out of the way of the police and being careful not to touch anything so as not to convolute any evidence that they might need in order to prosecute the criminals they had just captured. There was a sense of camaraderie and jubilation among the officers as they exchanged expressions of surprise and joy when they discovered bag after bag of drugs. They were obviously elated that their investigations had paid off. This was bound to be one of the biggest drug busts in Dade County. "I think we got us a kingpin this time," he heard one officer shout.

Suddenly, Mark wheeled around and headed outside. In his haste to get inside of the building to look for Olivia, he had momentarily forgotten about Teresa and the sedan driver. He arrived just in time to see the medics lift Teresa into the emergency squad. From the bags and tubes dangling above her on the stretcher, Mark realized she was obviously still alive. He knew that she would certainly be able to tell him where Olivia was. "Wait," he yelled to the medics loading her into the van. "I need to ask her some questions," he shouted.

"Sorry, buddy," answered one of the medics. "She's unconscious—hasn't made a sound since we found her."

Mark could see the small trickle of blood coming from a wound on her forehead. "What about the other guy, where's he?"

"Didn't make it," said the medic pointing to the body bag still lying on the ground where Mark had first seen the man fall.

"Dammit," he yelled. He whirled around and glanced up at the side of the warehouse. For a moment, he just stood there staring at the building.

"Are you okay, sir?" asked the medic who was trying to close the rear door of the van.

"Yeah, I'm fine," muttered Mark.

"Well, then would you mind moving over, so I can close the door, and we can transport this lady to the hospital," the medic asked.

"Oh, sorry, of course," said Mark moving out of the way as he continued to stare at the side of the building. *I know that the exterior of the sides of this building are bigger than the interior space*, he observed. He moved to the front of the building and started stepping off the distance from the front to the back of the warehouse.

222

"Considering buying the building?" asked Bill, startling Mark as he approached him out of the darkness.

"Does that interior space seem smaller to you than the outside width?" asked Mark losing count of how many steps he had taken.

"I'm not sure what you're getting at," responded Bill. "But, there's only one way to find out, go ahead and step it off."

Mark started once again to step off the distance from the front to the back of the building. "Okay, the building is approximately two-hundred fifty feet wide. Let's check the inside," Mark yelled from the back edge of the building.

Inside the building there continued to be a hub of activity as police wearing gloves carefully examined boxes, tires, and everything and anything that might contain hidden compartments for stashing drugs. Mark moved to the side out of their way and began stepping off the interior width of the room. Bill counted as Mark methodically measured the space. When he had reached the outer back wall, Mark whirled around, and they stared at each other from across the room. Mark was right. The exterior of the building was more than twenty feet wider than the interior width.

Bill quickly surveyed the back wall of the interior space as he hurried across the room to reach Mark. There were shelves across the entire length of the wall, but there was about a three foot break in the shelving before they continued the remaining distance to the end of the wall. The gap in the shelving was easy to dismiss unless you

223

were looking for it. Bill called to one of the police officers wearing gloves and asked him to remove the objects from the shelves on both sides of the gap between the shelving. The policeman frowned but continued to do as Bill had asked.

Bill and Mark spotted the electrical box at the same time. Mark started to open the small metal covering on the box, but Bill grabbed his hand. "Rule number four—don't screw up potential finger prints," he warned. Bill asked the officer who had cleared off the shelves to open the box. Inside, it looked like any standard electrical box. As Mark moved in closer, he noticed a barely-visible, white button located in the corner below the metal housing. The button wasn't noticeable unless you were actually looking for something unusual.

The policeman looked at them with questioning eyes. "Mind if I call the Sergeant over here to take a look at this," he asked.

"Do whatever you have to do, but do it quickly," said Mark impatiently.

"Hang in there, Mark," said Bill. "This may not be anything."

"Or, it may be everything," Mark retorted, anxiously shifting his weight from foot to foot and wringing his hands. "Where in the hell is that Sergeant?" he cursed.

"What's going on here, Bill?" asked the Sergeant slowly sauntering over to the two observers.

"Push that damn button," ordered Mark impatiently.

The Sergeant cast Bill an inquisitive look, before answering. "Son, hopefully, before you just start pushing buttons when you're out there protecting me and the others back here at home, you'll get some patience and take the time to consider the possible consequences of every move you make. Let me ask you a question," he continued. "How do you know that hidden button isn't hooked up to some explosive device that would send all of us hurling through space with fire streaming out of our pants?" he asked.

"I don't know that. You're right," said Mark. "But, what I do know is that the exterior width of this building is twenty feet wider than the width of this room, and that button will more than likely swing open this clear space between this long, row of shelves. And then, once we are on the other side of this fake wall, I have no doubt that we will find the girl we are looking for, probably locked up in some disgusting cell or cage. I'm sure of it," he asserted. "Now, please, just push the damn button."

"I appreciate your frustration," said the Sergeant, "but, I'm gonna have our explosive expert get over here and assure me that I won't be risking the lives of everyone in this room before I push it," he asserted. He turned around and walked to the bottom of the stairs leading to the overhead office. "Burton, get yourself down here," he ordered.

A thin, young police officer slid down the twisting railing and strolled with the Sergeant across the room to where Mark was impatiently pacing back and forth. Bill was pushing against the wall in the clear space but couldn't feel any give in it. He tried to examine the wall around the space for cracks or hinges, but the metal strips for

225

the shelving hid any spot where he thought the cracks might be.

"Burton, take a look at this button and tell me if you think it might be connected to an explosive device or something," instructed the Sergeant.

"Nah," said Burton, reaching in and pushing the button. "There you go," he said, "It's just an opener for a secret wall. Pretty cool," he said. "I wonder how much stashe is hidden back there?"

Mark pushed passed the others and began yelling for Olivia. He groped along the wall until he located a light switch. "Oh, my god," muttered the Sergeant. "It must be 120 degrees in here, and what is the smell?" he said gagging as a pungent odor spread out over the entire room.

"How could anyone be so inhumane?" groaned Bill, as he looked down the row of wooden boxes lined up against the wall. He tried to ignore the stench streaming from each cell. He counted ten boxes that were about the length and width of his dining room table. He immediately began helping Mark lift the heavy metal bars that held the doors closed. The Sergeant and Burton quickly joined in the search as Mark continued to scream for Olivia.

"Oh, my god," cried Mark. "Here she is, thank God; thank God. Here she is," he repeated, lifting Olivia's lifeless body into his arms.

Bill quickly pressed two fingers against her neck. "She's alive, but barely," he shouted. "Let's get her out of here
226

and into some air," he said pushing Burton and the Sergeant out of his way. "Call for more emergency equipment," he yelled over his shoulder.

Mark rushed through the warehouse carrying Olivia as stunned police investigators stared in silence. Outside, in the open air he laid her on the ground and immediately began to administer mouth-to-mouth resuscitation. In the background, he could hear the sirens of the approaching emergency vehicles as he counted the seconds between his breaths.

The medics quickly ran to where Olivia was lying on the ground. "We'll take over," one of the medics said as he expertly slipped an oxygen mask over Olivia's mouth and nose. Mark moved out of the way of the medics and stood helplessly by as they checked her heart and blood pressure. Another medic slipped an IV into her arm, and Mark noticed the bruises inside the crook of her elbow, probably from the drugs that her captors had injected into her.

He heard the medics call out the readings from the various machines they had attached to her. He tried desperately to recall the minimums and maximums of vital signs but couldn't unscramble them in his mind. Bill approached him and laid his hand on his shoulder. "Her vitals are weak, but if she's a fighter, she should recover. She was the only one in there, but there were signs that some of the other cells had been recently occupied. The Sergeant told me that they had already found an accounting of all Gutierrez's clients on one of his computers and had dispatched cars to the locations of several local massage parlors that were probably fronts for brothels."

"Those dirty, rotten bastards," yelled Mark, punching his fist against the side of the emergency squad.

"Rule number five, don't get mad, get even," said Bill grabbing Mark's fist. "They're going to pay. There's enough evidence here to keep them locked up for life."

"That's not good enough for them. They should be publicly castrated," shouted Mark angrily.

"Come on, Marine," said Bill firmly. "Keep the code."

Mark whirled around to face Bill with hatred blazing in his eyes. "How can you be so cool with all of this? Do you have any idea what they intended to do with her, if by chance she survived?"

"Of course, I know. I was a cop in New York, remember? I've scraped up young girls who have plunged out of windows to their deaths to escape from some pimp. I've dug them out of trash cans with dozens of holes in their veins and a bullet in their head. But, I was an honorable Cop. Sure, I wanted to bash the heads of the pimps, but I realized they weren't worth wasting my life and my family's on. You need to focus on getting this girl and her mom through this. Stop thinking about your own damn feelings," he shouted.

Mark stared in stunned silence as he saw his own hatred and anger reflected in the eyes of his earlier calm, mellow friend. He spontaneously reached out and grabbed Bill hugging him tightly. "I'm sorry, man," said Mark. "I've got a lot to learn. I'm sorry."

Bill patted him on the back and stepped aside. "Now get

228

over there and see what you can do to help her."

Mark whirled around and headed toward the spot where the medics were frantically hooking Olivia up to the last of the monitoring equipment. He kneeled down next to the stretcher and took her hand. Leaning in close to her, he softly whispered. "Olivia, it's Mark, Frank's nephew from the diner. You're going to be all right. I promise I'll keep you safe, but you have to fight. You're strong, I know you are—just like Gina and your mom." He glanced quickly down at his hand as he felt the light squeeze from Olivia's delicate fingers.

"Why don't you come with us to the hospital?" suggested one of the medics. "I'm sure she'll be less fretful if you stay with her."

"Did you hear that, Olivia? I'm not going to leave you. I'm going to stay right beside you until your mom gets here." Olivia squeezed his hand again as a tear trickled across her bruised cheek.

"Now you're learning," said Bill as Mark started to climb into the back of the ambulance. "I'll let you call the folks up North once you find out more of the details about her condition, but don't forget to call by eight, or I'll be getting a call from Meredith at 8:01." He laughed. "And, by the way, rule number six—always follow your hunches! But, I guess you already have that one mastered," he said as he patted Mark on the back. "Well, done, Marine," he said as he walked away.

Chapter 17

Mark glanced at his watch—seven-thirty in the morning and still no word from the doctor's examination of Olivia. He felt guilty about not immediately telling the folks in Ohio that she was safe, but things had been happening so fast that he hadn't thought about calling them until now. Besides, he'd lost his cell phone somehow in the fray of last night, and he knew he'd have to leave Olivia to find a phone—something he definitely didn't intend to do.

He looked down at her frail body, finally lying peacefully in the emergency room. While they had been examining her earlier, they had asked him to leave the room, and he had to let go of her hand. She immediately had become highly agitated, tossing her head from side to side and reaching her arms toward him. The nurses had to restrain her. He'd tried to reassure her that he was still there by talking to her calmly from behind the curtain. He talked to her about her mom, Gina, Sam, and the others who had helped him to find her. Hearing his voice gradually calmed her again. He told her about how Sam had gotten information from the Internet and that Meredith had given him the keys to her condo. He also told her how Unabomber 2, or Kenneth, had copied down the license plate of Teresa's car, which helped him find her so quickly. The doctors and nurses in the room had encouraged him to continue to tell her more about the diner and her family back in Ohio, and he had wondered if it was for Olivia's sake or for their own interests that they wanted to hear more about the *Frank's Diner* family. When they were finally through with their examination, he came back into her room and held her hand once again; she weakly responded with a light squeeze of his fingers.

Although he'd only briefly seen her the other morning in the diner, he had immediately felt a connection to her. At that time, he assumed that it was just a physical attraction to her as a beautiful, young woman. But now, as he stared at her, strange sensations stirred in the pit of his stomach and made it difficult for him to breathe normally. He gazed at her fine, delicate facial features and the long eyelashes that rested on her cheeks, concealing the deep blue eyes that he remembered from their first meeting. Her slightly curly, blonde hair fell in ringlets around her face. *She probably hates her hair,* he thought. *All women seem to hate their hair. I wonder why that it is.*

"I apologize that it has taken us so long to get back to you," said the doctor, jolting him out of his weird thoughts about women's hair. "Since you aren't her next of kin, by law, I can't disclose much of what we've learned about her condition from this cursory examination. But, because you're obviously important to her, I'm going to bend the rules a little and tell you as much as I can about what we know so far."

"I appreciate that," said Mark nervously.

"She's in serious condition because of critical dehydration and the effects of a drug overdose," continued the doctor. "If you're right that she's only been given the drug since Monday night, her recovery from the drugs will be short, although there's always the potential of flashbacks forever. Treating the dehydration is another matter; there may be serious kidney damage and damage to other vital organs. Time will tell about that. We've already begun hydration therapy for her, but I need to talk to someone who can give us consent for her continued treatment and can give us some information for the required insurance forms."

"Will you give me a number where her mother can reach you this morning?" interrupted Mark. "I'll call her right away."

The doctor wrote his number on a prescription pad and handed it to him. "Have her call me as soon as possible," he said. "We need that insurance information and other details about her to proceed with additional treatment."

"Is there a possibility that I can get a phone in here?" asked Mark. "I seem to have lost my cell phone, and I don't want to leave her alone, even for a few minutes."

"We may have your phone out at the desk," answered the doctor. "The medics found a cell phone in their van and gave it to one of the nurses. I'll have her bring it to you right away. Although we discourage the use of cell phones back here, I'll again bend the rules for you." He smiled and quickly left the room.

By the time the nurse brought him his phone, it was just a few minutes before eight. He immediately called the diner. This time it was Jan, who answered on the first ring.

"I have her," he shouted as his throat tightened, making it impossible for him to say any more. He was surprised by the relief he felt as he uttered those words, and he
232

was amazed at the sudden rush of emotion that the words stirred in him.

"Oh my god, oh my god," cried Jan. "He has her," she screamed. "He has her," she repeated. As the diner phone crashed against the floor, Mark could hear the shouts and cheers in the background.

"Hey, Marine," said Gina, finally picking up the phone. "You did okay, buddy. Are you all right?"

"Yeah, I am now," said Mark trying to conceal the emotion in his voice.

"Well, when you pull yourself together, tell me how Olivia is, and I want to hear every tiny detail about how you found her, and I mean a minute by minute accounting not a bland summary. And speak up—everyone is screaming and crying around here, so it's hard to hear."

Gina had a way of making everyone feel better, even from far away on the phone. But as Mark listened to her forced, light tone, he didn't miss the shaky quality in her voice that betrayed her own emotional response to his news. *She's tough, but not hard.* He smiled.

"I've got it all together, now," he whispered. "Olivia is here with me, although she isn't awake right now. So, I'd rather not talk too long. It might bother her."

"What do you mean that she isn't awake—is she just sleeping or is something else going on with her?" asked Gina, obviously upset. "Hey, quiet down out there," she yelled to the crowd in the diner. "I want to hear what the man has to say. Okay, Mark, go ahead, tell me what's

233

going on with Olivia."

"All I know is that she's suffering from severe dehydration and seems to be slipping in and out of consciousness. I'm really worried, but don't tell Jan all of this. Maybe she'll be better by the time she gets here." When there was nothing but silence from the other end of the phone, Mark finally asked, "Gina, are you still there?" as he checked his phone to make sure he hadn't dropped the call.

"Yeah, I'm still here," she whispered, and Mark knew that she was crying but thought it wise not to mention it.

"I need for you to give Jan a number to call right away," he said.

"Okay, go ahead," she whispered.

Mark read the number to her then quietly asked, "Are you okay?"

"What do you mean by that? Of course, I'm not okay. Are you actually okay? But I'll be fine by the time I turn around and face the others. I just need to pretend that I'm still talking to you. Tell me some good news for god's sake."

"Well, they caught the bad guys just like on those TV shows you're always talking about," he answered.

"That is good news, and don't make fun of my TV shows, although I'm not sure I can watch them anymore with quite the same amount of detachment. Okay, That's

234

enough. I'm fine now. Take care of Olivia, and don't you dare leave her until Jan gets there," she warned.

"You don't have to worry about that," said Mark. "There's no way I'll leave her alone again."

When he finally ended their conversation, it was agreed that Jan would get on the next plane for Miami and meet him at the hospital around noon. He closed up his phone and noticed that the battery was nearly gone. *Why don't they build chargers into the damn phone,* he wondered.

"I don't know how much you heard of that," he whispered, leaning close to Olivia. "But your mom will be here real soon, and I'll be right here until she arrives. You never have to worry about someone taking you from us ever again. I promise."

Olivia squeezed his hand as a single tear once again trickled down her cheek.

For the next several hours, Mark dowsed off, sitting in the uncomfortable metal chair in the emergency room with his head resting against the bars of the metal rail surrounding Olivia's bed. He was suddenly awakened when Olivia screamed. She pulled her knees up to her chest and grasped her stomach while she rolled back and forth crashing against the metal bars surrounding her bed. She repeatedly gagged and strained so hard that it looked like she might explode. Mark quickly pushed the *Call* button and tried to soothe her by talking to her and stroking her hand and arm. Beads of sweat peppered her forehead.

A nurse quickly responded to the alarm and immediately

injected Olivia with something through her IV. After several minutes, Olivia began to relax, straightening her legs as the pain began to subside, and the vomiting stopped.

"She's going through drug withdrawal," explained the nurse. "It's not unusual with heroin even after a few doses. Typically, we provide an oral liquid containing a synthetic opiate, methadone, in increasingly smaller amounts over time until the body's nervous system is able to function normally as the excessive dopamine diminishes from the system. Unfortunately, as you've no doubt noticed, the extent of her dehydration is causing her to fade in and out of consciousness, so we can't risk having her choke on the liquid. Once she gets more fluids in her body and is more alert, we'll be able to start the typical detoxification process. She should be able to detox quickly since she probably hasn't developed a strong emotional dependency on the drug."

"It's scary to watch," said Mark. "She looked like she was in terrible pain."

"I understand that the stomach and muscle pains are severe," said the nurse. "That's why it's normally impossible for a person to try to detoxify without assistance. The cold-turkey approach typically never works," she explained. As she continued to check Olivia's blood pressure and other vitals, she frowned. "I'm going to send the doctor in right away," she said quickly leaving the room.

Mark stared at the machines monitoring Olivia's heart and blood pressure. Since the episode of the pain and vomiting, the lines indicating her heartbeat had become erratic, and her blood pressure had dropped. He began gently stroking Olivia's hand once again. "Olivia," he whispered. "Come on. You've got to fight this. Please squeeze my fingers to let me know you can hear me." He stared anxiously at her hand, watching for any sign of motion, but there was none. She lay completely still.

The doctor who had examined her earlier, burst into the room, looking extremely concerned. "Is her mother on her way," he asked.

"She should be here in about an hour, why?" asked Mark.

"I was just hoping that we would see some improvement with the intravenous hydration, but she's not responding as I had hoped."

"What do you mean? Are you saying she might die? How can that be?"

"Severe hydration can be fatal if not treated soon enough," replied the doctor. "Her exposure to intense heat and the recurrent vomiting induced by the drugs, plus the lack of any fluid intake, are all working against her recovery right now. We are doing all we can for her, but we have to monitor carefully the amount of fluids that we can give her through the IV. Too much fluid, too quickly can make the cells in her body absorb too much water too fast, causing them to rupture. That would be especially catastrophic if the rupture occurs in the cells of the brain."

"Oh, my god," responded Mark, squeezing Olivia's hand a little tighter, trying to get a response from her. Once

237

again, he stared anxiously at her fingers to see if he could detect any movement—even a slight twinge, but there was still no response from her at all.

"A few more hours in the heat and conditions you described without any fluids, and she would have been dead when you found her," said the doctor.

"This whole thing doesn't make any sense to me. Why would they abduct her with the intention of selling her as a sex slave and then just let her die?" muttered Mark.

"More than likely, they were distracted by the capture of the others that you told me about, and they just ignored her. I agree with you, it wouldn't make sense to let her die if their intentions were as you described, but then I don't pretend to understand the minds of people like that. The whole thing makes no sense to me," he said. "The nurse will be back in a few minutes to check her vitals again. I need to go check on the other woman that they brought in from the same drug bust that you were involved in."

"You mean she's in this hospital too?" asked Mark, frightened by the possibility that Teresa would be near Olivia.

"Next door," replied the doctor. "They've stationed a police guard at her door, but she's not a threat to anyone anymore. She'll probably live but never be able to function on her own. There won't be much quality to her life."

"She never lived a quality life in the first place," snarled Mark. "I just want to make sure that she never gets near
238

Olivia or that Olivia ever finds out that she's in the same hospital. And, what about the thugs that the police pulled from the wreckage of the car—are they in here, too?" Mark asked.

"One of them is in here. I understand that the others were treated at the scene and released to the police."

"What's the name of the one they brought in here, do you know?" asked Mark.

"No. I wouldn't be able to give out that information anyway. Don't worry; I take it that you haven't noticed the guard outside your door. The police want to ensure that no one gets to Olivia. She's an important witness in this whole mess, you know."

"That's what scares me. You don't know these people; they're vicious. I'm sure they'd do anything to make sure she can't testify against them."

"I understand," sighed the doctor. "But, let's just worry about getting her well—not just so she can testify, but so she can enjoy the life that a young girl like her should enjoy. I have a daughter about her age, and I can't even imagine the fear and anger that her mother must be feeling and will probably feel forever. It'll be a long time before she'll be able to believe that Olivia is safe again—and with good reason. They're both going to need some strong support and tons of compassion, but from what you were saying to her earlier, when we were examining her, it sounds like they have that kind of support back in Ohio."

"Yeah, they do," sighed Mark. "But I hate that they'll have

239

to go through all the investigation and relive the whole thing again in court. God, this really isn't over, is it?"

"No. Unfortunately, it isn't." said the doctor as he left the room.

Mark turned back toward Olivia, again starring at her for a long time. *My god,* he thought, *she looks so fragile. How is she ever going to have the strength and courage to face what's ahead for her? Will she ever be able to have a normal life,* he wondered. *How can anyone who's experienced what she has, be able to ever feel safe again?* "Oh, Olivia," he said aloud. "I am so, so sorry."

He sat back down next to her, still holding her hand. He stared at the monitors and watched as her heartbeat became slower and her blood pressure continued to drop. The nurse came in several times when an alarm went off signaling that the saline drip bag had gone dry. He questioned her about Olivia's slowing pulse and sinking blood pressure, but she would only assure him that they were doing all they could. "The rest is up to Olivia and God," she said.

Another hour had ticked slowly by when Mark heard a rustling of activity outside Olivia's room. *What was going on? Who was out there*, he wondered, as he prepared for the worse. Yanking back the curtains, he was relieved to see Jan impatiently trying to push past the guard to get to her daughter. Bill Fleming stood next to her, patiently trying to explain the situation to the guard.

"It's okay, Officer. She's Olivia's mother, and Mr. Fleming is a close friend," said Mark as Jan pushed past him to get to Olivia.

240

"Oh my god, Mark. She's so pale and lifeless. What's going on?" begged Jan with tears flooding her eyes.

Mark explained as best he could the complications of the dehydration and the drugs, trying to sound hopeful, even though he was beginning to feel less so as time went on without any response from Olivia.

"Olivia, sweetheart, it's me," said Jan, lowering the rail on Olivia's bed and lifting her into her arms. "Come on, baby, you can beat this, but you have to fight. I promise I won't leave you alone, not for a second. Come on, baby, fight," she pleaded rocking Olivia gently back and forth.

The two men stood helplessly watching Jan as she seemed to be trying to pour her own strength into Olivia.

"Mark," whispered Bill after several minutes. "I have strict orders from the headquarters in Ohio to take you back to the condo where Meredith is fixing you a feast."

"Meredith?" asked Mark.

"She flew down here with Jan. She wanted to make sure that she got to the hospital and had someone down here to help her until Olivia is well enough to go home. I picked them up at the airport, but Meredith insisted on taking a cab to the condo, so Jan could come straight to the hospital."

"I'm not sure I should leave," said Mark. Even though he was starving and feeling totally spent, he suddenly couldn't imagine leaving Olivia.

"It's okay, Mark," said Jan, gently laying Olivia back on the pillow and tucking in the sheet tightly around her. "I know it's hard to decide where to be," she said reaching up to hug him tightly. "But I'm fine now that I'm here, and I know Olivia's a fighter. Everything will be okay; you'll see," she comforted. "Go with Bill, eat some decent food, and get some rest. I promise I'll call you the minute there's any change," she assured him.

"Every once in a while, Olivia has some horrible reaction to the drugs, so don't panic. Just push that *Call* button there on the bed, and a nurse will come right away. Just make sure you put that rail back up on her bed, and keep holding her hand. I promised her that I would keep holding her hand," he said.

Jan smiled at his earnest fear that she wouldn't be able to take care of her own daughter. "I promise I'll take care of her while you're gone. I'll never be able to repay you for all you did; you know that, don't you? I think an angel must have sent you to us."

The thought of his grandfather as an angel caused Mark to chuckle. "Well, actually, it was a pretty, crusty old man that sent me, but I'll always be thankful to him for that." He quickly turned away to hide the tears that swelled in his eyes. "Okay, Bill, let's go see what kind of cook Meredith is, and I can't wait to get a shower," he called over his shoulder. "I've had these clothes on for three days now."

Bill chuckled. "I can tell," he said, throwing his arm around Mark's shoulders as they walked out of the Emergency Room.

Chapter 18

With Jan and Mark in Florida and Kelley in Germany with Carl, Gina felt lonely and out of sorts as she headed toward Edith and Kenneth Talbert's house for dinner. She was restless and even more flighty than normal. Frank was constantly telling her to settle somewhere. Earlier today, he had yelled at her, saying *'You're making us all nervous. You flit around in here like a fly looking for some morsel to devour.'*

He was right. She wasn't content anywhere. Yesterday, she had even gone out looking for a new apartment because her current one made her mad every time she walked into her empty living room. She still didn't have the money to replace the DVD and other media players that Greg had stolen from her. She did buy a cheap, small screen TV, but she had to put it in her bedroom because she didn't have enough money to replace the couch missing from her living room.

Greg finally tripped himself up when Jeff questioned him the second time. Jeff had checked out his alibi about his whereabouts between the time he left Gina's apartment and the time he was arrested. Greg had lied, saying that he had spent the night in a local motel. When Jeff told him that they knew he never checked in to any of the local hotels or motels, he finally admitted to stealing everything with the help of a friend.

Now at least Gina knew what had happened to her stuff,

243

but the recovery of the stolen things was just not going anywhere. According to Greg, he had sold them to some dealer from out of state who was still out there somewhere re-selling them to god knows who. Greg claimed that he was robbed immediately after receiving the money for the stolen goods and suspected that the man he sold them to was responsible for his robbery. *He is such stupid jerk*, she thought.

What she missed most were her Karaoke CDs and her CD player. Singing along with the CDs helped her to hold on to her dream of getting to Nashville. She hadn't sung once this entire week, not even in her car where she always sang along with the radio. She just didn't feel like singing—certainly, nothing that happened this week was worth singing about.

As she turned into the Talbert's driveway, she slowed down and opened her windows to let the soft evening breeze perfume her car with the sweet smell from hundreds of roses that lined the long drive. *Now this is what life should be about: Beautiful colors, delicate flowers, sweet aromas, and warm breezes that tickle your head as they gently rearrange your hair.* She sighed. Unfortunately, this whole week had been full of things so removed from the joy of this moment that it was hard to believe that what she was enjoying right now was actually real. *Such a shame*, she thought, *we're all so busy chasing after artificial nonsense that what is natural, real, and forever is what actually seems surreal to us. We spend our lives pursuing expensive junk that ultimately never satisfies us and leaves us worrying about theft, destruction, and loss—when the real pleasures in life are free. These beautiful roses expect nothing from us except to respect their right to be. Who was it that once encouraged us to 'stop and smell the*
244

roses,' she wondered. Well, whoever they were, they knew what they were talking about; they had obviously found the key to true happiness.

Strange, she thought as she glanced around at the beautiful landscaping surrounding the front of the Talbert's home, *I've always felt sorry for Kenneth all this time because he wasn't able to enjoy life the same way I thought he should enjoy it. Now I realize that he's the lucky one; he knows what he loves, and he has perfected it and surrounded himself with it. I'm the one who's so busy trying to figure life out that I'm missing it. I always felt bad that he couldn't or wouldn't talk. But, I was wrong. He says a lot; he just says it through his lovely roses.*

"Hello, Gina," shouted Edith Talbert from the front door. "I saw you coming up the drive. I noticed you took the time to enjoy the roses as you drove past them—good for you. You'd be surprised at how many people just speed past them without ever noticing them."

"Actually, I wouldn't be surprised at all. I think most of us pass by what really matters in life with blinders on. I know I've been blind to what really matters, until lately." Gina smiled and presented Edith with a bottle of red wine that she hoped would be an appropriate gift.

"Thank you," said Edith. "This will be perfect with the meal that Kenneth has planned for us."

"Kenneth is doing the cooking?" questioned Gina.

"Yes, he's a wonderful cook—the master of the grill—I call him. Tonight he has something special planned for you. He's very excited about your coming, and I appreciate you taking the time for us."

"I've been looking forward to this all week," said Gina. "I want to learn more about Kenneth. I'm discovering that he's a young man with lots of talents."

"He is," answered Edith. "But before we go out to the patio, I wanted to ask about Olivia; that is, if it doesn't bother you to talk about it. What a terrible ordeal for such a young person to experience," she lamented.

"Well, she's starting to respond to the hydration therapy, but they really won't know if there was any damage to her kidneys and other organs for several weeks. At least, she's more alert and is able to respond to Jan and Mark a little more. The doctor has begun the detoxification from the drugs that she was given, and that seems to be going just fine. But she has a long way to go, and she'll probably never be the same emotionally again. She certainly has lost her innocence, and she's still extremely fearful. Jan and Mark never leave her. They take turns coming and going to the hospital, so there's always one of them with her day and night."

"How horrible," sighed Edith. "And, what about the creeps who abducted her? Did they capture them all?"

"Who knows?" answered Gina. "They had contacts all across the United States and in foreign countries too. The police in Miami have arrested more than thirty people involved in either drugs or prostitution, and I understand that even more are being held in New York, LA, and Detroit. The Miami police are also keeping twenty or more young girls under protective custody until

246

they are able to build their case against the jerks that forced them into prostitution. They have to make sure that the girls are safe from the possibility of harm from other thugs involved in the prostitution and drug cartel of this Gutierrez jerk."

"Were the two young coeds who were missing from our campus among the girls they found?" asked Edith.

"Yes. They did find them. Unfortunately, they weren't as lucky as Olivia. They had been used as sex slaves for several weeks. One of the girls is in the same hospital as Olivia. She tried to commit suicide and is in bad shape. Her parents visited Mark to thank him for helping to find her and the others."

"Oh, my," sighed Edith. "It's hard to believe that there's such evil out there, especially when I live in this beautiful environment. I'm really blessed. I know that." Then, noticing the sadness in Gina's eyes, she added, "Come on, let me take you outside, you deserve a change of realities. Kenneth has designed a special garden just for you. Let's go out before he begins to worry that you're not coming."

Gina was astounded when she walked outside onto the patio. The backyard spread out over several acres and tall pine trees surrounded it, providing complete privacy. Adjacent to the house was a large greenhouse outlined in tiny twinkle lights. Spotlights cast flares of light on small islands of roses, herbs, and other flowers arranged in different patterns and designs that were connected by meandering streams of white pebbles. Lanterns of every shape and size illuminated the paths between the individual beds of flowers and plants.

When the two women came out onto the patio, Kenneth actually greeted her. "Welcome, Gina," he said shyly.

"Oh my goodness, Kenneth. I feel like I'm standing at the entrance to the Garden of Eden," she praised. "This must have been what it looked like. This is absolutely the most amazing place I've ever seen in my life. What a landscape artist you are. Thank you, thank you so much for letting me share this with you and your grandmother. I'm completely blown away."

Kenneth dropped his head, but she could see the smile on his face. *Strange*, she thought, *I don't think I've ever seen him smile before.*

"Come," he said, motioning for her to follow him.

"You're going to love this," said Edith. "He started it on Tuesday, as soon as he learned that you would be coming here tonight. He even skipped going to the park the past two days, so it would be finished for you tonight."

Gina followed Kenneth down a twisting path. They passed by beautiful arrangements that she wanted to stop and admire, but Kenneth was walking so fast that she practically had to run to keep up with him. Then she saw it, all lit up in front of her. "Oh, my gosh, Kenneth. It's the diner," she shouted. Gina stared in disbelief at the huge garden of flowers arranged as a giant portrait of the diner. "You've actually painted a giant picture of the diner in flowers. It's perfect. It looks just like it, even down to the signs that we have in the windows and your bike and Sam's truck outside. Kenneth, you are so talented. I don't know how to thank you for this. It's so life-like. I brought a camera, will you let me take a picture?" she

248

asked.

"OK," he said. "Time to eat now."

"I'm so excited," she said, "but I don't think my excitement will interfere with my appetite. What are you fixing? It smells delicious. I didn't realize you were a gourmet cook too. You should give Frank some cooking lessons," she added.

Kenneth actually chuckled. "Frank cooks okay," he said.

Gina stared in awe at the variety of food beautifully arranged on a sideboard near a large built-in grille. Kenneth had roasted a small chicken on the rotisserie attached to the grill. The chicken was stuffed with all sorts of fruits, vegetables, and herbs—apricots, oranges, garlic, and a small bouquet of herbs were nestled inside the cavity of the chicken. The sweet aroma from the chicken, mixing with the perfumed smell of the flowers surrounding the patio was intoxicating.

Next to the chicken, there was a platter with three bacon-wrapped filets of beef topped with mushrooms and caramelized onions. A large platter of roasted vegetables was lightly covered with a balsamic sauce and sprinkled with roasted almonds. The salad was almost too beautiful to eat. A mixture of edible flowers, herbs, and fresh Bibb lettuce was splashed lightly with raspberry vinaigrette that was both sweet and savory. Every dish was delicately decorated with a spray of small rosebuds or an herbal bouquet.

Gina tasted everything, finding each new flavor more delicious than the one before. She finished her meal off

249

with two desserts: a piece of mile-high chocolate cake with thick, creamy chocolate frosting and an apple dumpling, each topped with homemade vanilla ice cream. She thought she might actually explode as she chased the last crumb of the light and moist cake around on her plate.

"My goodness, Kenneth, if you can cook like this, why do you bother to come to our little diner?" she asked.

"Friends," Kenneth quickly responded, causing Gina to feel a wave of shame and guilt, as she recalled how they had nicknamed him after someone as insensitive and crazy as Ted Kaczynski.

"You're a good friend, Kenneth. I'm so glad that you do come to the diner. We're lucky to have a friend like you." She smiled, wanting to reach out and touch him but remembering Mark's warning about him possibly not liking it. "If it hadn't been for you, we may never have found Olivia. I promise I'll be a better friend to you," she said, trying hard to swallow the tears that were threatening to expose her deep felt remorse for her former attitudes about him. *What's wrong with me this week,* she thought—I *never cry, and I've been crying all week.*

After dinner, Kenneth accompanied her as she wandered through the gardens. Each of the variously shaped plots had a specific theme, but as a whole, he had managed to create a color scheme that demonstrated the nuances of the effect of light spreading out across the garden. Standing at the front of the garden, near the patio, Gina noticed that he had used soft pastels in his designs illustrating the effects of the

250

bright lights streaming from the house. But, as she looked out away from the patio, he had used deeper, complementary shades of color. Finally, at the very farthest edge of the garden, he had chosen vibrant, dark colors creating the impression that the tall pines had cast a shadow across the outer gardens, and the light from the house had diminished.

"It's like walking through a painting," sighed Gina.

"Monet," said Kenneth.

"Yes," said Gina. "I remember studying about him in school. He was an Impressionist, just like you. I love his paintings, and I love your gardens. You've managed to use the effects of color and pattern to produce the impression of light diminishing as it spreads out to the edges of the garden.

"You understand me," said Kenneth. "Come," he said, leading her toward the greenhouse.

Gina didn't pretend to understand what was happening with the flowers in the greenhouse, and though he tried, Kenneth had trouble telling her about what each of the experiments was trying to accomplish. But though she didn't understand the science involved, what she did know was that she was seeing colors that she didn't realize existed, and flowers that were the most unusual she had ever seen.

"I wish I could understand all of this, Kenneth. I'm sure you do, but I never paid a lot of attention to science in school. But I have to tell you—I've never seen such gorgeous colors, not even in pictures of birds and plants

251

in the Rain Forest. And I've never seen such tiny, delicate rosebuds or such gigantic ones in my life. It's amazing what you've been able to create. You must really be proud of your work."

"Yes," nodded Kenneth. "It's hard for me to talk about it."

"I'm sorry about that, but really, talking is overrated. You're a wonderful listener and observer, and those are the best things. You learn a lot more when you're quiet, like you. I know I should listen more, but I just can't help myself—I chatter constantly."

"I like your chatter," said Kenneth. "Come," he said again, leading her back to the patio.

Edith had finished putting away the left-over food and clearing away the dishes. She was just coming back out of the house onto the patio carrying a large box, beautifully wrapped with a small bouquet of red roses attached to the top of it. "This is for you," she said. "Kenneth and I wanted to do something nice for you because you've been so kind to him."

"You didn't have to do that. I don't really deserve such kindness," said Gina, dropping her eyes, as the guilt of her past impressions of Kenneth once again blew through her mind.

"Please, take it. Kenneth told me what to buy," responded Edith.

"It's too pretty to open," said Gina.

252

Lifting the beautiful bouquet off the top of the package, she held the roses close to her face and inhaled deeply, letting their sweet aroma fill her lungs. "I'll take these and put them in water right away." Then noticing that each rose was already placed in a tiny tube of water, she laughed, "I should've known that you would have already kept them safe."

She gently lifted the precisely folded corners of the wrapping paper. When she finally uncovered the box, she shouted with joy. "You're kidding. I can't believe this—you bought me my own karaoke machine. How did you know I've always wanted one of these," she asked looking at Kenneth.

"I listen," he said.

"Yes, you do. And, I promise you that I'm going to be a much better listener from now on," she said jumping up and hugging him. "Oh, I'm sorry," she said immediately as she felt him flinch. "I forgot. I won't do that again," she said.

"It's okay," interrupted Edith. "I hug him all the time. I've explained to him that women just need to hug."

Kenneth smiled and dropped his head. "Did I do right?" he asked quietly.

"You did better than all right. You gave me the perfect gift—one that I didn't really deserve, but one that I will treasure, forever. I don't know how to thank you."

"Sing a song," answered Kenneth.

"Here? Now?"

"I'd love to hear you sing," said Edith, "if you don't mind, that is. Kenneth tells me that you sometimes sing as you clean off his table at the diner."

"I do, don't I. I sometimes forget where I am. I just love to sing," she said, remembering that she hadn't sung all week. But now, she knew there was always something to sing about, so she began unpacking the Karaoke machine. "This comes with a CD, let me see if I can find a song that I know," she said scanning the list of songs on the CD. "Ah, here's one I like; it's an old country song by Eddy Arnold, but I think it will be just perfect out here in this beautiful garden." She slipped the CD into the player and picked up the mike as the music from "A Big Bouquet of Roses" flooded the night air, and she began to softly sing the lyrics.

Chapter 19

Frank was relieved that it was Sunday, and the week from hell was finally behind them. He realized that the fallout from Olivia's ordeal was far from over, but at least she was in safe hands now. He was physically and emotionally exhausted from everything that had happened, and he missed seeing Jan. Even though he talked to her every night on the phone, it wasn't the same as seeing her every day.

In just seven short days, the life of practically everyone in the *Diner* family was drastically changed somehow. Besides worrying about how Olivia and Jan would cope with the changes to their lives, he was sorry that Mark was spending his last free summer bound up in their problems instead of being able to take—perhaps his last trip—across the country as an unencumbered, young man. He worried also about how Kelley and her family were going to cope with the months of physical therapy that were facing Carl.

Gina, he wasn't worried about. Of all the members of the *Diner* family, he knew she would always land on her feet, no matter what life threw at her. Yesterday, she seemed to have rebounded from her mess with Greg and was her same, chatty self. She was so excited about everything that she had learned about Kenneth that she couldn't stop bragging about him all day.

Frank wondered about how her date went with Jeff last
255

night. He had watched Jeff fight his attraction to her for several years. He was glad that he finally got up enough courage to ask her out.

Yesterday, Gina still insisted that Jeff saw her as a charity case and that his interest in her was more as a big brother than as a potential lover. Sam had made a bet with her that she would be singing a different tune today. *I'm betting that Sam will win*, he thought.

Already done with the morning prep work, Frank started sifting through the stack of mail that he had ignored all week. He stood over the waste can tossing the catalogs, brochures, and other junk mail into it without a thought about them being of any value to him. When he reached the bottom of the pile, he uncovered the letter from his leasing company that he had received earlier in the week. Assuming that he knew what the contents of the letter would be—a reminder of his need to renew his lease—he absent mindedly tore open the envelope as he watched Gina wheel her rusty clunker into her parking spot. He moved the letter back and forth trying to get the small print into focus, reminding himself that he had to make an appointment for an eye exam—one more sign that he was rapidly reaching fifty.

Gina walked through the door just as the content of the letter sunk in. "What the hell?" he shouted. "They can't do that."

"Well, good morning to you too," chirped Gina.

"I can't believe this," he muttered waving the letter in the air. "They're selling the center and may tear down the building."

256

Gina reached over the counter and snatched the letter from his trembling hands. She quickly scanned the first paragraph and tossed the letter back onto the counter. "They can't do that to you, can they?" she asked. "We have to fight this."

"How?" moaned Frank. "Do you happen to have a million bucks that Greg didn't steal?"

"What's going on?" asked Sam as he bustled through the door. "You two look like you've just had horrible news. Is Olivia okay? What is it?"

Frank slid the letter to him, and Sam let out a slow whistle as he read the first paragraph. "My good god, can they do this?" he asked.

"It looks like they can," sighed Frank.

"What's going on?" Tom asked as he walked into the diner. "Bad news from Florida?"

"No. Take a gander at this," said Sam passing him the letter.

Tom took the letter. When he saw who it was from, he immediately knew what its contents were. However, he hadn't expected the proposal offered in the last paragraph. "Hmm," he said.

"Hmm?" repeated Gina. "That's all you have to say?"

Tom smiled at her and continued to read the rest of the letter. After he was finished, he simply tossed it back on

257

the counter. "Wow, what an opportunity!" he said as he headed for the back room to grab an apron.

"Opportunity?" said Frank irritated by Tom's flippant attitude. "They're going to sell this strip center and possibly knock down this building. They will only give me a month-to-month lease until it's sold and the new owners decide what they want to do with it. Just how is that a great opportunity?"

"Did you read the rest of the letter?" asked Tom, coming back into the diner, tying on his apron. "They're offering you the *First Right of Refusal*. Essentially, their offering you the chance to never have to worry again about a lease. But, you only have until Monday to make them an offer? How long have you had the letter, anyway? Surely you didn't just get it yesterday."

"What the heck does it matter when he got it?" asked Gina, obviously irritated at Tom's callous attitude. "None of us has that kind of money or enough collateral to entice any legitimate bank to give us a loan, even if we combine everything that we own. I suppose you're going to tell us that, from the huge tips we get in here, we can raise the million plus they're asking for this dump by five o'clock tomorrow evening. Sorry, Frank, no offense, but you have to admit that the place is about to fall down around us."

"Actually, Gina," replied Tom, "the structure of this building is sound. It needs a new roof and a little sprucing up, but the building is fine. They don't make them like this anymore."

"How would you know about the structure of the

258

building?" she mocked.

"I majored in Engineering in college," he said, as he handed Sam his cup of coffee and rye toast, light on the butter. "Two or three eggs today, Sam?" he asked.

"You're simply amazing," interrupted Gina. "Here you are working in a diner and acting like raising over a million dollars in twenty-four hours is an opportunity that you obviously think is actually doable. If you think it so easy to do, let's see you pull it off."

"First, I'm volunteering here, not working here," he reminded her. "And, I may just take you up on that challenge."

"Well, be my guest," she retorted. "This is like some joke to you, isn't it?

"No, believe me, I know this isn't a joke," defended Tom. "I realize the seriousness of this, but maybe I can…oh, never mind; forget it. We need to get to work. Here comes the early church crowd."

"He drives me nuts," said Gina. "He never finishes a sentence, and we don't really know anything about him, except that he runs everywhere he goes, he likes steak and eggs, and he waited on tables at some time in his past."

"Well, now we know he went to college and majored in Engineering," Sam added.

"Big deal," snapped Gina. "And besides, if he actually

graduated in Engineering, why isn't he an engineer?" she said.

"Who knows?" said Sam. "Maybe he is."

"Yeah, right," muttered Gina. "Not likely," she said.

"Anyway, let's change the subject. How'd your date go last night?" Sam asked.

Gina smiled and walked away. "None of your business," she called over her shoulder.

" Hey, we had a bet, and it looks like I won." He laughed. "Just look at her over there, Frank. You've gotta love her. She bounces back like a rubber ball," continued Sam.

Frank simply sighed, and mumbled, "Yeah. Some things are easier than others to bounce back from."

"I don't know what to say, Frank," said Sam. "Closing this place will affect all of us."

"Especially me," muttered Frank.

"Morning, Sam, Frank," said Leroy as he came into the diner and headed for his counter stool.

"Morning, Leroy" muttered Frank.

"What's going on?" asked Sam. "You're mighty early today."

"I know. So much has been going on around here lately
260

that it has got me off my schedule. I'm afraid that I'm going to miss something," responded Leroy. "From the looks of Frank, it appears that I may have already missed something this morning. Why the long face, Frank? What's the news from Florida and Germany? Everyone doing okay?" asked Leroy, looking at Sam for some indication of the reason for Frank's despondency.

Sam slid him the letter from the leasing company.

"What?" yelled Leroy. "How're we going to solve this one? You'd better call Meredith down in Florida, and tell her we need her back up here right away—tonight if possible."

"Tom says this is Frank's opportunity," said Sam.

"Well, it is," said Leroy. "That is, if he can come up with the money. Tom seems like a smart guy, and I've never bought into the idea that he's just a drifter. Maybe he's actually one of those trust-fund babies with so much money he doesn't have to work."

"Yeah," said Frank, finally joining the conversation. "Like he's the rich playboy who is playing the role of the Pauper, concealing that he's actually a Prince. That's why he dresses in running clothes from the thrift store down the street, doesn't own a car, and lives somewhere nearby. There aren't too many mansions within running distance around here in case you haven't noticed," he pouted.

"Frank's right. Sorry, Leroy, but I don't believe in *Cinderella* stories; not anymore," scoffed Sam.

"Like heck you don't," argued Leroy. "What about the surprise you're planning for Gina. If that's not hoping for a *Cinderella* ending, then I don't remember the story."

"Keep your voice down," whispered Sam. "I intend to keep it a secret until the time comes, so she won't be able to make up any excuse for not going."

"Going? Going where?" asked Frank. "Is there something else that I should know about?"

"Not really," mumbled Sam. "Just don't mention to Gina that I'm trying to surprise her with something."

"Whatever," muttered Frank. "I don't want to hear about any more surprises anyway. This week has been too full of them already."

"What are we going to do about the diner?" asked Leroy again. "We can't just sit here and not try to do something."

"Forget it, Leroy," said Frank. "I would really rather not talk about it right now. Who knows? Tom said he had some ideas; maybe he can suggest a solution. I'll get with him after we close and see what he thinks I should do. Let's talk about something else, if you don't mind." He turned back around to flip the pancakes that he'd almost let overcook.

Sam and Leroy looked at each other and shook their heads. As usual, Sam was the first to start a new conversation. "Hey, what do you think about me asking Kenneth to help me out at the farm? I would like to do some landscaping around the house. I've never paid
262

much attention to it, but I've been thinking about sprucing the place up a little bit."

"Good idea," muttered Frank, trying to sound enthusiastic.

When Kenneth came in, Sam invited him to sit up at the counter, assigning him a seat next to Meredith's currently vacant stool. Though Kenneth never made eye contact with them, he quietly slid on to the stool assigned to him.

Gina flew to the counter and hovered around Kenneth like a watchful mother hen. "Are you okay," she whispered to him. "You can move to your booth if you'd rather. Everyone will understand."

"Counter is fine," he muttered.

"Kenneth, what do you say to you coming out to my farm some day this week?" asked Sam. "I could use some help with replanting some of the flower beds in front of my house."

"Okay," muttered Kenneth.

"Do you mind if I tag along?" asked Gina quickly. "I would like to get a glimpse at some of those prize cattle you're raising out there, Sam."

Before Sam could answer, Kenneth blurted out, "Good."

"Fine by me," said Sam, understanding Gina's real reason for volunteering to join them. She was obviously taking on the role as protector of Kenneth.

Frank looked up from the grill and smiled at Gina. *That girl will go to her grave taking care of someone else. What in the heck will happen to her if I have to close the diner?* He shook his head trying to put the thought out of his mind. *There has to be a solution to this lease thing, somehow,* he decided.

~~~~~

Tom was busy all morning, but his mind was on other things. He was finally excited about something—an emotion that he hadn't felt for a long time. When the diner closed at two, he slipped out before Frank and Gina realized he had gone. He wanted to be sure that he could work everything out before he told Frank his plan. When he arrived at his apartment, he immediately called John Humphries in California. He realized that it was Sunday, but he didn't care. He was sure that John would answer his private number.

"Mr. Humphries," he said when John answered the phone. "This is Tom McGinnis."

"Yes, Tom. I wondered who would be calling me on my private number on Sunday. I haven't heard from you in months."

"Yes, sir. I know," answered Tom.

"Have you finally given up on the '*I'm gonna make it on my own,*' nonsense, and decided to take advantage of what is rightfully yours?" asked John.

"No, sir, not totally," answered Tom. "But, I am going to need access to a rather large sum of money quickly, and
264

I want to make sure that I won't have to jump through a bunch of hoops when I ask for the check."

"I doubt that you could withdraw enough from your account to cause a dent in its balance, even if you were trying to buy a third-world country. What do you need?" asked Mr. Humphries.

"Good," said Tom, failing to respond directly to John's question. "I'll call you tomorrow afternoon at the bank. Thanks for taking my call," he said, quickly hanging up before John could ask him any more about what his plans were.

After he hung up, he paced back and forth trying to figure out his next step. He couldn't decide whether he should call Frank today and tell him what he hoped to do, or if he should simply go ahead with his plans and let Frank discover later what he had done. He knew that his father would simply have told him to '*act don't ask*.' On the other hand, his grandfather would have reminded him that '*the wise man listens to the opinions of all those who will be affected by whatever he intends to do, and only then does he develop his own plan. You'll avoid a lot of surprises and disappointments if you gather the information you need before you decide what to do.*'

Although his grandfather died when Tom was only eight years old, he remembered him well. His grandfather was his best friend during his early years. He had retired by the time Tom was born and lived with them in the house that he had designed and built. Even though Tom was very young, he admired his grandfather and sensed his greatness.

The elder McGinnis had moved to California as a young man of sixteen in the early 1900's. He worked in the shipping yards of the Port of Los Angeles, loading freight onto the huge freighters that delivered cargo to places all over the world. While working there, he had observed the amount of man-hours and effort it took to unload cargo from the trucks and railroad cars onto the huge ships, and he began to think about ways to expedite the transfer. Eventually, he drew up plans for large containers that could fit on the backs of trucks and on flatbed railroad cars. Giant cranes would lift the containers from the trucks and trains, and they would then be securely locked onto the ships in one smooth motion. He took his plan to one of the largest shipping companies along the dock and convinced the company's owner to let him construct his system.

By the mid 1920's, his grandfather went from being a young, sixteen-year-old boy who slept in the bunkhouse of a rundown rooming house, to an entrepreneur living in one of the most magnificent homes in Los Angeles. He had laid the groundwork for later standardization of multi-modal shipping and had amassed a huge fortune, which Tom ultimately had inherited.

Tom grabbed his phone and dialed Frank's number, choosing to follow the advice of his grandfather. "Frank, this is Tom. I was wondering if we might meet somewhere for dinner. I have some things I'd like to talk over with you."

"Sure. I wondered what happened to you this afternoon at closing. You just disappeared without giving me a chance to talk to you about your thoughts on the lease problem. Hopefully, that's what you want to discuss over

266

dinner," said Frank.

"It is. Actually, why don't you come to my place, and I'll order some pizza. I have some things I'd like to show you, but I can't exactly bring them with me."

"Sure, I'll be there at six o'clock. Will that work?" Frank asked. "Jan usually calls me around eight o'clock, and I'd rather be home to get her call on my land line. Will that give us enough time to discuss my '*opportunity*'?" He chuckled sarcastically.

"It will indeed. It shouldn't take too long. What kind of pizza do you like?"

"I like anything but anchovies," replied Frank, "the more toppings the better."

"Great, me too. See you about six. Do you need directions?"

"Not directions, just your address," responded Frank.

As soon as he hung up the phone, Tom began mapping out the details of his plan for the strip center and for the diner. When he finally felt he had outlined the main idea sufficiently to explain everything to Frank, he glanced up at the kitchen clock. "Shit, I'd better order the pizza, or we won't have anything to eat," he said, whipping out his phone and pushing the speed dial to call his favorite pizza parlor.

The pizza and Frank arrived at his door at the same time. "Good timing." He smiled at Frank. "Come on in."

267

~~~~~

Frank glanced around at the half-empty apartment but was impressed with the quality of furniture that Tom did have. He obviously didn't buy his furniture from the same place he bought his clothes. "That desk is the most beautifully crafted piece of oak I've ever seen; and this table looks too fine to put a greasy old pizza box on top of it. Don't you want to put something under it to protect its beautiful finish?" he asked as he sat down at the table.

"It's okay. It has a special finish that resists damage from liquids and heat. So, you like the desk and the table?" asked Tom.

"My god, they're gorgeous, and this chair feels like it was made to fit me. They all look like they belong in some expensive mansion, not in a cheap apartment—no insult intended."

Tom laughed. "I'm not at all insulted. Believe it or not, I made every piece of furniture in this apartment."

"What? You made this table and that desk?"

"Yes. In fact, this furniture is part of what I want to talk to you about," said Tom.

"I'm not sure I'm following you," said Frank totally confused.

"Well," continued Tom, handing Frank a paper plate, "I guess I should begin by telling you a little about myself."

Frank chuckled, remembering the conversation at the diner with Sam and Leroy. "Leroy thinks you're a wealthy, trust-fund baby pretending to be a Pauper." He reached into the pizza box and pulled a piece onto his paper plate.

"Leroy is very perceptive," Tom answered seriously.

Frank glanced across the table and stared intently at Tom. "You're not laughing," he said.

"That's because I do come from a very wealthy family," replied Tom.

"What? You're joking, right?"

"No. It's true. I do have access to a huge fortune, but I've tried to live by my own means since I was old enough to figure out what that meant."

"Why?" asked Frank. "Why would you live like this, if you could live surrounded by luxury?"

"I'm sure a psychiatrist would have a heyday trying to uncover some deep, psychological quirk for why I have chosen to deny my inheritance, but, actually, my reasoning is pretty straightforward and simple. I had a grandfather that I loved dearly. He was the one who earned my family's fortune, but he started out with nothing. I want to make it in life the way he did—through my own ingenuity, blood, sweat, and tears."

"I admire you for that and believe it or not, I understand it," said Frank.

"I knew you would," said Tom. "People like you who have made it on their own understand my thinking. Most of my former acquaintances, including my banker, think I'm nuts—or at least eccentric."

"But, most people who '*make it on their own*' don't really have a choice. They do what they have to do to survive, but you do have a choice, or so you just said. And, to be honest, that is a little harder to understand. What about your family, Tom? You referred to former acquaintances and your banker..."

"I don't have any family," Tom interrupted. "I was an only child, and my parents were killed in an automobile accident when I was ten years old." He dropped his head and stared at his empty paper plate. "My grandfather had died two years earlier, and I don't have any other living relatives that I know about."

"I'm sorry," said Frank. "I didn't mean to pry or to bring up painful memories."

After several minutes of twirling around the paper plate with his finger, Tom continued. "My parents were on their way home from a party on Christmas Eve when their car skidded off the road and careened down a rocky slope in the mountains of California. They had obviously had too much to drink to maneuver the steep, twisted road that wound around the treacherous curves leading to our sprawling home located high in the mountains, overlooking the Pacific Ocean far below."

"How terrible," whispered Frank. "You were just a little older than I was, when my mom and brother disappeared."

270

"When they died," continued Tom, "I became a ward of a Trustee by the name of John Humphries, who had been appointed for me in my parent's Will. Although John was an excellent financial advisor, he was a bachelor who had no idea what to do with a ten-year-old boy, so I was sent off to multiple prep schools spread out across the United States and Europe. I became a belligerent, hateful kid and was kicked out of one school after another for bad grades or bad behavior. After I finally finished high school, by the grace of a huge donation from my trust fund, Mr. Humphries managed to get me into a college in Germany, where I studied Engineering. Luckily, I finally found something that interested me, and I actually graduated with honors."

"When you told us today that your major in college was Engineering," interrupted Frank, "we were curious as to whether or not you are still working as an engineer."

"I did go into engineering immediately after college, and I was very successful," replied Tom. "I traveled throughout Europe and the Middle East, designing major projects in Paris, Germany, and Dubai. Within a very short time, I gained international recognition for my unique structural designs and innovative approaches to the sound construction of buildings situated along ocean fronts. This type of building, as I'm sure you realize, is, subject to intense weather and storm conditions. I enjoyed my work and was proud of living off my own money, instead of depending on my inheritance."

"Why did you come back to the States if you were so successful overseas?" asked Frank.

"Unfortunately, tragedy reared its ugly head again," said

271

Tom. "Four years ago, one of the projects I was working on in Germany suddenly collapsed, killing thirteen workers. Although I was cleared of any blame for the collapse, which had nothing to do with my design but rather with a faulty mixture of concrete, I was ashamed that I wasn't there the day of the collapse."

"Why? asked Frank. "What could you have done?"

"Probably nothing," admitted Tom. "But, my best friend, a college buddy, was overseeing the construction in Germany for me while I was in Dubai lining up our next project. He was among the thirteen who were killed, and even though the investigation cleared me of any fault, I still felt responsible for his death and the death of the others."

"But it wasn't your fault," insisted Frank.

"I don't know why I blamed myself," said Tom. "I simply was unable to accept the fact that I wasn't somehow to blame for the tragedies that resulted in the death of people I cared for, so I stopped believing in myself. Anyway, after the collapse in Germany, I wondered around Europe for the next two years gambling and drinking away all of the money I had earned and saved on my own. I became just another international playboy, rather than one of its rising stars. Finally, completely broke and disillusioned with life, I moved back to California two years ago to my family home, but I was unable to find any comfort in the house that had once brought me total happiness. I finally sold it and began hopping across the United States doing odd jobs, still refusing to tap any of the money from the sale of the house or from my inheritance—trying to prove to myself

272

again that I could live by my own means."

"But, how did you end up here, of all places?" asked Frank.

Tom laughed, "Running became my new obsession—not only to improve my well-being after years of abusing my body with rich foods, lots of alcohol, and occasional illegal drugs, but to prove to myself that I was able to stick with something—something I could do alone, without the responsibility for or the dependence upon anyone or anything else. When I run, I'm an independent, free spirit with no ties and with limits that only I control. I began running in every marathon I could in order to prove to myself I could accomplish something.

"Aha," said Frank, "the Columbus Marathon brought you to Columbus."

"Right," said Tom. "While I was training for the Columbus Marathon, I stumbled across the diner on a morning practice run. Every morning for the next three weeks, I planned my runs so that I would end up at the diner in time to listen to the conversations between Leroy, Sam, you, and Howard. I was immediately intrigued by all of you and enjoyed listening to your stories and arguments. You four were real, without any pretentiousness. I especially admired you, Frank."

"Me? Why?" asked Frank.

"You are a self-made man—like my grandfather. He started out with nothing and managed to amass a huge amount of wealth by inventing a method to expedite shipping procedures. Like him, you were someone

273

making it on your own in spite of a story that included heartbreak. Anyway," Tom continued, "the diner feels like home to me, and this is where I want to be."

"But how have you managed to rent an apartment and pay for your expenses without using the money from your trust?" asked Frank. "Not that it's any of my business," he added.

"I've been doing free-lance work at a local engineering company to pay for necessities, and I've made enough to rent a small unit in a modular building as a workshop for my furniture construction," answered Tom.

"Is your unit part of the huge industrial park a couple of miles west of the diner?" asked Frank.

"Yes. It's about two miles from the diner, so it's a short run for me and helps me work off my daily steak and eggs. By the way, you do make great steak and eggs." Tom laughed.

Frank smiled, still in disbelief of what Tom was telling him.

"A few months ago," Tom continued, "I hired my neighbor who teaches woodworking at the local high school and some of his students who really want to become craftsmen to help me after school to build my designs. I love working with the young kids. I'm teaching them not only to think about how to use the tools and to choose the wood to make the perfect final product but also to consider the ultimate function of the furniture so that the end product supports the needs of the human skeletal and muscular systems. It's great. I know I can

274

make a good living from the sale of my furniture, but I haven't found a place that could serve as a retail outlet. But now that we have the opportunity to buy the center, we can solve both of our problems."

"We?" said Frank. "I have some savings, but not enough to be a partner in buying the center."

"Just hear me out," said Tom. He pushed the paper containing the outline of his proposal over to Frank to let him read it. "Look this over before you say anything else."

Frank pulled out a pair of cheap reading glasses from his shirt pocket and studied the outline of the business partnership that Tom had written. After he had finished reading the proposal, he just sat there, starring at Tom.

"Well?" asked Tom, nervously.

"I don't know what to say, Tom. This kind of thing just doesn't happen to me. Nobody has ever offered to do anything like this for me. It sounds too good to be true— and if there's one thing I've learned over the years, if something is too good to be true, then it is."

"I know it's hard to believe, given what you've seen and know about me from the diner. But I promise you that everything I have just told you is true. I am who I told you I am, and I can do what I have spelled out on that paper."

"So, let me get this straight. You intend to use the vacant unit in the shopping center as a retail outlet for your furniture, and you are actually willing to give me part ownership of the shopping center if I simply promise that I will keep the diner there, and if I will manage the center itself."

"Yep, that's about it. What do you think, deal?" asked Tom.

"You don't do drugs anymore, do you?" asked Frank, causing Tom to burst out laughing.

"No, I don't do drugs or alcohol any more—they're bad for this efficient running machine I've spent the last two years perfecting," he said, thumping his chest. "If you don't have any major objections to everything I've explained, then I'll start the ball rolling tomorrow morning. Everything should be done in time to meet the deadline set by the leasing company."

"Objections?" said Frank. "Do you think I'm nuts or something? What's there not to like about such a proposal? But, won't you have to break your promise to yourself to make it on your own without tapping into your inheritance?"

"Some promises, are made to be broken, haven't you ever heard that old saying."

"Yes, I have heard that, but honestly, Tom, I have to say that I won't believe you can pull this off until I actually see the deed for the building. Here," he said handing Tom the letter from the leasing company. "You'll probably need this to get everything started."

"Great," said Tom jumping up and offering his hand to Frank. "I'm finally excited about something again," he
276

said. "I'll set up the closing for as soon as I can, hopefully by next week. Cash deals don't usually take too much time to close. Is there a day next week that will be better for you?"

"Any day after two o'clock will be perfect," responded Frank, grabbing Tom's hand with both of his, and shaking it vigorously. "I still can't believe that you're for real," he said again, "but I sure pray to God you are!"

"And, oh, by the way, do you mind just keeping this between the two of us?" asked Tom. "I'd rather that Sam and the others still see me as a poor, shiftless young man who runs in there every day for steak and eggs. I'm not sure why, but I just enjoy being that guy with them," he said.

"Whatever you say, partner," Frank answered. "But I'm pretty sure that it wouldn't make any difference to them who you are. They'll treat you just the same—what you see is what you get from them."

"I guess it's more about me than them. I just want to be someone who makes something happen by himself, like this furniture thing."

"For what it's worth, son," said Frank, "there's no doubt in my mind that you could've made the furniture thing happen on your own. It's only because of what you're doing for me that requires you to reach back into your inheritance. I know that, and I will never forget it. And, I'm quite sure that your grandfather would be impressed by what you're doing."

"I think he would too." Tom smiled. "You'd better get

277

going. You don't want to miss Jan's phone call.

"Just saying '*thank you*' doesn't seem enough for what you're doing, but I do thank you from the bottom of my heart," said Frank. "God, what a week this has been, huh?"

"The week from hell!" said Tom.

"Until this evening," Frank added, smiling.

"Before you take off," Tom said as they were headed for the door. "What happens next with Olivia? I mean with the court case and all?"

"She'll have to identify her captors, although one of them was killed during the bust. And, Teresa, I guess, will never stand trial because of the massive brain damage she had from the gunshot wound. But, the big guy, this Hasting Gutierrez, is in jail being held without bail, and it's not clear, at this point, whether they'll need Olivia's live testimony when his case finally gets to court, or not. Since she wasn't actually forced into prostitution, she might be able to just sign an affidavit about the kidnapping and assault charges filed against him.

I guess they have so much concrete evidence and so many other girls who have much more major charges against him and the others who ran the brothels, that her testimony may not be necessary to send him and the others away forever. It's my understanding that there are also murder charges being brought against Gutierrez and some of the members of his cartel, resulting from the deaths of some of the girls and from the death of Teresa's brother. So, hopefully, he'll receive the death

278

penalty. Thank God Florida reinstated it, and this governor has used it more than once."

"For Olivia's sake and Jan's, I hope that she can just sign the affidavit and be done with it. The sooner she is able to put this behind her, the better," said Tom.

"Either way, Jan intends to bring Olivia home as soon as she can. They're comfortable with the fact that she's not in danger of any retaliation given the wide net of thugs they've arrested. Jan wants her here where we can all help to get her back on her feet. It's certainly a tangled up mess that will take time and lots of strength to get through."

"Yeah, it is, but I'm sure that getting her back home will help," agreed Tom.

"She's got a counselor up here that was making some headway with her. Hopefully, she'll help Olivia to put this all behind her and to move on with her life. Olivia's a bright girl with lots of potential; she just needs to get rid of her self-destructive attitudes. I think this incident might have jarred some of that out of her."

"Yeah, hitting the bottom has a way of helping you understand that the only way left for you is up," said Tom, recalling his drinking and drug days in Europe.

"I think she'll be able to get her act together this time. For Jan's sake, I hope she does. It's really been hard on Jan to be on the outside looking in with Olivia. Olivia is all she has."

"You could change all of that, you know." Tom smiled.

"What do you mean?"

"Come on now. Are you the only one at the diner that hasn't noticed how Jan feels about you? I noticed it the first day I came in."

"If we're going to be partners," warned Frank, smiling, "I suggest we keep our personal relationships out of the mix."

"I just want my new partner to be happy."

"Well, he is. Thanks to you!" said Frank, slapping Tom on the shoulder as he headed for the car.

"Coward!" called Tom, laughing.

Chapter 20

Mark tucked the blanket around Olivia's knees to make sure it didn't get caught in the wheel chair as he got ready to push her out into the hallway. "Are you ready?" he asked, smiling down at her.

"Am I ever," said Olivia. "After two long weeks in here, I can't wait to get to Meredith's to enjoy some real food again. Mom said on the phone that she and Meredith had been in the kitchen all morning making all my favorites."

"What?" said her nurse, laughing. "You didn't like our food here?"

"I didn't mean to sound ungrateful. Actually, what I got to eat wasn't all that bad," apologized Olivia.

"You've never been ungrateful," replied the nurse. "All of the staff agreed that you've been the model patient. You even thanked us every time we had to wake you up in the middle of the night to give you that nasty tasting cocktail and those painful shots."

"I'm glad I wasn't too demanding, but do you think that you could do just one more thing for me before I leave?" asked Olivia.

"Sure, what's that?" asked the nurse.

"I want to see Teresa," said Olivia.

"What?" asked Mark, glaring at the nurse, who responded by throwing her hands up and mouthing '*not me*'. "How did you know she was in here?"

"What makes the difference how I found out that she was in here? Please, Mark. I need to put closure on this thing if I am going to put it behind me."

"If you're sure you want to do this," said the nurse. "I'll check at the desk. It isn't the hospital that's screening her visitors—it's the police. Are you sure you want to see her?" she asked, looking over at Mark and then at Olivia.

Mark bent down in front of the wheel chair so he could see directly into Olivia's eyes. "I don't think this is a good idea," he said.

"This is important to me," whispered Olivia, "very important."

"Wait here," said the nurse.

Olivia and Mark waited in silence watching the nurse as she called up to the floor where Teresa was being cared for. Mark shifted his weight from side to side and paced in small circles behind the wheel chair. He wasn't sure that Jan would approve of this. *Should I call her,* he wondered. *No, probably not. After all, Olivia is a grown woman, not some teenager. Well, she is actually only nineteen, but she is old enough to make her own decisions. Only nineteen,* he reminded himself, *and I'm twenty-four—five years older than she is. What difference does that make here,* he wondered. *Why am I thinking about the difference in our ages anyway?*

282

"I got the clearance for you to visit her, but there will be a guard in the room with you," said the nurse.

Olivia laughed. "Why? Are they afraid I might try to harm her? From what I hear, she's been punished enough."

"Hmm. I'm not sure I would agree with that," Mark said as he pushed Olivia toward the elevator.

They were greeted on the fifth floor by one of the police officers guarding Teresa's room. "Sorry, Miss," she said, "but, I have to make sure that you're not carrying any hidden weapons."

Olivia laughed. "Go ahead," she said, lifting the blanket that Mark had so carefully tucked around her.

"Oh, for heaven's sake," moaned Mark. "Olivia, this is ridiculous. Let's just get out of here."

"Please, Mark. It's okay. I don't mind. They're just doing their job."

Mark threw up his hands and shook his head. "Satisfied?" he asked the police officer sarcastically.

"Yes sir," she said. "You may come with her to the room, but you'll need to wait outside."

"Fine," stormed Mark shoving the wheel chair down the hall where another police officer was stationed outside Teresa's door. "Look, Olivia," he said, once again crouching down in front of her. "Please think about this. What good will it do for you to see her again? It might

283

trigger some awful flashback, and then what?"

"I want to do this, Mark," she said firmly, causing him to throw up his hands as the police officer grabbed hold of the wheel chair.

"I don't need the wheel chair," said Olivia pushing herself up. "It's just the policy of the hospital that patients use one while they're leaving. Thank God, I can still get around by myself; that's something she'll never be able to do again," she said pointing to Teresa.

Mark watched as Olivia drew in a deep breath, and the officer followed her into Teresa's room. Through the open door, he had a clear view of Olivia and Teresa. Teresa was hooked up to all sorts of machines and was obviously not conscious. He watched in amazement as Olivia reached out and gently took Teresa's hand in hers, and then bowed her head for several minutes, obviously praying.

"I forgive you," Olivia finally muttered wiping a tear from her face.

Mark dropped his head. He had been wrong. Olivia was right. He could feel a release of his own pent up anger as he watched her gently place Teresa's hand back on the side of the bed. Olivia would be fine; he was sure of that now.

"Okay, now let's go eat," said Olivia as the police officer followed her back into the hall. "Are you okay, Mark?" she asked noticing the tears in his eyes.

"I'm fine—just fine," he muttered. *Rule number seven*,
284

he said to himself, *forgive your enemies.*

~~~~~

Jan and Meredith rushed to the car as Mark and Olivia pulled into the drive. Olivia jumped out to meet them. "Here, let me help you," offered Jan.

"It's okay, mom," said Olivia, kissing Jan on the cheek. "I'm really able to walk on my own. I'm not handicapped, just starved!"

The phone was ringing when they walked back into the house, and Meredith hurried to answer it.

"Hey, Meredith. It's Gina. Is she there yet?"

"She just walked in, Gina. Hold on. I'll get her." She handed the phone to Olivia. "It's Gina," she said.

"Hey, Gina," said Olivia. "You're right on time. I've really appreciated you calling me every day."

"How are you doing, sweetie. I've been worried about you this morning. Did you do what I suggested?"

"Yes. I did. Thanks, Gina. It helped. I think it even helped Mark."

"How is our young Marine? Has he proposed to you yet?"

"Gina. You're nuts. I'm sure I don't know what you're talking about."

285

"Oh yeah, right. I know you better than that. You know exactly what I'm talking about."

"Can we change the subject here? I do have an audience, you know." Olivia laughed.

"Let me talk to the poor guy. I'm sure he's not letting you get too far out of his sight, so he must be close by," she said.

"Sure, hold on." Olivia turned around and bumped smack into Mark. "Here, Mark," she said laughing, "Gina wants to talk to you."

"Now what have I done?" he moaned.

"I heard that," said Gina. "It's what you haven't done that's the problem."

"What's that?" he asked.

"Never mind," said Gina, "I'm sure you'll get around to it eventually. Look, when are you guys heading back up here?"

"I'm not sure, why?"

"Sam wanted me to ask you."

"Sam?"

"I'm not sure what he has up his sleeve, but he wants to know how soon Jan would be coming back to work."

286

"She has tickets to fly home on Thursday, but I don't know what her plans are for going back to work. The doctors here want Olivia to have frequent blood tests when she gets home to make sure that everything is functioning as it should. But other than that, she has no restrictions. She intends to enroll in school for next semester, so I guess Jan can start living her own life again whenever she decides she wants to."

"I've no doubt that she'll be back in here as soon as she gets home. I know she misses being with Frank."

"Speaking of Uncle Frank," said Mark. "What's happening with his lease?"

"I don't know what happened, but all of a sudden that issue was magically solved—something to do with new owners of the center offering him a lifetime lease or some such nonsense. Since last week, he's been a changed man. He even whistles now while he works instead of heaving those deep, horrible sighs."

"Wow, that's great—it was kind of a fast turnaround, wasn't it?"

"I have my own theory about what happened, but I think it's not something that I should share, at least, not yet." Gina laughed.

"You and your theories! But, I have to admit your hunches have been pretty much on target," said Mark. "Anyway, I'm glad for him. Tell him I intend to head his way in a week or so. I promised Bill Fleming I'd go deep sea fishing with him tomorrow, and I want to see some of Florida and the coast on my way back home. I'll

287

probably come the long way, up the coast, then cut over somewhere in Virginia toward home. I'll let him know my plans once I see Olivia and Jan off."

"Do you realize that you just called Ohio *home*?"

"I did say that, didn't I? I guess I do see you guys as family and the diner as my home base. So, listen here, little sis, don't be filling Olivia's mind with your romantic notions. And by the way, how's your new love? I understand you two are inseparable."

"That's none of your business," responded Gina.

"Just as I thought—you can dish it out, but you can't take it."

"This conversation is over," said Gina. "Give my love to those down there who deserve it!"

~~~~~

Gina smiled as she closed her phone and put it back into the pocket of her apron. Walking over to the large front window, she stared at the cars speeding past the diner. *I wonder where they're all hurrying to*, she thought. She touched the heart-shaped, gold necklace hanging around her neck that Jeff had given her last night. *I am one happy girl,* she decided. *Everyone I care about is safe, including me. We've all been very lucky. Things could have ended tragically for all of us; but they didn't.*

If she hadn't actually been part of everything that had happened during the past several weeks, she knew that she would never have believed how it all turned out. *I would have complained about a movie of our past month as being a far-fetched farce.* She laughed. *Actually, I'm going to start watching more movies with happy endings,* she decided. *Ordinary people, like those of us here at the diner, can do extraordinary things. We just proved it.*

"Hey, Gina," shouted Frank, interrupting her reverie. "Do you mind coming back from wherever you are, and putting the chairs up, so we can get out of here?"

She smiled. "I'm on it, Captain," she said, turning to face Frank. *Some things just never change; and that's a good thing,* she thought. She blew Frank a kiss and thoroughly enjoyed his startled look.

As she started piling the chairs on to the tables with Tom's help, she suddenly began to laugh. Her contagious laughter quickly spread to Tom and to Frank. The three of them just stood there looking at one another and laughing hysterically without any of them really knowing why.

"I think this is what you call sheer joy," she giggled.

Epilogue

Edith Talbert watched out the window as Kenneth, Sam, and Leroy fussed with the arrangement of the patio furniture to make sure that everyone would have a clear view of the big screen TV that they had rented for the occasion. What a summer this had been; so many lives changed in such a short time, and more changes on the way. *The ebb and flow of life is amazing—and a little scary,* she thought. She wished she could just freeze time at this very moment. Right now, everyone was content and full of anticipation of wonderful things to follow. Of course, life was never still—only memories of magical moments could be captured and held—not life. "Look at them out there," she said to Meredith. "They're as nervous as expectant fathers."

"They are, aren't they? Sam has been on edge for the past two weeks. He's called Gina every night to check on her," said Meredith as she put the final touches on the cake that she had carefully decorated for the occasion.

"I'm thrilled for her. I can't believe that Sam was able to make this happen for her," said Edith.

"Sam just started the ball rolling. Gina did the rest."

"Yes, but still it was thoughtful of him to lay the groundwork and to fund her way through the whole audition process."

"Sam is very grateful for what Gina did for him. I guess it was Gina who helped him make it after his wife was
290

killed in a car accident. He told me once that if it hadn't been for her, he would have committed suicide," said Meredith heaving a deep sigh.

"I can't even begin to tell you how much she's helped Kenneth. Look at him out there. He's even arguing with them about where the flowers should be placed around the patio. He's no longer afraid to talk when they're around. Did you know that Gina made the appointment and took him to his enrollment interview on campus? She's convinced him that he can get his degree and can get someone to help him publish his research. It's remarkable. He's a completely different person—much more confident and more accepting of his autism."

"I can't believe how talented he is. That flower painting of the diner is so lifelike that it looks like you could step inside and sit down and order breakfast," said Meredith.

"What about you, Meredith. How are you coping?" asked Edith.

"It's hard being alone, but thanks to Sam and the others, I've had so much to occupy my mind that I haven't had time to feel lonely," said Meredith. "I've decided not to sell the house up here. I'm just going to go back to Florida for the winter months, like we always did. I've gotten too attached to everyone up here to ever give them up."

"How's Frank adjusting to Gina's absence at the diner?" asked Edith.

"Now that he and Jan are engaged—again thanks to Gina's nudging, or more like shoving—he's happy as a

291

lark. Kelley will be coming back to work in a couple of weeks, and in the meantime, Tom and Olivia are filling in. I know he dreads having Mark leave next week—and so does Olivia. It will be hard for all of them."

"I know," said Edith. "I just pray that the good Lord keeps Mark safe. He's such a wonderful young man and has become such an integral part of the fabric of the *Diner Family*. There are going to be so many changes this fall—exciting, but also a little daunting. This is the perfect moment, here and now."

"It is; most certainly, it is," agreed Meredith.

The door bell rang and Edith hurried through the kitchen to the entranceway with Meredith right behind her. "Come on in," said Edith, greeting the diner crowd. Frank, Jan, Olivia, Tom, and Kelley and her husband and kids poured through the open door. "Here come the O'Connors and Colin, too. We're all here now," said Edith.

"Your driveway is gorgeous," said Jan. "I've never seen so many lovely roses."

"You haven't seen anything yet," said Meredith. "Wait until you see the backyard."

"This is so generous of you to have us all here," said Olivia. "I can't wait to see the floral picture of the diner that Gina bragged about."

"Just follow the hallway straight on back," responded Edith. "The guys are out there fussing over the arrangement for the chairs. Maybe you could give them
292

some pointers."

"Hurry up you guys," yelled Sam. "It's about to start."

They all rushed out onto the patio as the familiar theme song of the Grand Ole Opry filled the night air.

"Look, look, there's Jeff and Mark sitting in the front row," shouted Olivia.

"Oh. I'm not so sure they should have sat that close. They might make her nervous," worried Sam.

"Nothing makes Gina nervous," said Frank as he reached out for Jan's hand. "She's the one who got them the front row seats. She told them that she'd be a lot more relaxed if she could sing to someone she knew."

Jan smiled as she noticed that Frank's hands were clammy and as cold as ice. Obviously, he was the nervous one.

Edith glanced around at the group of friends, all sitting on the edge of their seats, staring intently at the TV. *Strange*, she thought. *How different we are, yet how close we've become.*

"There she is," yelled Sam. "Everyone keep their fingers crossed," he whispered, his voice husky with emotion.

"Take it easy, pal," soothed Leroy. "You don't have to worry about Gina. She'll knock 'em dead."

"She will," agreed Kenneth.

"Ladies and Gentleman," said the announcer. "It's a pleasure to introduce an up and coming new star, Miss Gina Meyers, who hails here from the Buckeye State of Ohio." The camera panned the audience and the *Frank's Diner* group broke out in laughter as they saw Mark and Jeff whistling and stomping their feet on the floor.

"It looks like you have a small, but extremely vocal following out there in the audience," remarked the announcer, smiling at Gina.

"I do, indeed." Gina chuckled and tossed a kiss to Jeff.

"Look at that, would you," yelled Sam. "She's as cool as a cucumber."

"Only on the outside, I bet," said Olivia.

"Gina, why don't you tell the audience about how you ended up here tonight. It's a remarkable story."

"How long did you say your program was?" she responded, smiling into the camera. "Well, let me just say that I am very grateful to my friend Sam Weston, who sent you the CD that I had given him for Christmas. He arranged for me to participate in your contest and paid all my expenses. And, somehow, by the grace of God, I won, and here I am.

"You're being modest," said the announcer. "I've heard you sing. So, what are you singing for us tonight?"

"The song I'm singing tonight is one of those songs that reminds us of the importance of others in our life. I want

294

to dedicate it to my two vocal friends in the front row, and to my breakfast friends back home, who are all huddled around a big TV in my good friend Kenneth's beautiful rose garden. Just for them, I've chosen one of Kenny Chesney's greatest songs: *Because of Your Love.*"

Edith sat back, tears welling in her eyes, as she listened to Gina's beautiful voice sing out with such sincere feelings of love. *What a gift that young lady has been to all of us*, she thought. She looked around at her new friends and at her grandson, leaning so far forward in his chair that she thought he might topple to the ground. She allowed the grateful tears to trickle slowly onto her cheeks, thankful that she, too, was now a part of the *Breakfast Friends*.

****

Other Books by The Author

The Mansion

Raven's Call

Raven's Son (2012)

www.ingramcontent.com/pod-product-compliance
Lightning Source LLC
Chambersburg PA
CBHW021947170626
46808CB00001B/52